slightly south
of simple

slightly south
of simple

A NOVEL

Kristy Woodson Harvey

G

GALLERY BOOKS

New York   London   Toronto   Sydney   New Delhi

G

Gallery Books
An Imprint of Simon & Schuster, Inc.
1230 Avenue of the Americas
New York, NY 10020

First Gallery Books trade paperback edition April 2017

GALLERY BOOKS and colophon are registered trademarks of Simon & Schuster, Inc.

For information about special discounts for bulk purchases, please contact Simon & Schuster Special Sales at 1-866-506-1949 or business@simonandschuster.com.

The Simon & Schuster Speakers Bureau can bring authors to your live event. For more information or to book an event, contact the Simon & Schuster Speakers Bureau at 1-866-248-3049 or visit our website at www.simonspeakers.com.

Interior design by Davina Mock-Maniscalco

Manufactured in the United States of America

10   9   8   7   6   5   4   3   2   1

Library of Congress Cataloging-in-Publication Data

Names: Woodson Harvey, Kristy, author.
Title: Slightly south of simple / Kristy Woodson Harvey.
Description: First Gallery Books trade paperback edition. | New York : Gallery Books, 2017. | Series: The peachtree bluff series ; 1
Identifiers: LCCN 2016049826 (print) | LCCN 2017003143 (ebook) | ISBN 9781501158056 (paperback) | ISBN 9781501158063 (ebook)
Subjects: LCSH: Domestic fiction. | BISAC: FICTION / Contemporary Women. | FICTION / Family Life. | FICTION / Romance / Contemporary.
Classification: LCC PS3623.O6785 S55 2017 (print) | LCC PS3623.O6785 (ebook) | DDC 813/.6—dc23
LC record available at https://lccn.loc.gov/2016049826

ISBN 978-1-5011-5805-6
ISBN 978-1-5011-5806-3 (ebook)

To my parents, Paul and Beth Woodson,
who always told me I could.

seagulls

ansley

I still have dreams about that yellow-and-white-striped bikini, the one I was wearing the night I met Jack, my first bona fide summer love. I was fifteen going on sixteen, the perfect age, when your hair tints that summer blond that hairstylists become superstars for emulating. You have filled out enough not to be gangly but not so much that you can imagine a one-piece being in your future.

We spent those bikini summers in Peachtree Bluff, my family and I, at my grandmother's waterfront home, the one that I didn't realize until years later was truly something special. It was always blissful, always enchanted, but that summer, Sandra and Emily, my two best friends, and I spent nearly every day at Starlite Island across from Grandmother's house. It was only a few boat lengths across the sound, but you couldn't swim there and needed at least a kayak to go. It felt like freedom.

Those summers were all about seeing how close we could get to the wild horses on our favorite island and gauging if any of us could tame the wild boys who seemed as native to the beach as the crabs scurrying about. Skin tanned dark and hair sun-bleached, they sipped Pabst Blue Ribbon all afternoon, throwing footballs and telling (mostly false) stories about how cool they were back home, wherever they had come from.

I imagined then that no matter where my life took me, Peachtree Bluff would always be a part of my story. But it never crossed my mind that one day things would change so quickly and so fiercely that I would end up moving to my childhood paradise, my sanctuary from the real world, full time.

Wherever it may be, you always tell your kids that they can come home again. It's the thing that, as a parent, you're supposed to say. But maybe this is why so many people downsize when their children go off to college. Maybe this is why they move to condos on the lake, not the sweeping clapboard home that their grandmother left them in a harbor town in Georgia. If you don't have five bedrooms and a three-bedroom guesthouse, there is no way that all of your children—families in tow—can descend on you like seagulls on the day-old bread the grandkids throw out on the dock.

But change is the only thing I've ever been able to count on in this life, the only thing that hasn't let me down. And I am quite proud to say that although I may not always have done the right thing, I have survived it all. Hit after hit, storm after storm, I have weathered, I have protected. Like that dock across the narrow street from my house, I have withstood hurricanes, tornadoes, and even the occasional hailstorm.

When I was too scared to go on, too shaken to stand, too rattled to know which way was up, I carried on for the three best parts of me, for the girls who almost ruined my life yet somehow ended up saving it.

As I hear the voices upstairs, some happy, some mad—they are sisters, after all—I open the refrigerator door and wonder, not for the first time, how I got here. How is it possible that a couple of months ago, I was in my grandmother's house on the sound, enjoying the splendor of the silence? I would open my fridge to find exactly three Smartwaters, one canister of coffee, two yogurts, and some old ketchup.

Now I open that same fridge in that same house to find it nearly spilling over, each item a reminder of one of my girls. The bottles of breast milk are the biggest surprise, the choice to nurse at all an unlikely one for my beautiful, smart, but somewhat selfish Caroline. But it is these very bottles that helped her gain back her trim, toned figure nearly instantly, the prenatal vitamins making her long dark hair even silkier and shinier.

The chocolate milk that you would think was for Sloane's young sons, but actually is for her, comes next. That middle daughter, doe-eyed like her older sister, her hair a light brown, as though the dark hair gene got lighter with each girl until it eventually gave up and allowed Emerson, the youngest, to be fully blond, has loved chocolate milk since her first taste. Sloane is the least concerned with appearances and has adapted to the role of mother easily, as the hot dogs, grapes, string cheese, and Capri Suns will attest.

The fresh-squeezed green juice beside those bottles, stored in an unusually narrow yet still shapely carafe, reminds me of its blond-haired, blue-eyed owner, Emerson, with her high, sculpted cheekbones that still manage to make her look soft and feminine. Her looks and talent have combined to put her on her way to the acting career she's always dreamed of. She is the one that, finally, looked like me. Though my hair is now clipped to right at my shoulders, the way hers runs long and free down her back reminds me of my younger days.

The takeout containers and the wine? Well, those could be for any one of my girls. The rows and the list go on and on.

But this is how it is, I've come to see. Sometimes you don't know how empty your fridge—or your heart—can be. You don't realize it, that is, until at long last, you find them full again.

civilization

caroline

I was the only one who wasn't really into the whole Peachtree Bluff thing. It's kind of like being the Grinch at Christmas. My sisters would be beside themselves about riding on the boat, shrimp boils on the beach, and roasting marshmallows all summer long, but I was more in a severe depression because I had to leave my friends in Manhattan and the subway and the lights and, well, you know, civilization. There were no museums—unless you count that pitiful excuse for a boat warehouse they call a museum. There was no theater—unless you count the high school's horrific performance of *Fiddler on the Roof* or the annual drag queen fashion show. I'll admit, that one was fairly Manhattan. But *Rent* on Broadway it was not.

Most of all, I couldn't stand the idea of missing out on an entire summer's worth of fun and gossip, even if it was just sitting around Jenna Franklin's mom's house when she was at work, talking about boys and painting our toes. All summer, every summer, I missed *everything*. And don't get me started on the year my mom kidnapped us and made me move down there for a whole semester. It was like prison. Well, prison with a good view, I mean.

Looking back, I realize that most of the reason I didn't want to leave Manhattan was that I didn't want people to talk about me when I was gone. I couldn't deal with feeling left out of the circle that I had worked so hard to insert myself into.

Because, I'll admit it, I've always cared a hell of a lot about what other people think. I used to believe it was human nature, but now I've realized it's more akin to the nature of a New York City social climber. I call myself that affectionately, now that I'm back in New York, back in my apartment, back in my old life, yet somehow a completely different person. I've never felt that it was a bad thing to want to better your station in life. Which is why after my father was killed and my mother moved us to Podunk City,

USA, I felt that, geographically and socially, I had moved in the wrong direction in a big way.

I used to thank God every night that I only had to live in that hick hellhole for six months. Only six months before I could escape back to NYU, aka civilization. I got that my mom was scared and all of that after 9/11. But honestly. The city rebuilt. Why couldn't she?

I felt guilty leaving my two sisters to rot there. Emerson especially. She was only a baby, for heaven's sake. Well, I guess ten isn't a baby. But it's young enough that you don't know what you don't know. And what she didn't know was that our selfish mother had taken her out of the city of action and opportunity and dropped her into the cultural desert.

So I made it my life's mission to encourage her passion for art and acting. And I guess somewhere in there, I forgot to work on my middle sister, Sloane. Bless her heart, as those degenerates say with their slow accents, she stayed in the damn place. Went to college in Georgia with all those peaches and practically no teeth. Married a guy in the military, which, I mean, yeah, is admirable and all that.

But we're Murphys. We were destined for greatness.

Greatness was what I thought I was getting when I met James. His hair was great. His plane was great. His 57th Street apartment was great. Even his mother was great. For thirteen whole blissful years, we were great, too. Just great. Until he decided to come home and tell me, six months pregnant, no less, that he was no longer in love with me. He was no longer in love with me, you see, because he was now in love with a twenty-year-old supermodel who subsisted on squeezy applesauce and whipped cream vodka.

This is what you should expect when nothing in your life is ever good enough. You should expect that your husband will eventually trade you in for something better. Truth be told, sometimes I'm surprised I hadn't traded *him* in, as hard as I was scraping to reach the top. But, well, it's harder to climb when you're pregnant in heels.

And so, when I decided to take a short sabbatical with my sweet, beautiful, fated for a Nobel Peace Prize daughter, Vivi, I figured I'd already fallen about as far as I could. Might as well fall all the way down to "my momma's house," as they would say in Peachtree, a town with too many mullets and too few chromosomes.

Had I known that we'd be Murphy, party of eight, I might have rethought my decision. But there are no people in the world to make you realize what a spoiled, selfish bitch you've become and put you right back in your place quite like sisters. All I can say is that for the state I was in, thank God I have two.

the tide rolls in

ansley

I love pretty much every quirky thing about my town. The weird people and the weirder traditions, the over-the-top celebrations and beautiful old homes. I love that I can feel like I am completely at the end of the earth but then, two bridges and twenty minutes later, enter an adjacent town large enough to have everything I need. I thrive on the quiet and privacy of the off-season but the summer vacationers who feel free to photograph my home and sometimes even peek in through my windows have never been my favorite thing.

And Caroline has never been my favorite child. I know that's not nice to say, but it's nicer than saying she's my least favorite child, which is really the truth. I love her to pieces. I'd take a bullet for her. I'd sooner die than see something bad happen to her, and I would never, ever want to live without her. But she is . . . tricky.

So I guess that's why I didn't answer the first time she called. I was in Sloane Emerson, my interior design shop, which, yes, I did name after my other two, more favored children. It's a bit of a family joke, actually. When we moved to Peachtree Bluff, Caroline kicking and screaming in her designer jeans the whole way, I acted casual about opening my store. I acted like it was something I was doing to take my mind off of my beloved husband dying, like it was something I was doing to assert myself. In actuality, I'd had to go back to work because, while we were told we would be receiving millions of dollars in life insurance, we hadn't. I thought it would intensify the general panic and nightmares and PTSD around our new, very large, very potentially haunted home if my girls knew that.

So when I announced that I was getting back into decorating, my darling jewel of a daughter Caroline had said, "Oh, good. I hear the camper-trailer design business is really flourishing right now."

And when I enthused that the business was going so well that I thought I would open a storefront, my sweet-tempered, well-adjusted child snapped, "If you name it Caroline's, I will die."

So I didn't name it Caroline's. I named it Sloane Emerson. It was the first thing I had done in quite some time that my eldest daughter thought was funny.

It was quiet around town that January morning, the tourists hiding wherever they had come from, not to return until April, despite it being my favorite time of year. Maybe it was the temperatures in the mid- to high sixties that made me love the winter so much. Maybe it was that only the locals remained. It was hard to tell.

I was pulling some Pine Cone Hill matelassé samples for two regular clients who needed to spruce up their yachts—in a town of three thousand people, boat owners had become my bread and butter—when the bell above the door rang.

Ah, yes. I would know that beard anywhere. Hippie Hal, reporting for duty.

"What's up, Hal?"

"Oh, not much, Ansley. You know. The tide rolls in, the tide rolls out."

"Sure does, Hal."

This was a part of the morning. Whether it was forty degrees or 140, Hal wore rumpled jeans and a meticulously pressed white oxford. But depending on the heat, he'd layer a few of the shirts. It was his signature look. Hal, who had sold the three McDonald's he owned in Tennessee and headed for the shore, lived in a small house two streets over that was always a subject of heated debate at town meetings. You see, Hal refurbished bicycles, saved them from the landfill, as he put it. So there were always a few on his front lawn to entice tourists ready to bike around town.

And the historical association, Mrs. McClasky in particular, had a fit about it. Every month.

But it took a lot to ruffle Hal, and until she came over in her crop pants and Keds and made him remove those bikes, they were staying put.

In the meantime, Hal made his morning rounds, said hello

to all the shop owners, and rode one of those front-yard bikes back home. He had a big garage. Biggest in town, in fact. I asked him one time, "Hal, why don't you put those bikes in the garage, and then we could quit having to talk about them every single town meeting?"

He got a far-off look in his eye and said, "That's not a bad idea. But you see, here's the problem. If I put those bikes in my garage, Mrs. McClasky wouldn't have anything to do anymore. She'd have no purpose. Then she'd be miserable. And I feel like it's my job to spread happiness wherever I go." He grinned then.

That seemed about right to me.

I smiled at Hal, and he asked, "Want me to send Coffee Kyle down here?"

I nodded, samples in hand. "Sure, Hal. That would be great. I could use a little caffeine." He turned to walk out, and I said, "Hey, Hal. Wait a minute."

"What's that? You need some produce? I can get Kimmy down here, too."

"No. I don't need any produce." I held up two blue shades of matelassé. "Which one do you like better?"

He pointed to the lighter shade on the left. Hippie Hal might have worn a piece of rope as a belt, but the man had taste.

"Boyfriend Sky it is," I said out loud, even though he had gone.

I looked down at the sample again, thinking of Caroline and how I needed to return her call. She would love this matelassé. Maybe I would send her one. Things were good between us now that she had forgiven me for stealing a whole half-year of city life from her, now that she had still married one of the most eligible bachelors in town and had Vivi and this new baby on the way and that big life she had always dreamed of.

I picked up the phone to dial her—my daughters found it hilarious that I still dialed their numbers as often as I searched for their contacts. As I did, I realized that, yet again, my finger joint was sort of sticking when I tried to bend it, like a door swollen from the rain. I had quit doing my Trigger Finger exercises for a couple of days and the annoying condition had come back with a vengeance. I sighed. Aging is not for the faint of heart. Before I could hit the green button, Kimmy walked in. Her hair got weirder and weirder. She had a severe spiky haircut that was half black, half blue. It looked like a Smurf gone Goth.

"Hey, Ansley."

"Kimmy."

"Hal said you wanted Swiss chard?"

This was the only problem with Hal. He was really helpful, except that he had smoked away every brain cell he had long, long ago. Kimmy was the owner of a hydroponic farm, but you didn't have to be part of the Drug Enforcement Administration to put together that vegetables weren't the only thing she was growing hydroponically. Hence the friendship between Hal and her.

"That wasn't me," I said.

"Didn't think so. You hate chard."

I do. I thought of my youngest daughter, Emerson, and smiled. She was in LA pursuing her acting dream, like thousands and thousands of other talented, beautiful women and men. I was proud of her for following her heart, but it still bugged me that she hadn't gone to college. What was she going to do when she got her first wrinkle and lost all job possibilities? She would land on her feet. Probably.

Emerson loved Swiss chard. She put it in the blender with a handful of grapes and half an orange and some ice and thought it was the most delicious thing ever. But that was LA for you.

"That's OK." I pulled a five-dollar bill out of my wallet. "Can you leave me something I do like to cook for dinner?"

I knew what she was going to say, and it annoyed me every day. Every single day. But she asked it anyway, like it was a fresh question. "You eating alone tonight, Ansley?"

I pretended I didn't hear her and said, very loudly, "Coffee Kyle!"

Coffee Kyle was smoking hot. I was a fifty-something-year-old woman whose children would taunt her mercilessly if they heard her utter the phrase "smoking hot." And it was inappropriate for me to think that way about a kid in his mid-twenties. But he was, and there was no way around that. He looked like one of those really versatile actors in the Hallmark movies Emerson had done. He was tall, dark, and handsome and could play the mechanic in one video, the lawyer in the next, and the serial killer in the third without skipping a beat.

"Well, hey there, Miss Ansley. I brought a skinny soy vanilla latte for you today." He winked at me. "Although you don't need the skinny."

I laughed in spite of myself. He really was so cute. Something in his good nature reminded me of Sloane's husband, Adam. I hadn't seen it at first, but Adam was the perfect man for Sloane. She was kind and loving, my easiest child by far. It had hit her the hardest when her father died, made her afraid and, for a while, anxiety ridden. I worried that a man would overpower her, take advantage of her gentle nature. But Adam knew how to love her, how to make her feel safe and special. I always taught my girls that they didn't need a man to save them. They needed to be able to save themselves. And Sloane could. But, confident in the knowledge that she could stand on her own two feet, I adored how Adam had positively swept her off of them.

"So what you got going on today, Miss Ansley?" Kyle asked as I handed him his money and he handed me my latte.

"Page and Stage has a new Southern writer coming in today. I thought I'd run down and pick up her book." I hated TV. I thought it was the downfall of civilization. I didn't have one. So I read. A lot. I guessed I would have to get one when Emerson's next TV movie came out. "Other than that, just work. I've got two new yachts down there I'm designing if you want to go check in on them. I'm sure they'd love some coffee."

He saluted me. "Yes, ma'am. I believe I will."

I was pretty sure that Coffee Kyle was the only barista in the known universe who left his coffee shop wide open and unattended while he made deliveries to his locals. You could buy regular and decaf on the honor system by leaving your dollar in the basket. If you wanted something fancy, Kyle came back every thirty minutes to serve you. But if you lived in town, he knew what you wanted and was probably going to bring it to you anyway, which made it pretty rare to have people in the shop unless they were there for the atmosphere—which, frankly, the place was a little low on, if you asked me.

Kyle hugged me, which was the best part of my day, sadly.

I looked down to see a text from Emerson. Call me when you get a few minutes. That really was strange. It was only seven a.m. in LA. My little Emmy was never up that early. She had probably started some new aerial yoga or zum-barre-lates something or other. I had started to dial her when I heard the bell tinkle yet again and had to end the call.

At first, I thought the man walking through the door was a tourist, which was rare this time of year. He was a little bit over-weight, and had a ruddy, dark complexion, that particular mix-ture of too much sun and too much alcohol that makes a face look aged yet somehow youthful, as though the wearer of said face was still squeezing every square inch of fun out of life. "I'm Sheldon," he said. I instantly remembered the phone conversa-tion from the day before and realized that while, no, he wasn't someone I would call a friend, I had definitely seen Sheldon around.

"Oh, of course," I said, walking out from behind the counter. "The fifty-three Huckins Linwood. Thanks so much for getting in touch with me." Sheldon had called to let me know he had a boat coming in for an extensive rebuild. It had been badly damaged in a recent hurricane off the Florida coast, and Sheldon was one of the foremost experts in the country in its particular make and model. While he was taking care of the structure of things, he asked me if I'd like to come alongside and take care of the, as he put them, "girly parts" of the boat. I would have preferred the term "aesthetic elements," but, quite frankly, it was winter, business was slow, and I could use the cash.

I could tell already that my new buddy Sheldon was a man of few words. He motioned his head to the door and said, "Well, you want to see it?"

"Oh, now?" I said, grabbing for my jacket and hanging my camera around my neck, thinking that now wasn't really great, as I had two daughters to call. But this shouldn't take too long. I could redesign three staterooms and a salon in my sleep.

Little did I know that, after today, sleep wasn't something I would be getting much of for a long, long time.

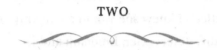

supermodel husband stealer

caroline

I have always, always, for my entire life, wanted to be a mother and nothing more. My sisters find this odd, which I find odd. I mean, sure, I'm honest. But that doesn't make me unmaternal. I don't say things to my daughter Vivi like "Don't eat those Oreos, or you'll turn into a big fat cow." I say things like "Sweetheart, too much sugar isn't healthy for you. It will ruin those beautiful teeth and that perfect complexion." It's still true, but it isn't quite as cutting.

From the time I was a baby, I was always dragging a doll around with me. So when Sloane was born, even though I was only two, I was probably the most excited anyone has ever been. I still remember going to the hospital, climbing into bed with Mom and tiny Sloane, seeing her for the first time, and knowing that my whole life had changed in the best way. Mom says I can't possibly remember. I've just seen so many pictures that I think I remember. But she is wrong. I remember.

Sloane and I have always been close, despite the fact that our lives are scarcely relevant to each other.

So Sloane was the perfect person to drop the bomb on first. She was so selfless. I knew she would soothe my very damaged nerves. We didn't deserve her, Emerson and I.

The problem was, I couldn't quite find a way to tell her about James. Instead, I heard myself saying, "I found this little indoor tent that I thought the boys would love, but I didn't want to spring it on you because I know it will take up a lot of room."

"Oh, they would love that," Sloane gushed. "There's plenty of space in the playroom."

My phone beeped. "Oh, wait!" I said. "There's Emmy." This would be better. I'd tell them together, only have to taste the terrible news in my mouth once. "Hang on a minute, and I'll merge us all together."

"OK," Sloane said. "But don't cut me off, because I have to tell you—"

Too late.

"Hi there, little Em," I said. Oh, I loved that girl.

"The best thing has happened!" You could practically hear her glowing from across the miles.

That could mean that she had downloaded a great new song or had found the best new manicurist. Em was overly dramatic on both sides of the spectrum, which is a good quality for an actress. I've often envied her ability to get so excited over the smallest things, but the joy wouldn't be worth how upset she also gets over practically nothing.

"Hold that thought," I said. "I have Sloane on the other line."

I merged the calls and knew they were both there when I could hear Emerson's giggles and Sloane saying, "I know, love bug. But we don't eat candy in the morning."

The woman was a saint.

I looked out the window of my apartment. The view of Central Park was going to be hard to leave. I still couldn't believe I was actually going to do this, move back to a place I couldn't stand and couldn't get out of fast enough. But I would love to be in a place for a while where no one had ever heard the name Edie Fitzgerald—or at least didn't care who she was. Bitch. With her three feet of shiny black hair and eight-foot-long legs.

"What's going on?" I heard Sloane say.

"I have to leave LA." Emerson practically cheered, although I couldn't figure out why that would be a good thing, unless, of course, she was leaving LA for New York. Then it would be the best move ever.

"Oh, my gosh!" I exclaimed. "I'm leaving New York!"

"What?" Sloane chimed in. "Can you breathe if you aren't in Manhattan?"

When I laughed, it felt like a reflex, not true joy. I knew I could be real with my sisters. I knew I could relay my devastation to them, that they would be able to feel it no matter how nonchalant I acted. But I couldn't go there yet. I had to be strong just a little bit longer. "We'll see," I said breezily. "I'm flying south. I have been the victim of a supermodel husband stealer."

"No!" Emerson gasped. "But Caroline!" Her elation had turned to devastation on a dime. "You're *pregnant*."

The baby kicked right at that moment, as if knowing that he or she was being talked about. I rubbed my belly. I was excited that we didn't know what this one was. We. It was depressing to realize that "we" just meant Vivi and me now. No more James. I felt my throat go thick. Nope. He didn't deserve my tears.

I looked down at my shoes, wondering if they were actually as cute as I'd thought they were in the store. Of course they were, I decided. But once the man who is supposed to be your forever leaves you for a supermodel, you start to doubt every choice you make. What if I've been drinking almond milk but I should have been drinking cashew? What if we find out in twenty years that casein really *is* good for you? Every small decision is suddenly under the microscope, another example of how acutely I have mismanaged our lives.

Because, it's awful to admit, even to myself, but I knew James was having an affair.

I may not be exactly tactful. And there's probably no good way to hear your husband is cheating. But honestly, there had to have been a better way than the one he chose. James sat me down in our sun-filled living room on our white banquette, the one I had gotten from Mom when Vivi was eight and I had finally felt like I could redo the house because she wasn't going to spill chocolate milk—the love of which I am certain she inherited from Sloane—on everything anymore. He took my hand and said, "Baby, I know this isn't the best timing." He looked down at my stomach. I knew what was coming, really, but I tried to avoid it. In those seconds, I pretended that he was going to say he thought we should move or he was going on a big trip the week before my due date or something, anything that would be bad timing except for this.

"I'm so sorry," he said. "And I don't really know how to tell you this. But I'm not in love with you anymore."

I'm not in love with you anymore. I'm not in love with you anymore. It ran through my mind all day, every day, like the refrain of a horrible pop song you wished the radio would quit playing. Twelve years of marriage, thirteen years of being together, an eleven-year-old daughter, another baby on the way. How could he not love me anymore?

Of course, it was only a couple of hours before Jenna Franklin, my "friend," called and said, "Oh, Caroline, I don't know how you're coping. I don't know how you can stand to stay here when he's gallivanting all over town with her."

My heart sank. I couldn't act like I didn't know what was going on. Especially not to *her*. Which was when I said, "Got to run! I'm late to pick Vivi up from swim practice."

It was perfect, because it rubbed in the fact that we were members of Central Park Swim Club, which would not let Jenna in.

So I called my *real* friend, Sarah Peters.

"Is it true?" she asked breathlessly. "Please tell me it isn't true."

"I have no idea," I said. "I am somehow totally in the dark. James has told me he's leaving me. But who is he leaving me for?"

"Oh, Caroline. Please don't make me say."

That was when I knew it had to be one of our friends. Probably that whore Alex Martin. Everyone knew she had only married that old man husband of hers because she was going to have to go back to waiting tables if she didn't find someone soon after her previous husband had caught her cheating with her high school boyfriend. But I always saw the way she eyed James. I actually kind of liked it. Because I believed that he loved me so much he would never leave me.

I was a lot. I knew it. I had a sassy attitude and a bad temper, but I loved him. *Loved* him. And he always said that was what he loved most about me. I challenged him. I put him in his place. I made him work. And the way he looked at me, like I was the only woman in the world . . . Well, let's just say I never imagined that he would do this to me. It made me want to crawl into a hole and die.

But when Sarah said "Edie Fitzgerald," I about fell out.

I mean, James was good-looking, sure. He still worked out every day and had that gray around his temples, which I thought was sexy once a man hit forty or so. Honestly, I only assumed that since he was eleven years older than I was, there was no way he could trade me in for a newer version.

Evidently, I was wrong. Edie Fitzgerald was the hottest up-and-coming model in the city. She was on every billboard in town and a magazine darling. They ate up the fact that she was, ironically, from Georgia.

"And Caroline . . ." Sarah added, keeping her voice conspicu-ously calm, "I found out from my producer friend, you know that one over at HBO?" She cleared her throat. "Well—apparently James is going to appear with Edie on *Ladies Who Lunch*."

When I broke the news to Vivi that night, thinking it was better she hear it from me than those gossipy, middle school socialites-in-training she called friends, the poor thing was to-tally inconsolable. I'd never been much of a shrinking violet, as Grammy would say, but I had a baby to birth in a couple of months and this daughter to tend to, and for God's sake, *Ladies Who Lunch*? The man really had no tact. Unbelievable. Truly. I blamed his mother. I know I said I liked her. But she was the one that made him so weak.

Suddenly this warm, golden feeling washed over me, like I'd been cold in the air-conditioning all day and stepped out-side to warm sun blanketing my body. It hadn't even occurred to me: We could leave. We really could. At least for a little while. I could get out of town, take Vivi. But where to go?

I can't explain why Peachtree Bluff popped into my head. But suddenly, all the things I had hated about it—its tiny size, the quiet streets, my mom not having a TV—seemed incredibly appealing. No TV. Nowhere to watch the damn *Ladies Who Lunch*. It was perfect, actually. I was sure I could talk that sweet headmistress Mrs. Stewart into giving Vivi a spot in her cute private school.

I sat down beside Vivi and rubbed her back. She was lying listlessly on the bed like the brokenhearted ex-girlfriend in some teen movie.

People can say what they want to about me, but I am a terrific mother. I've never doubted that. I momentarily wondered if escaping would be teaching Vivi to run away from her problems. But instead, I realized that running away for a couple of months would help to keep her young just a little bit longer.

"I know this is horrible, sweetheart. And we can talk about it all you want to. There's nothing you can't ask. OK?"

She sat up and nodded. "I hate Dad."

I hate Dad, too. No. I didn't hate James. Not really. Not even in that moment. James had broken my heart. Shattered my world. Shattered my child's world. There was a difference.

"I've been thinking," I said, as though this was an idea I'd been mulling over for months, not the past ninety seconds. "You know how we always say we're going to spend the summer at Gransley's? Go out on the boat, learn to fish, take surfing lessons?"

She nodded sulkily. I couldn't blame the kid.

"Well, what if we do that now? We could spend the spring there instead."

She jumped up and threw her arms around my neck. "Mom! No, you're kidding me!"

I shook my head. "I am not kidding you. Not at all. Every good New York girl knows when to take a break from the fast pace."

She squealed. "You are the best mom in the whole world."

I relayed the entire scene to Sloane and Emerson on the phone that day and was met with total silence on the other end, suddenly punctuated by a loud sob. I rolled my eyes. Oh, Emerson. "Look," I said, "I love you both, and we'll have plenty of time for family therapy, but right now, I need to keep it together and just get home. OK?"

Nothing.

"Guys, I mean it. I can't fall apart, for Vivi's sake."

"OK." Emerson sniffed.

I heard Sloane take a deep breath. "I understand, Caroline."

She paused. I could tell, even from across the miles, that there was so much she wanted to say. It was killing her.

But instead of grilling me, Sloane said, "Wait. Emerson, why are you leaving LA?"

"Oh, right," she said, sniffing again. "I'm filming in Atlanta and around Georgia for a few months. I found this awesome town house to rent."

This was the best news I'd heard in a long time. Maybe this wouldn't just be the pathetic divorcée coming home. It would be fun sisterly bonding. "Wait! No! You should come live in Peachtree Bluff, too!"

"Well . . ."

She sounded skeptical. "Come on, Emerson," I coaxed. "It will be so fun. We can paddleboard and swim and go over to Starlite Island like old times."

"You guys know I have major FOMO," Sloane said.

"You should bring the kids for a couple of weeks," Emerson said. "To visit Caroline, Vivi . . ." She paused dramatically. "And me!"

"Yay!" I cheered.

"Actually," Sloane said, "Adam just got deployed for nine months."

"Oh, Sloane," I said, feeling my heart break for my sister. I didn't know how she did it. "Un-yay."

I could hear the tears in Emerson's voice as she said, "Sloane, no. Not again."

"Girls," Sloane said. "Yes. Again. This is his career. Buck up." In this regard, Sloane was just like me. She never let anyone see her sweat.

"So you come, too!" I said. "Bring the kids, and come to Peachtree Bluff. It will be like a fun sisters' retreat!"

"I guess I could," Sloane said. "At least for a month or so. That will be so much better than sitting around here worrying by myself."

That was when my heart began to race. Mom's guesthouse was plenty big for Vivi, the new baby, and me. It had two stories; the upstairs had two bedrooms, and the downstairs had one, with its own kitchen and living room. It was almost as big as our apartment in New York.

But if Emerson and Sloane were coming home, I wouldn't be the only one who wanted that prime location. And now it was more essential than ever, because if I didn't get the guesthouse, Sloane's germ-ridden children would be near my baby all the time. I couldn't have that happening. I cringed at the mere thought of those noses, always a little runny like the drip hoses Mom kept on her roses.

"Girls," I said casually, "don't worry a bit. We will stay in the guesthouse so no one has to hear any of that pesky middle-of-the-night crying."

There was a long pause. I knew Sloane wouldn't say anything. And what could Emerson say? It wasn't like she could justify taking the guesthouse with its three bedrooms when she didn't have any children.

But I didn't want to risk it. So I said, "Oh, my goodness. I have to run. My lawyer is calling."

I hit *End* abruptly. I hadn't hired a lawyer, so my lawyer wasn't calling. But my credit cards were. Better put those babies to good use before the separation was finalized.

In reality, I was lucky. James couldn't cut me off. New York was a fault state, and he had cheated on me. Even if the settlement didn't go the way I thought, I knew I had the nest egg Dad had left for us to fall back on.

I felt it again. That lump in my throat. I cleared it. Only three shopping hours left before Vivi would be home from a birthday party. A spa birthday party. I rolled my eyes. I'm not sure I had realized how ridiculous our lives had become.

It was increasingly evident that we needed to get to Peachtree. And fast. Plus, I had to stake my claim to that guesthouse before anyone else could.

It occurred to me, briefly, that I didn't know what Emerson's new role was. No matter. I'd find out soon enough. Maybe she would get to play the lead this time. Maybe this would be her big break.

I wondered briefly if you actually recognized your big break as it was happening to you or if it was only in hindsight.

Then I grabbed my tote and walked out the door, calling the mover to pack up all our things as I did. Really, when you thought about it, this was going to be the best thing that ever happened to my mom. She obviously didn't have anything going on in that sleepy town of hers.

It was a sucky time any way you sliced it. But it made it a little bit better to think that Mom was going to be so happy.

THREE

this side of the mason-dixon

ansley

I'm not sure why my grandmother chose to leave her Peachtree Bluff home to me. It didn't make sense that she wouldn't have left it to her children. Or at least to all of her grandchildren. I've never been quite so shocked as when my mom told me the news after the funeral, with a bit of a put-off air, that I was the new owner of the Peachtree compound. My cousins never went to Peachtree anyway, but my brothers, Scott and John, did. Scott, in true Scott fashion, couldn't have cared less. He was off on his next adventure before it had time to be a blip on his radar screen. But John had a fit.

It was so childish, as though I had gone to Grandmother and begged her to leave me the house, as though I had tricked her into rewriting her will and held the pen while she was doped up on morphine. I had no control over her actions and promised my siblings and cousins that they could use the house anytime they wanted to. But that wasn't enough for John. In fact, he quit speaking to me altogether for quite some time. Over the years, I had received a terse sympathy phone call from him when Carter was killed and had talked to him a few other times. I thought it would blow over quickly, be no big deal. My brother was going to disown me over a *house*? It didn't seem possible. But he had. Since the day after Grandmother's funeral, nothing much between us had changed.

In similar fashion, I was pretty sure nothing about this boat had changed since 1974 when it was built—at least, nothing for the better.

This was a beautiful old motor yacht, no doubt about that. If it had been a house I would have said it had great bones. But houses didn't have to float on water. Or run. I was unconvinced that this once-proud vessel could competently do either.

The white boat had huge flecks of paint missing from its sides and two of the windows were broken.

"Yikes."

"Bad hurricane," Sheldon said, unconcerned.

I could tell from the look on his face that this project meant a lot to him.

"Hey there, Ansley, Sheldon," I heard Dockmaster Dan call from behind us. It really was uncanny. It was as though you had to have a name that would alliterate well with your chosen profession in order to live here. No one could believe I wasn't an architect. Kimmy had been Kale Kimmy for an entire hour. But she wasn't having it. And she has a lot of tattoos, which makes people uneasy. So everyone dropped it.

"Good morning, Dan. Looks like you've got a full house today." He was tall and sinewy, as darkly tanned as Sheldon with deep lines accentuating his face. He was wearing a hat that said, "No Thinkin', Just Drinkin'." Charming.

"Sure do," he said. "If I get any rich-looking ones I'll send 'em your way."

I laughed.

"Got you a doozy here," Dan said. "But she'll be right purty when you get her all shined up."

Sheldon only nodded.

"Am I safe to climb on?" I asked.

"Oh, yeah," Sheldon said. "She won't bite ya."

"I was more worried about falling through the deck."

Sheldon said nothing but helped me climb aboard, so I could only assume that he felt safe. Inside, the carpet was mildewed, and the captain's chair was missing. A thin layer of silt covered everything from the teak-and-stainless steering wheel to the berths where mattresses should have been. Everything in the galley had a singed look about it. I looked at Sheldon questioningly.

"Small kitchen fire," he said.

I shook my head. "Poor girl." Then added, "Who in his right mind would buy this thing?"

Sheldon grinned. "Nobody said he's in his right mind."

We both laughed.

"I'll be back," Sheldon said. "But you take your time."

"What about the owner?" I asked. "Shouldn't I get an idea of what he wants?"

Sheldon looked at me like I was dense and "girly parts" passed through my mind again. "Right," I said. "He probably doesn't care what it looks like. But he does probably care what it costs."

Sheldon nodded. "Yup. I'll see if I can round him up. Ain't like there are too many places to hide in this town." He laughed.

I took a moment to pull out my phone and call Emerson. "Mom!" she said breathlessly. "I have the best news!"

I've learned over the past couple decades or so, ever since Emerson became competent at speaking in full sentences, that sometimes her "best news" and my "best news" were different. So I took it in stride in case the news was that a new juice bar opened up right across the street from her.

"Well, don't keep me in suspense, love bug!" I ran my hand across the shelf in the master stateroom. My hand was black. Yuck.

"I got the lead in a new TV movie. You'll love it. It's so Southern."

I gasped. This was a dream come true for my Emmy. I knew that. I was, as I think mothers often are, ambivalent at best about her becoming famous. But it was what she wanted. And so, again, as mothers do, I reveled in her joy. "Emerson, no! That is amazing!" This was so much better than the juice bar opening I had anticipated.

"Mom, that's not even the best part."

I was crouching down, peeking into the kitchen cabinets hesitantly, afraid of what might potentially jump out at me. The teak had been immaculate. You could tell that. But they would all need to be replaced. "What's the best part, sweetie?"

"We're filming in Georgia. I'm coming home for like six months!"

"Wow!" I said, feeling excited but also a little nervous. I hadn't had a child living with me in quite some time. "That's great."

"We're all coming," she said, and for a brief second, I had an image of the entire cast of her new movie bunking with me. Until she added, "Mom, it's bad. Adam is getting deployed again and Caroline's husband left her"—her voice broke—"for Edie Fitzgerald."

"Oh my gosh," I said. Even *I* knew who Edie Fitzgerald was. That was really saying something. "What happened? Is she OK? Is she getting divorced? Is Vivi OK—"

"Mom," Emerson interrupted. "I don't know any of that."

"Right. Sorry. But all of you means all of my girls?"

My heart began to race. I was stressed and sad for Caroline, worried for Sloane, excited for Emerson. Everything.

"And the kids, too!"

"Amazing," I said. "I need to go call Caroline, hon."

"Yeah," she said. "But she doesn't want to talk about it, just so you know. She said she has to be tough until she gets home."

I nodded, though Emerson couldn't see. I stood up, not wanting to notice the creak in my knees as I did, and looked out the window to the glittering sea beyond.

"Okay, Em. Well, I love you. Let me know when you're planning to arrive."

"Love you too, Mom."

Before I could even dial Caroline, my phone buzzed in my hand.

Caroline: You were right. That asshole James is going to be on TV with his supermodel girlfriend. Vivi wants to start school there this semester. We call the guesthouse. Don't call me. I can't talk about it until I get home.

Now I really felt like a heel for not answering Caroline's call. Of course, all I wanted to do was talk to her. But I understood her point of view. When you call your mom, you fall apart. She couldn't fall apart. My heart was breaking for her. And for Vivi. And the new baby. So many questions. I just needed to get her home.

And I didn't hate James. I simply knew he was trouble from the start. But mothers don't say "I told you so." Well, at least the good ones. Instead, we bring our children home, soothe their wounds, and tell them how wonderful they are until they're ready to go back into the world. And so that was what I would do. Gladly. But that didn't keep a tiny feeling of uncertainty from creeping in. Things between Caroline and me could be great or not so great. I realized I had been holding my breath when I exhaled while reading the next message.

Caroline: At Barney's. Bringing you a new wardrobe. And new antiaging skin-care line. When I saw you a few weeks ago, you looked . . . tired. And 50. Need to spruce up.

I shook my head. *Oh, Caroline.* I was actually fifty-eight, so I didn't think looking fifty was such a bad thing. Caroline viewed my aging with disdain like older children viewed younger children's youth and ridiculed them for it. It wasn't something we could help, but it was distasteful nonetheless.

I laughed. No doubt about it. For better or worse, my simple life as I knew it was over. I didn't care what she said. She was my daughter, and I was calling her. I felt like I needed to hear her voice.

I walked out onto the deck. The teak stain was peeling and damaged, but this part was salvageable. The sun was so bright it took my eyes a few minutes to adjust, and I couldn't see the screen of my phone at all. As I was telling Siri, "Call Caroline," I saw someone walking down the dock, toward the boat. I figured it must have been the owner. As he got closer I almost thought he looked like . . .

"Oh my God, Jack," I said. The phone slipped out of my hand and fell to the deck with a crunch.

Because that's what happens when your heart stops beating.

"Ansley?"

The blood was rushing to my face so fiercely I couldn't hear anything but my own heartbeat in my ears. But it registered with me that he definitely wasn't expecting to see me, either. Jack was as shocked as I was.

"What are you doing here?" I asked, too frantic and frazzled to worry that my face was, I was certain, a telltale shade of beet. But his was a ghastly white, so we were even.

"This is my boat," he said. "I just picked it up and brought it to Sheldon to be reconstructed."

I thought about saying something witty about the boat. Wanted to. Tried to. But nothing would come out. So then I tried for something, if not witty, at least normal. Maybe, "How are you?" But the words were stuck in my throat. I felt light-headed, like I couldn't breathe.

All I could think of was the last time I had seen Jack, decades earlier, and the last words I had said to him: *You can't flip the script on me now, Jack. You agreed to this. This is what you asked for. You didn't want children, I did. We couldn't be together. Remember? I have Carter. I'm happy. I have a whole life. I won't let you ruin it.*

I'll never forget the way he looked at me that day, the sun beating down on half of his face. Betrayed. That was the best way to describe it. As though I had taken all of our history, all of our years together, all of our past and used it to slap him across the face.

"I'm not going to ruin your life, Ansley," he had said, emotion lacing his voice. "I love you far too much to ever hurt you." I remember sadness being in there, maybe a touch of anger, an incredulousness that made me feel terribly guilty.

That last moment hung between us. No, not hung. Stood. Grew as tall and dense and wide as a cinderblock wall.

All I could do all those years ago was run away. I hadn't even been able to let him finish talking, to have an adult conversation, because everything in my body was telling me to run. And so I did. I ran then and I knew I would run now. I picked up my phone, which was, predictably, shattered into a million pieces, and rushed past him, walking quickly down the dock.

I could see Sheldon just ahead, and as I passed him, I

called, "You're going to have to find someone else to take the job."

He didn't say anything. I wanted to run but I also wanted to breathe, so I settled on the fastest I could walk until I got to my house where, finally, I sat down on the brick front steps, closed my eyes, put my hand on my heart, and focused on deep, slow breaths.

I had almost calmed down when I realized that Jack was here. Jack was in Peachtree Bluff, only blocks away from my house. My girls were coming home, I remembered. Jack and my girls would both be here for who knew how long. And I had only one thought: I had to get him out of here.

FOUR

a normal life

caroline

I was the first person to realize there was something special about Emerson. Or I was, at least, the first person to admit that I knew there was something special about Emerson. She was always so talented. She had this presence about her even as a child. When Emerson walked into a room, everyone turned to look.

But she wasn't only beautiful; she was smart as a whip, too. We were all good in school, all made good grades, but Em was on a whole different level. Like when I was in high school and had to memorize Shakespeare's sonnets, she would memorize them, too, much faster than I ever could, and then act them out, preparing her own monologues. I always knew she was going to be famous.

Whenever I would say that, my mom would brush it off. I could never figure out why she suppressed Emmy's talent, so finally, one day, I asked her.

She sighed, sitting at the kitchen table in our apartment, hands wrapped around a coffee mug. "I just don't want her out there in the world, in the spotlight. It's such a hard place to be. A normal life is so much easier."

"But Mom," I said, "a normal life is so boring." I paused. "I know you grew up in the South, and it's sleepy and quaint and all that. But you're raising New Yorkers. We are going to be different."

Ansley Murphy was not the kind to be swayed by her children, but I noticed that when Emerson asked to try out for the school play, this time she didn't say no. And I noticed that when Emerson got the lead role as the littlest angel, even though she was only nine and there were ten- and eleven-year-olds vying for the part, Mom was proud of her.

So proud, in fact, that she let Sloane and me skip school that early morning to see Emerson's dress rehearsal. I still can't think about it without feeling sick. She was up there, acting her little heart out, and even though she was my sister, she wasn't, you know? She became that littlest angel who didn't want to leave her earthly home. The only sad thing was that Dad, who was supposed to be there, had an emergency at work and couldn't leave. But he promised Mom he would go to the show the next night.

It was more of a poignant moment than any of us could have imagined.

When Mom's phone rang, Sloane and I gave her the evil eye. She wouldn't let us have cell phones, and hers was going off in the middle of Emmy's play. She picked it up and rushed out the door.

I looked questioningly at Sloane and started to get an uneasy feeling in the pit of my stomach.

You could hear this murmur in the audience and then people starting to get up. At first, I thought it was so rude, these people ignoring my little sister's Tony-worthy performance. But then I realized it wasn't only rude. It was concerning.

I walked out into the front lobby of the school, and everywhere people were on their phones, chattering and gesticulating wildly with their hands.

Mom was saying, "I understand, but I think you should try to get out of there. It isn't safe. It can't be safe." It was the first time I had ever seen my always calm and pulled-together mother on the border of hysteria. "I love you," she said. "Please come home. The girls and I are going now."

Then the lights came back on in the auditorium, and I still didn't know what was happening, but I knew it wasn't good. I ran up to the stage and grabbed Emmy, who looked bewildered in her wings and halo. She was too big to carry on my hip, but I did anyway, Sloane following close behind. We found Mom, which was when I finally said, "What is going on?"

"A plane hit the World Trade Center," she said. "But it was the other tower. Dad is OK," she added, her voice sounding confident, her face betraying that she was anything but. "And we are all going home."

We didn't understand yet what had really happened. At least, Sloane, Emmy, and I didn't. I brushed it off, like *Oh, that's weird. How would a plane hit the World Trade Center? It must have been flying too low.* I remember my mom calling the airline and learning that all flights going in and out were canceled. I know now that she had a bad feeling and she wanted to get us all out of the city. But when she found out that she couldn't, she took my hand and Sloane's, something she hadn't done in years. I was still holding Emerson, who was a good fifty-five pounds by then. At my barely 110, I can't explain how I carried her, with the blush on those tiny cheeks, for the five blocks from school to home.

I remember the astonishment in her big blue eyes. Even back then, you could tell that she was the most beautiful one. As vain as I was, it didn't bother me. She was my pet. I was proud that she was beautiful. I felt like somehow, when people stopped on the street to comment about how stunning she was, it was as though I had done something good.

We didn't know what was going to happen. In fact, looking back now, I wish we could have stayed on that sidewalk, me holding Emmy, Mom holding our hands, forever. We could have stayed in that moment and never gotten to the next one. Our lives would never be shattered. Our daddy would get to come home. And Emmy, my little Emmy, could stay that sheet-and-tinsel-clad angel for the rest of her life.

miss fancy pants

ansley

Every Wednesday since what must be the beginning of time it-self, Peachtreeans have gathered in the parish hall of St. Timothy's church for the town meeting. But the year when Jackson Thomp-son was mayor—note how I say *year*, singular—he decided that a parish hall was too religious a place to hold a town meeting. It conflicted with the idea of separation of church and state.

The only problem was that Peachtree Bluff was a tiny place. There weren't many buildings that could hold so many of us. So Jackson decided to start holding the meetings in the park downtown. Everyone would bring his or her own lounge chair and enjoy the beautiful weather. The day of the first meeting, it rained, so everyone had to sit under umbrellas. For the second meeting, there were so many mosquitoes that ev-eryone left looking like he or she had the measles. We all joked that God was mad that we had moved from St. Timothy's and sent a modern-day swarm of locusts. By the third meeting, it had turned chilly. That was when Jackson Thompson decided that maybe the parish hall wasn't so bad after all. You see, holding weekly meetings outside with no backup plan for weather or other unforeseen situations is not a good idea.

It's also not a good idea to make a giant scene when you are solidly middle-aged if you would rather not obsess about said scene for days. Unable to sleep, I got up at five a.m. It was a chilly morning, so I put on the leggings and long-sleeved tee I paddled in when it was too cold for a swimsuit.

The quiet, still water eased my mind. This was what I loved most about the winter in Peachtree Bluff. The water was so clear and slick it looked almost like a painting. At night, if you didn't know it was there, you might walk right into it thinking it was a continuation of the street. Usually, when I wanted to do my morning yoga outdoors I paddled over to Starlite Island, right across from my house. But I needed to go farther this morning, clear my mind, let the tide carry my troubles away, transform my thoughts from a roaring bundle of waves into a slick, crestless calm.

I looked at my watch. The tide should be low enough now that I would have hours. The tide always lent me serenity. It was constant, changeless. Every day it had its highs and its lows, but, like clockwork, it continued on. That was how I needed to be too. Sometimes low, sometimes high, but always steady. Always there for my children. Always there for my friends. The constant in other people's lives. That was my role. I knew how to play it well.

As the sun began to rise I bumped my paddleboard into the sandbar. I knew I could kiss my little board goodbye because as soon as the girls got here . . . Well, no matter. I'd rather have them than the paddleboard—or the defined arms and core it had lent me. It crossed my mind that this sandbar was where I'd first met Jack. But this sandbar held a million good memories, past and present. And it would hold a million more. I convinced myself that it wasn't Jack that had led me there that morning, that it wasn't thoughts of how much he loved to fish here at sunrise that had beckoned me.

Saluting the sun as the sun rose was perhaps the most cleansed a human could get. Inhale, rise up, exhale, swan dive forward, inhale, plank, exhale, chaturanga, inhale, up dog, exhale, down dog. And so on and so forth, as if I was the one helping the sun to chart its course into the sky. I have always been able to lose myself in that combination of body and breath. And I have always been able to find myself once again along a stretch of sand surrounded by water.

The puttering of a small engine didn't cause my thoughts to wander. I simply incorporated it into my motion and my mantra. It was as natural a sound as the birds calling or the waves crashing, as much a part of life on the water as any other.

I looked up to see a small craft coming toward my sandbar that was quite unlike any I had ever seen before. It was the size and shape of a paddleboard, but with shallow sides, a tiny engine, a Carolina blue Yeti cooler for a seat, a lovely teak steering wheel and rod holders behind the cooler. It was small and functional, but even I knew it was very, very expensive.

As the boat came closer, I started to wonder . . . It couldn't be. Certainly not.

Only, it was. Jack didn't notice me. I considered slipping away unseen, paddling silently home. I was mortified over how I had acted when I had seen him last. But I found myself watching as he opened his cooler, removed a fish, baited his hook, and cast. It was a gentle motion, a smooth one, a rhythmic one, with as much finesse as my own yoga flow. I remembered the days that I spent baiting hooks with Jack, offshore or in. I never cared much for fishing. But I did care for Jack. And there was a time when I would have done most anything to be close to him.

As I remembered, he turned and, finally, saw me. He laughed. What else could you do, really? But he stopped before the sound fully escaped, reeling it back into his mouth. He didn't say anything and neither did I. We both just looked. It should have felt incredibly odd, standing there in the silence. But there was something about the stillness of that morning that you couldn't bear to interrupt, something that felt natural about our quiet.

"I swear I won't try to talk to you," he said finally. "You can go. I'll pretend like I didn't even see you."

I looked for the sarcasm, but found none. That wasn't Jack. Not now. Not ever. There had been times I wanted him to be angry with me, times he certainly should have been. But, mostly, to a fault, he was kind. My face flushed with the memory of my running away. Coming face to face with the man that featured so prominently in the highlight reel of my past had caught me so off guard, so unprepared. I had imagined seeing him again for years, what that moment would be like. I never would have anticipated acting that way. I noticed that my heart was beating only a little wildly now, which was growth. Yoga must have calmed me.

"I'm sorry I acted like that," I said. "It was awful of me. I was just so surprised."

He ventured a small smile. "You and me both."

"Yeah?"

He nodded. "Truth be told, I was glad you ran away. I felt like I couldn't breathe when I saw you."

I could feel my heartbeat relaxing back to normal. "Me, too."

I took a few steps until I was close enough to see his face. It still had that childish roundness to it, and his eyes were still measured, steady, black as ink stains.

Jack grinned at me. That same old grin like we were teenagers sneaking out to smooch on the dock. But we weren't. We were all grown up now. I wasn't sure why, but it pained me to remember that.

"How are you?" I asked, cheering in my mind that I had said something, anything normal.

He nodded. "Fine. You?"

I shrugged. "The girls are coming home."

He smiled. "How wonderful." He looked out at his line. "Ansley, listen. We have each lived a lifetime since we last saw one another. There's nothing that hasn't changed." He paused. "Well, I mean, I still have great hair, but otherwise . . ." We both laughed, and I could have hugged him for lightening the moment. "Sheldon is redoing my boat. I'd love it if you'd decorate it while I'm here. It would make my life so much easier."

My face moved in a way that made us both know that I was about to say "no."

"You don't even have to see me," he said. "You can do whatever you want."

I didn't say anything, and he added, "Sheldon says you're the best yacht designer this side of the Mason-Dixon."

I put my hands on my hips. "You mean he thinks there are better ones on the other side of the Mason-Dixon?"

I think that's when we both knew I was going to say yes. I sighed. "I'll come look at it later in the week." I added under my breath, "I'll show Sheldon which side of the Mason-Dixon is better."

Jack laughed. We both saw the tug on his line. The way he moved when reeling it in was so familiar that, for an instant, it was as if we had rewound the clock forty years.

"I hope you caught a good one," I said.

He reeled it in, glanced at it, and then held his gaze on me a little too long as he said, "Oh, I did."

My mind was miraculously still as I paddled home. Once inside, I didn't have long to consider the ramifications of Jack being in Peachtree before my phone beeped. From beneath the glass screen cover that my store manager, Leah, had given me to keep my fingers from looking as though I had taken them to a mandolin until I could get to the phone store, I saw: Caroline: Plane leaving in 5. Flight 791. Will grab an Uber when we get there.

I laughed. *Grab an Uber.* Oh, that child. Did she honestly think we had Uber here? I checked her flight status and saw that she and Vivi would be arriving in an hour and a half.

I texted Leah: Any chance you could open today? My daughter is arriving at 10:30 . . .

She pinged back immediately: Sure. Be there at quarter to 10.

The good thing about a town this small was that you couldn't live more than a ten-minute walk from anywhere. So when you needed someone, it didn't take long to track her down.

I turned the shower on, stepping onto the mosaic marble tile, the steam fogging the solid glass door. I didn't think of it often, but this morning I remembered the putrid harvest-gold color this entire bathroom had been. After Carter's death, when we moved here, I didn't have the money to change it. I think Sloane started to realize then that something was up. But not Caroline. She was so wrapped up in being mad at me—to deflect the pain and anguish of her father dying in such a sudden and gruesome way, I think—that she hadn't realized my spending habits had drastically changed.

At least her bathroom tile was white. I would have heard about that, too.

I felt that familiar pain around my heart even thinking about that time in my life, that pulsating feeling like it was literally breaking in two. It was a feeling I had never known until Carter died, one I had believed to be something that sounded romantic, a figment of some gifted writer's imagination. But once you've felt it, once you know what it's like for your emotional pain to be so deep that it becomes physical, you never forget it. Nearly every day for sixteen years, I had felt that pain. Not all day every day, like I once did. But every day, in some small way, that pain was there.

I tied my hair up on top of my head to avoid getting it wet while I washed my body. There was no time for drying and styling. The airport was thirty minutes away, and more than anything, I needed coffee. And maybe a little bit of Kyle. But definitely coffee.

I stepped out of the shower and stood in front of my mirror, examining the lines around my eyes and mouth, pulling and poking at them a bit, wondering if I should try some of those fillers my best friends Sandra and Emily were always raving about, immediately deciding I couldn't possibly watch a needle coming at my face. I took longer than usual with my makeup, knowing that it would be heavily criticized by Caroline no matter how good I thought it looked. I believed in my heart that she was trying to help. But our lives didn't remotely resemble each other. She was a New York City socialite. I designed beach houses in flip-flops. We were apples and oranges.

While I was getting ready, I instructed Siri, "Call Mom."

Much to my surprise, Siri did call Mom, as opposed to getting directions to the mall or searching the Web for pillows.

"Hello-o," Mom sang.

"Hi, Mom." I loved it when she was chipper like this. "How's Florida?"

"Darling, Florida is as fabulous as ever. It's warm, it's sunny, the eligible men keep coming."

I laughed. That was the difference between my mom and me. After my dad died, she was sad, of course. She did her year as the dutiful mourning widow, and then she got back in the saddle. I, on the other hand, had spent sixteen years too paralyzed to move forward.

"Well, you won't believe this," I said.

"Try me."

I swiped blush on my cheeks, thinking that my mom and my daughter would both be happy about that. "All three of the girls are coming home."

She laughed. "You're kidding me. Are you happy? Terrified?"

I paused. "Yes."

We both laughed.

"I heard James was going to be a television star," Mom said.

I cleared my throat. "Um. Yeah. You could say that."

"Oh, darling," she said. "This, too, shall pass. I'll come down to visit while all my girls are there."

I heard a muffled sound in the background, followed by "Oh, goodness. I'm almost late for bridge. Love you!"

"Love you, too," I said. But she was already gone.

I wondered how she did it. I worried about my children and my life and what was going to happen every minute. She had never seemed terribly concerned about any of it. I had definitely gotten the worrying from my dad. And then, with no warning, in the midst of my smile, there it was again, that tinge of resentment, that tiny stab that made me realize I still wasn't over it. I still hadn't fully forgiven my mother.

As I stepped out the back door, shutting it behind me and not bothering with the key—no one in Peachtree locked their doors, as there was no reason to—I stopped dead in my tracks. Standing at the door to the screened porch was Mr. Solomon, aka the neighbor from hell. He had on khakis and a short-sleeved, button-down, lime-green shirt. I could see a sleeveless undershirt beneath it. He had his pants pulled up high enough that his stomach protruded from between his belt and his pant legs like a basketball half stuck in the sand. He was nearly bald and had these wet, beady eyes that always reminded me of a lizard. I couldn't stand the man. Truly.

I consider myself to be a nice person. But even I have my limits. And Mr. Solomon was my limit. "I don't have time today for whatever sort of ambush this is, Mr. Solomon. I have to pick up my daughter at the airport." I smiled wickedly at him. "In fact, all three of my daughters and my three, soon to be four, grandchildren will be here for months and months. Doesn't that sound great to you? The sounds of children's laughter in the yard again?" So no, I wasn't sure I was 100 percent enthused about the idea of having them all under one roof. But making Frank Solomon mad had to be a silver lining.

I swear he snarled. "Ansley, you keep your sprinkler water out of my yard."

This might have been the stupidest complaint yet. "Oh, you

mean the dirt lot behind your house where nothing can live? Sure. I'll make sure nothing touches that. We wouldn't want to go crazy and let a blade of grass grow or anything."

He cut his eyes at me. "I mean it. I will call Bob."

Bob had been mayor for forty-seven years, except for that one lost year where we'd taken a chance on Jackson the meeting mover. And Bob had had the hots for my mom for all of those years, thank goodness. So he always took my side in these squabbles with Mr. Solomon.

I crossed my arms. "That's good news for me, Frank, because you know he always agrees with me."

"Not when I have the law on my side, Miss Fancy Pants."

I laughed. "Yeah. Because there is a law saying my sprinkler water can't hit your lawn. Don't worry. I'll keep the water on my side of the fence." Peachtree had so many inane rules there probably *was* a law saying that.

His beady eyes got beadier. He turned around and walked the two dozen steps between his house and mine.

One of the things I loved most about Peachtree was how close together the houses were. It was a historic town, and the homes were built side by side for protection and safety back in the pirate days. Each home had a picket fence around its front yard. To increase the privacy and create defined parking, I had also added a picket fence around the back.

Mr. Solomon and I had never been friendly, exactly. He would gripe about our construction noise keeping him up, bemoan that a painter left a cigarette butt in his yard. But we weren't sworn enemies or anything—until the fence.

He claimed that the fence was five inches over his property line. I said my survey said it was inside mine. Which it was, by the way. Most people would have let it go. What's five inches, for heaven's sake? But not Mr. Solomon.

He served me with a certified letter from his attorney. I served him with one right back from my attorney, saying that if he wanted to pay for a new survey, I would consider moving my fence.

He wouldn't pay. I wouldn't move. And we'd been fighting about it ever since. That was fourteen years ago. No amount of yoga or meditation could make it so that my insides didn't seethe every time he shuffled out his back door. I wished I could handle it more like Hal handled Mrs. McClasky and those bikes. But I just couldn't. The man drove me up the wall. It was so stupid to the outside world. I realized that. But it felt very personal and extremely irritating to me.

I consoled myself with the fact that Mr. Solomon had to die someday. So far, it wasn't looking good. He had to be nearly eighty-five. And I still saw him leave his house every day, with his insipid yippy dog, for a walk. I immediately felt guilty. It wasn't the dog's fault. The dog was adorable. In fact, sometimes I had fantasies of kidnapping little Biscuit and rescuing her from her terrible owner. But she'd be pretty hard to hide right next door.

I knew Mr. Solomon had to be lonely over there all by himself. He rarely had visitors. And I would have been nice to him, taken him dinner, had him over for a glass of wine, if he wasn't such a vile little man.

I got into the car and cranked the ignition. It was 9:42. Damn it! Now I had missed the window when Kyle was back at the coffee shop to make my latte. Mr. Solomon was going to pay for this.

I pulled up in front of the coffee shop anyway. It was one in a row of smaller white clapboard houses on a side street that had been converted into commercial space. I walked into the plain, one-room shop. It had built-in banquettes around the picture windows, small tables and chairs scattered throughout the back, and a simple counter running down the side. The walls were bare, weathered shiplap. Oh, how I longed to accessorize them. I expected to find the honor jar for my plain, boring coffee. No foam, no whip, no pizzazz.

Instead, I found a note from Kyle. "Check the microwave, Ans. Heat for exactly 27 seconds."

I almost cheered when I saw that latte waiting for me. And just like that, the calm and happy I had cultivated on the water that morning returned. I slid a ten-dollar bill into the slit in the locked cash register drawer. Kyle deserved an extra tip for this one. As I stepped back out onto the sidewalk, into the warm morning sun, and said hi to several neighbors walking by, it hit me that I had done this all on my own. I had created a new life for my girls and for myself. But as I took a sip of the perfect latte, I had to consider that just because I had done it on my own didn't mean I had to do it on my own forever.

come hell or high water

caroline

When I had left New York that morning, the group text from Sloane and Emerson chiming happily about how much fun we were going to have, all the great things we were going to do, had bolstered my spirits and helped me walk out that door. But simply stepping into the airport in Georgia a few hours later made me realize what a mistake this had been. Two gates. Almost no way out. But then I looked over at Vivi. She was smiling ear to ear like I hadn't seen her do in quite some time.

"Mom, it's so warm," she said. "Isn't that awesome?"

Or eerie, I thought. It was January. Shouldn't it be colder? It wasn't tropical or anything. But it was at least in the high sixties, which was practically balmy considering we had left that morning in our down parkas.

"I hope our stuff gets here tonight," I said. Vivi and I had packed only enough clothes for a couple of days.

The fear that I had perhaps kidnapped my child rippled through me. An image of an AMBER Alert ran through my mind. But no, I was sure James would be too busy with Edie Fitzgerald to notice that we were gone.

"Me, too," Vivi said. "I can't wait to give Gransley all the stuff we got her!"

I nodded. "She'd better be able to fit into it." I could not tolerate it when women got older and started putting on weight and blamed it on their metabolism. Um, yeah. Your metabolism changed. So eat less. Work out more.

Vivi shot me a look. "Mom, I'm not sure you can talk right now."

I put one hand on my hip as I walked toward the door. Yes. The door. Which you could see from the gate. It was kind of hilarious. "Excuse me. I am growing your brother or sister. I am still in size two maternity clothes, I'll have you know." But honestly, being pregnant was the only time I didn't obsess about my weight. I wanted my baby to be healthy even more than I wanted to be sample-size thin. That was really saying something.

We walked out into the sunny day, and you could almost taste the salt in the air. The humidity wrapped around me and clung to my skin like a toddler who didn't want to be left at preschool.

I pulled out my phone and hit the Uber app. Something I'd never seen popped up on the screen: Uber not available in your area. I toggled back to the home screen and tried again.

"What is this?" I asked, genuinely stunned.

Vivi took the phone from me. She rolled her eyes. "Mom, seriously? It means they don't have Uber here."

I looked around the desolate parking lot. I racked my brain. I couldn't ever remember seeing a cab around here in that lost half-year I had whittled away in Peachtree. "OK," I said. "We can call Gransley, but she lives like half an hour from here." I remembered seeing a customer service desk inside. They'd know what to do.

As I turned to walk back inside, Vivi squealed, "Gransley!"

I was about to say, "Gransley will take forever to get here." But when I turned, there she was, running to my daughter.

She wrapped her up in her arms and said, "Oh, Vivi! You are so grown-up and so gorgeous!" She kissed both of Vivi's cheeks, held on to her shoulder, and said, "Let me look at you. How have you turned from eleven to eighteen in the two months since I last saw you?" She squeezed her again.

Then she lifted her very stylish, I must admit, sunglasses and said, "You look absolutely beautiful, my girl."

I smiled. That was always a nice thing to hear. She hugged me and then put her hands on my stomach. "You are looking well, too, grandchild."

"Hi, Mom. Thanks for letting us come in our time of need." I smiled pitifully.

"Chin up, darling. You're in Peachtree now. This is where people come to heal." She pulled her glasses down her nose. "Trust me, I know."

Um. Yeah. Sure. I could tell she had really healed. The

woman hadn't been on a date in sixteen years. That was real moving-on type stuff.

She put her arms around Vivi and me and said, "All right, girls. Let's get you home so I can show you off!"

We dropped our bags in the back of her SUV and slid into the backseat.

"Am I your chauffeur now?"

Vivi and I looked at each other and laughed. "Just habit, Mom. Sorry. But I'm such a whale. Can I stay back here?"

She waved her arm at me and started the car.

"Mom," I said, looking out the window. I had forgotten how empty it was here. I mean, yeah, there were a few cars on the highway, but how could a place be so unpopulated? It felt like an undiscovered colony. "Your arms look amazing."

"Do they?" she asked.

"You know they do," I responded.

"When someone sends you an e-mail every day with a new arm workout and an entire case of cellulite-reducing cream that costs more per tube than most people's car payment, you get the hint."

I smiled. Subtlety might not have been my strong point. But I got results. Her arms looked terrific. I was happy. She was happy. It was a win-win.

"Mom," Vivi scolded. "Why would you do that to Gransley?"

I patted her leg. "It was a gift, darling. A well-intentioned gift." I paused. "And Mom, you look amazing. Like seriously awesome."

"Yes," she said, looking over her shoulder to change lanes. "I also received your e-mail about my slowing metabolism and how I needed to cut all carbs and sugar."

Vivi looked at me, mouth open.

"Oh, what?" I hissed at her. "Like this surprises you?"

"Not with other people but with your own *mother*?" she whispered.

"Well," I piped up, "you won't get cancer, and you'll live a long time, too. So wasn't that nice? I'm worried about your health. You should be grateful."

"Thank goodness," she said. "Because I am quite elderly."

We passed a shopping center, and Mom said, "Girls, do you need anything before we get to Peachtree? This is the last specialty shopping enclave."

"You have a Vitamix, right?" I asked.

"And some sort of gluten-free flour?" Vivi chimed in. "I've really gotten into baking lately."

Mom hit her blinker. I could see her shaking her head.

"What?" Vivi asked.

"Nothing," she said. "I've never met an eleven-year-old quite like you."

"Gransley." Vivi sighed. "Do you understand how inflammatory wheat can be?"

Mom pulled into a parking spot and rested her head on the steering wheel.

"What?" It was my turn to ask.

"You girls are going to be the death of me."

What used to be a standard strip mall had been completely

renovated with a new façade that made it look vintage and almost charming, which was no small feat. It contained a kitchen store, a health-food store, a women's shop, a gift shop, and a baby store, which would be good to remember down the road. I walked into the brightly lit kitchen store, where a woman was whipping up something on a small stove in the middle of the room while people gathered around to watch.

I ended up filling my cart with a Baby Brezza for making baby food, two Vitamixes, one for the main house and one for the guesthouse, an entire set of All-Clad, every Calphalon baking pan known to man, a set of Wüsthof knives, a KitchenAid mixer, a Hurom juicer, a Crock-Pot that I would never use, a toaster that I would *really* never use, eleven containers of soap, and sixteen bottles of cleaning spray that were organically antibacterial. Charge it to James Beaumont, please, and thank you very much.

It would have made me feel even better if I thought he would see the credit-card bill. But we had made a pact long, long ago that the accountant paid my bills, and we didn't discuss them. It was better for our marriage. That had worked like a charm, obviously.

About the time I was done, Mom and Vivi appeared, weighted down with bags from the health-food store next door.

"Is any of this food?" Mom asked me, nodding her head toward the bags.

I shrugged. "That really depends on your definition of food, I think."

I gestured for the three men behind me to follow us to the car.

Mom gave me an annoyed look. "Caroline. Honestly. My house isn't in the Serengeti."

"Well . . ."

We all laughed. Well, all of us except the three men with the muscles schlepping all my crap. They did not laugh at all. But they smiled very big when I gave them their very large tip. So that was something.

I had to sit in the front seat this time, because our packages filled the entire trunk and backseat of the car. But I felt much more relaxed knowing that we would have a well-appointed kitchen. Not as relaxed as I would have felt if we had had a personal chef. But pretty relaxed.

Vivi put in her earbuds in the backseat.

I smiled and said, "So Mom, what's up with the hot bod? Is there a man?"

She scowled at me. "Don't be ridiculous. You know your father was the only man for me," she snapped, defensively enough to make me think she was lying.

Her face looked weird when she said it, and I thought I should change the subject.

"Actually," she said, "I figured I'd better keep myself in good shape since it appears that all of my daughters still need me from time to time."

I leaned back on the headrest, putting my hands protectively over my stomach. In the rush of the day, it was the first time I had remembered to panic. I had Vivi, and the new baby was coming in a few weeks, and my husband was gone. Gone. I was going to be all alone. I mean, as alone as you could be with your mother, your two sisters, and your two nephews.

Mom looked at me briefly. "It's going to be OK, you know."

I was never one for showing weakness. I never acted anything less than totally confident in my abilities and my choices. But on this point, I wavered a bit. "Do you really believe that?" I whispered.

"Sure I do. As tough as you are, you can handle anything."

I was tough. She was right. But sometimes you don't want to have to be tough. I got that strength from my mother. I knew that. I had given her such a hard time the year she took us away from Manhattan, and I felt guilty for that every day. I understood her better now that I was on my own. Sometimes you have to have a fresh start to even be able to get out of bed. Truth be told, selfishly, I didn't hate that she never remarried, because she was always there for us.

"Mom," I said, "just so you know, you don't have to be alone forever. Emerson and Sloane and I wouldn't care. We wouldn't think badly of you."

"Carter was the love of my life. It's hard to move on."

She had never called him Carter to me before. It was jarring, though I couldn't quite figure out why.

Mom looked at me briefly, right before we started on the bridge that crossed over from the beach town into Peachtree. "But you should, Caroline. Going it alone is OK. It has its merits. But there's nothing like being with a man you love who loves you back. It's worth everything."

I often wonder if her never dating, never finding anyone

new, was less about protecting us and more about being stuck in a holding pattern. I couldn't imagine moving on right now, but I also knew myself well enough to know that I never did well being alone. I would probably find someone new eventually. *And he'll be hotter than Edie Fitzgerald*, I couldn't help but think. I looked down at my stomach. The man could at least have had the decency to leave me after I got my figure back. No couth at all, that James.

I felt that queasy rumble in my stomach again, the uncertainty in my decision, as we drove over the Peachtree Bluff bridge. The sunlight on the water sparkled and shone like a million hand-sewn crystals on an Oscars gown. It was breathtaking. I knew I should have told James that I left Manhattan, that I took Vivi with me. But I'd be able to throw him off the scent for at least a couple of weeks. And I deserved that. Just a couple of weeks on my own, a couple of weeks that weren't about him.

Mothers have this sixth sense about things, so I shouldn't have been surprised when Mom asked, "So what did James say when you told him you were moving Vivi to Peachtree?" I was trying to formulate some sort of half-truth when she said, "Caroline!" in that scolding tone I hated.

I was about to respond when she pulled into the brick driveway. At first, it all looked the same. The white clapboard house, perfectly symmetrical, with the Charleston green shutters, so dark that they almost looked black. The guesthouse with the garage underneath and those beautiful wooden doors, not the standard ones with the four glass panes. The picket fence that Mom and Mr. Solomon had been fighting about for half of my life. But something felt off. I couldn't put my finger on it until I saw her. Emerson sauntered out of the front door of the guesthouse—over which Mom had grown a beautiful jasmine vine—like she owned the place. She waved at us, with one hand in the back pocket of her slightly baggy boyfriend jeans, which were rolled up to her calves.

I loved the girl like I had birthed her. I swear I did. But if she was trying to take that guesthouse, this meant war.

SEVEN

world war three

ansley

The Peachtree airport houses exactly three planes in its hangar. One is a Citation jet that belongs to Susan Henderson, the leading asbestos attorney in the country. One is a spiffy new Cirrus that Jerry Cross takes back and forth to his winter place in the Bahamas. The third and only one I have ever been asked to fly on is Henry Birman's. Henry is notoriously blind as a bat, and his old rust bucket belongs in an aviation museum. But those were only two of the reasons I never took him up on his offer to sweep me over to Florida to see my mom. The third and most important reason was that I was terrified of leaving three orphans.

After the horror of 9/11, I didn't fly without my children for years and years. Sloane was terrified to fly. Bless her heart, Sloane was terrified of everything for years after her father died. I didn't blame her. It was a terrifying event, one that shaped most of the people alive at the time. To be that close to it, to experience it the way we all did, took the fear to the next level. But I tried to show her every day, in small ways, that we had to carry on, we had to move forward. It saved me, having to be strong for those girls. I don't even like to think about what would have happened to me if I hadn't had them to live for.

The move to Peachtree was better for Sloane than my other girls because it allayed her fears somewhat. For her, New York was the center of the evil; Manhattan was the place where she was in jeopardy. So far away, on the water, in this tiny town that most people had never heard of, much less targeted, she was safe. She could breathe again—after a while, anyway.

But my fear went deeper than my girls' fear. I was a single parent now. I was all they had. If something happened to me, they were on their own, and I knew that couldn't happen. Not yet. By the time Emerson was eighteen, she was already in LA, out on her own, going to audition after audition. Plus, Caroline was settled enough that I knew she would take care of Emerson. In some ways, I felt like Caroline had had as big an impact on her life as I had. Caroline was certainly the one always pushing Emmy to follow her dreams.

That was the dichotomy of my eldest daughter, the thing you wouldn't expect. She's so brash and headstrong that you would assume she was selfish. But she wants everyone to do well and be happy. It took me a while to realize it, but when she does those things—like sending me the cellulite cream—that seem like the bitchiest things in the world, she does them because she knows you will be happier if your arms are more toned. I admire her for that. She is truly pleased to see the people in her life find success.

Maybe not Edie Fitzgerald. But I think anyone could agree that was warranted.

All the blood rushed to my head when I saw Emerson standing at the door to the guesthouse. *Oh, Emmy, no, please don't start out on this foot.* I wasn't insane. I knew my three daughters weren't all going to come home at the same time without some issues. But this wasn't a great time to ruffle Caroline's feathers. I was trying to keep her calm, not rile her up. Anyone could see that leaving your home and your husband behind, while pregnant, was a giant transition. I was never one to bow down to Caroline, thinking it only increased her power, but at this particular moment, some concessions should be made.

"I called it, Mom," Caroline said. "I have the text to prove it. I called the guesthouse before she even told you she was coming home."

"Honey," I said, "I'm sure she isn't trying to take the guest house."

"Then what does it look like she's trying to do?"

It looked like she was trying to take the guesthouse.

I stepped out of the car and said, "Hi, Em! I didn't know you were coming today!"

She skipped over and hugged me heartily. Well, as heartily as those bony arms could possibly hug. "Hi, Mom! I just couldn't wait to see you."

She was so thin. I loved thin. Thin was good in my book. But she was too thin. That was the part that scared me the most about her job. The pressure to be perfect was too much. I was always afraid it would get to her. Looking at her now, I couldn't help but think that it had. But this was a very sensitive topic with Emerson. You couldn't just bring it up.

"Emerson, no," Caroline said, a smug look on her face. "Go into the house and have a milk shake. I know you're trying to compete in Hollywood, but you have taken this weight thing too far."

I guess *someone* could just bring it up.

"Caroline!" I scolded.

"Nice to see you, too," Emerson said.

Vivi got out of the car. "Aunt Emmy!"

"Hi, my gorgeous girl!" Emerson said. "Come give me some love."

At that moment, Kyle walked out of the guesthouse.

Unbelievable. She had been here no more than two hours, and she was already sleeping with my barista. Good Lord. Children. I was wondering why I had agreed to this, but then I remembered that I hadn't agreed to it. Not at all. But I'm their mother. And this was my job.

Caroline crossed her arms. "If you think you can keep me out of *my* guesthouse by having sex in it, you've got another think coming."

"Caroline!" I scolded.

"It's OK, Gransley," Vivi said. "I know what sex is."

"Well, it's not nice to talk about it," I whispered to her.

"Are you serious?" Emerson asked, anger rising in her voice. "Is this what you think of me? I'm some whore who runs into town and sleeps with the first thing she sees?"

We all knew Emerson wasn't exactly demure. I was actually relieved when she moved to LA, so I wouldn't have to hear about her conquests around town anymore.

"Wouldn't be the first time," Caroline said, planting her feet in the driveway.

"Vivi, darling," I said, "why don't you and I go inside and get all your groceries organized in the fridge?"

"Oh, and I can show you how to use the Vitamix, too!" she said brightly, as if World War Three weren't happening on our manicured lawn. "Gransley," she said seriously, "it will change your life."

You couldn't help but smile. Eleven going on twenty-five.

As Vivi and I were unloading the car, that damn Mr. Solomon appeared. "What's all the commotion out here? Can you keep it down? The dog is trying to sleep."

"The dog?" Vivi whispered. "Seriously?"

I shook my head.

"You might want to invest in some earplugs, Mr. Solomon," I said. "The third one isn't even home yet." I paused, then, unable to help myself, added, "You'll be wishing that fence was longer, taller, and denser before long."

"I'll have you know," he said, "that I'll be running my tomato plants up that eyesore you call a fence. Since it's on *my* property."

"Great," I said, glaring at him. "I can't wait. I'll have fresh tomatoes all year long. Since they'll be growing on *my* property."

Caroline and Emerson were glaring at each other now, too. It hadn't been one minute. We hadn't made it one minute without a fight. But I couldn't help but think it was a little hypocritical to be mad, considering that I was doing exactly the same thing with Frank Solomon.

"Who is that?" Vivi asked.

"My horrible, rude neighbor." I practically yelled so that he would be sure to hear me. "Girls," I said, "why don't we talk the whole guesthouse thing out? This isn't worth fighting over. We're all going to be here together like old times, and it's going to be great." I paused. "I know," I said brightly. "Maybe Emerson could stay in the third bedroom of the guesthouse until the baby comes."

Win-win. They wouldn't fight, and that would be one fewer person in my house.

"I don't even want the guesthouse!" Emerson yelled. "I was doing something nice for my wicked witch of a sister. Now I see I shouldn't have bothered."

Poor Kyle was standing there totally flustered, as if these two bantering hyenas on the lawn were from a species he'd never encountered. He saluted me. "Ansley, I don't know much about this stuff. I sort of move the boxes and leave. I'll see you in the morning."

"The boxes!" Vivi exclaimed.

"Oh, my gosh!" Caroline yelled. "Emerson!" she called, running after her sister, which stressed me out because of her pregnant state. "I'm sorry, Emmy," she was calling. "I love you. You know you're my favorite."

But it was too late to apologize. Emerson was already in the house, halfway up to her room, I assumed. And all I could do was look apologetically at Kyle and hope that it was smooth sailing from here.

EIGHT

a total no-brainer

caroline

My sisters have always accused me of having the biggest mouth. They aren't wrong. Things fly out of it. It's like I don't know what I'm going to say. Mom says I should be able to control this, but I swear I can't. I blame it on the New Yorker in me. We don't filter like Southerners. If you can't take the truth, stay out of the Yankee's way. And the truth now was that Emerson, as much as I loved her, was kind of a slut and looked like she had an eating disorder. I didn't think I should be punished for pointing out these very true things.

To defend myself further, she looked like she was taking my house. And I was nesting. It was a very fragile time. I didn't need to be goaded during my fragile time.

"Emmy," I called. "I'm trying to apologize to you. I mis-judged the situation."

I tried her door. It was locked.

"I'm a hormonal, moody cow, and I have even less filter than usual, and I can't be trusted."

"No, you can't!" she called.

"Could you please unlock the door so I can apologize to you properly?"

The door flew open. She was wearing a gauzy white tank top that showed a hint of her practically nonexistent midriff when she moved just right. Her hair was that gorgeous LA blond, kind of wavy and very multidimensional, like she had spent a day on the beach and her hair had just happened. And she still had those eyes. Those big blue eyes, just like Mom's. When you saw her on-screen, she was stunning. In real life, she was almost so beautiful you had to look away. It was like a light so bright you're afraid it will burn your eyes.

I was thinking how insanely lovely she was, maybe more so than ever, when she said, "You are like twice the size you were when you were pregnant with Vivi."

Well, now. That stung. I nodded and bit my tongue. "OK. I deserved that. I probably am. I am old and alone and giant. And that's what I deserve, because I'm such a bitch to my sweet, loving sister."

She threw her arms around my neck. "No, you aren't! You aren't any of those things. You're positively glowing. You look better than I've ever seen you. I'm sorry I said that."

That was the difference between the two of us. She couldn't stand to be the least bit mean, even if she was telling the truth, which clearly she was.

"So did you really unpack my stuff for me?"

She nodded. "Yes. There wasn't nearly enough closet space, so Kyle and I set up some racks. I wanted you to feel settled and at home."

I put my hand on her cheek. "You're such a good, sweet sister and person."

She grinned. "I really am."

Emerson looked out the window. The only benefit her room had over mine was the glorious view of the harbor. She had a direct view of Starlite Island, the one we loved so much, with its few feet of sand, perfect for beach chairs and football, and the thick, dense tree line behind it. Those stunning horses that looked so gentle but were really so powerful would come and go, eating the grass and sea oats. Sailboats of all varieties— old and new, classic and shabby, large and small—occupied mooring balls in the harbor. Watching the sailboats was like a meditation on life. They made their way so gracefully.

"You should really rebound with Coffee Kyle," Emerson said, raising her eyebrows at me.

I laughed. "Yes. I'm sure the hottest twenty-something guy we've ever seen will be deeply interested in a mid-thirties pregnant divorcée. He will be crawling all over me."

She shrugged. "Stranger things have happened."

I couldn't imagine it, starting over again. I hadn't been on a date in fourteen years, hadn't slept with a man who wasn't my husband. I couldn't envision having to become that comfortable with someone again, having to get to know him, fall in love. In some ways, I couldn't fathom that it was possible. And so I guess I understood my mom a bit better. Opening your heart again, letting someone in after you knew what intense damage was possible . . . It was scary, to say the least.

"You don't want to sit around here forever and get old and dry up. Just saying. You might want to start hunting."

"Emerson, there are three thousand people in this town. How many single men could there be?"

An alarm buzzed on her phone. "Time for my green juice!" she cried, as if she were saying "Time for my seven-layer chocolate cake!"

I took her hand. "Look, hon, I know I was mean earlier about how thin you are. But my apology didn't change the fact that I mean it. You look sort of scarily emaciated."

"I'm sure I do. I had to lose ten pounds for this role. I'm playing a model."

"Promise that's all it is?"

She grinned at me. "Of course I promise. Caroline, it's my first starring role ever. And millions of people will actually be watching me!" she sort of half squealed.

I couldn't help but smile. I wanted it all for her. I always had.

"You know how much this job means to me." Emerson practically bounced up off the bed. I sort of lumbered off. We stood side by side, and she bumped her skinny hip with my heavily padded one. "I think this job means a little something to you, too."

She wasn't wrong. I loved saying that my sister was on her way to stardom. Rumor had it that she would be one of *People*'s 50 Most Beautiful People this year. That was a total no-brainer to me. She should be the one most beautiful person.

Well, maybe once she regained that ten pounds. It was an honor that we all believed would take her career to the next level.

We walked downstairs, and it made my heart happy to see my girl down there, so quiet and so demure, so unlike her mother and her aunt, baking with her grandmother. Mom said something to Vivi, and they both laughed. I couldn't help but think that while I certainly wouldn't say we belonged here, this was a good diversion from all the turmoil back home. Vivi deserved as normal a life as possible. That was what I would say to the judge when he was trying to put me in jail for kidnapping her.

I ran my hand along the railing—it was original to the house—and continued down the stairs. Mom had done such a beautiful job with this place. When we moved here, it was so old and out of date. And now it was the brightest jewel on a very shiny street, without a doubt. I remembered well when the kitchen had had layer after layer of green linoleum, outdated appliances, fake paneling on the walls, avocado-green laminate countertops with big chunks missing.

At the time, she had put tile on the counters and floors, bought white appliances, painted the walls yellow. Now the kitchen had been further updated to hardwoods, white marble, Thermador appliances, pale blue walls. She had added an island with huge, gorgeous white and gold pendant lights hanging over it. It was the perfect place to roll out cookie dough, which she and Vivi were currently doing.

"I had no idea," Mom said, "that you could make cookies

with no wheat, no eggs, and no dairy. Learn something new every day."

"None for me, thanks!" Emerson said. "If you guys haven't ever done a juice cleanse, you really should. You will feel amazing."

Mom gave me a withering look.

"I'm going to run to the farmers' market," Emerson said. "Anyone need anything while I'm out?"

"I think I'm good," I said.

"Me, too," Mom chimed in.

Emerson had barely closed the door before I said, "So what's up with that? Do we think she's OK?"

Mom shrugged. "I don't know. She is awfully thin."

On that note, I joined Vivi in scraping up bits of cookie dough. It was so good. I wasn't sure if it was because I hadn't had real cookie dough in so many years that I'd lost perspective or if this stuff really was delicious.

As I chewed, I said, "She says she's playing a model in this new movie, and she had to be thinner than usual for the part."

Mom nodded. "She has been awfully hush-hush about this role. Has she said anything to you about it?"

I shook my head. "Just that she is excited to be filming close to home for a while. I'm not sure I thought to ask what the movie was about."

"Oh, my gosh!" Vivi interjected. "Do you think I could be like an extra or something?"

Mom smiled at me, and I knew what she was thinking. A shudder of fear ran through me at the mere mention of my daughter being on any size screen, being a part of that world, living that life. It was cosmic payback for my encouraging Mom to let Emerson act all those years ago.

I ran my finger through Vivi's light hair. She had big brown eyes, but in some ways, she reminded me of Emerson. They both had Mom's bone structure, all sharp and angular. Sloane and I were much rounder in the face. When I was young, it made me furious. Now that I'm older, I realize a little padding isn't so bad. It hides the wrinkles.

"We'll see, sweetheart. I'm sure Emmy will get you a part if she can, but she might not have any control."

Vivi was cutting the dough with flower cookie cutters, setting each perfect one on the pan. She was so grown-up, so self-sufficient. The panic that I kept trying to push away rose to the surface. I was grateful, of course, to be pregnant again. After the years of fertility treatments after Vivi was born and nearly losing my mind with every negative pregnancy test, I would never have imagined that this little miracle would simply appear one day of his or her own volition. But I was starting all over. And this time, I wouldn't have James to hand the baby to after a long day. This time, it was all on me. It made me realize what a good thing it was that I was going to be home for a while. If I couldn't have my husband, at least I could have my mom.

My husband. I wasn't going to have a husband anymore. I wasn't going to be James Beaumont's wife. I was all alone.

While I knew how much Emerson valued her freedom, how her career had taken center stage and was all she could think about, I knew that would never be me. What James had done to me, that he could have just discarded me like that, hurt more than I could have imagined. Still, being without him was like becoming an entirely different person, rewriting the last fourteen years of my life and my entire future. And it occurred to me how much I wished I could stay in the same story. Rewind a few years and replay an old sweet song that I had come to love so very much.

NINE

bubble gum

ansley

As the sun began to set on Caroline and Emerson's fourth day back in Peachtree Bluff, as I remembered that Sloane would be joining us the next day, I realized that this was as good a time as any to take a peek at Jack's boat. I knew it needed a ton of work. What that work was exactly was as of yet unclear.

I turned left onto the sidewalk and right onto the boardwalk, my flats tapping on the wood beneath them, proud of myself that I hadn't even changed my clothes or fixed my hair. I was pretty sure that meant I was safe. Just work. Nothing else. I had thought of Jack more than I would like to admit over the past few days, but I rationalized that I think about all of my projects a lot.

I wasn't sure if Jack would even be there, but then I saw him, sitting in a plastic chair, sipping a beer, his feet propped up on the stern. "Oh, wow," he said when he spotted me. "You actually came."

I shrugged. I still felt uneasy around Jack. But at least it wasn't written all over my face now—and I could breathe, which was always good. He seemed more relaxed with me as well. But he was drinking, so it wasn't a fair fight. He tried to help me into the boat, but I avoided his hand, jumping onto the deck and landing with a thud.

Jack made a face. "That was optimistic."

"What?"

"Believing that you wouldn't fall through the deck."

I may have avoided his hand, but there was no way to shirk his wrapping me in that same hug he had all those years ago. I've never given much thought to hugs. But Jack's was one you never forgot. It was an earnest hug, a comforting one, like being wrapped in an afghan a beloved relative had knitted just for you. I inhaled deeply, remembering the smell of him, a mix of sunscreen, Old Spice, beer, and wood. I relaxed into him, as if by memory, and then scolded myself for it.

I held up my camera, and Jack said, "You take pictures. I'll get you some wine."

"Oh, that's OK," I said. "I don't really—"

But he was already gone before I could say "drink." And, honestly, between Mr. Solomon, the scene on the lawn with the girls, and seeing the interior of the boat that Jack swore was seaworthy but looked as though it had seen its best days half a century ago, when Jack offered me a drink, there was no way I could say no. It had definitely been a drink kind of day.

We sat on the back of the boat in plastic chairs, our feet

up on the stern, the teak worn and very, very vintage, and watched the most beautiful sunset in the world. It was pink and orange and so very vibrant, like someone had painted it by hand, mixing the colors just so, streaking the sky into a masterpiece. My husband, Carter, had been a wonderful artist, and when we first moved to Peachtree after he died, I would pretend that he was painting the sunset for me, sending it down from heaven to make me feel like all was not lost.

"So get me up to speed," I said. "What have I missed over the past, um, thirty-five years or so."

We both laughed. The wine was making my face warm already. On the bright side, I was decidedly less awkward. That was a plus.

"Well," he said. "Let's see. I retired last year."

"Retired?" I said, shocked. "How did you pull that off?"

He laughed. "I figured out something very useful early on in my career."

"Oh yeah? What's that?"

"Well, remember how I started a restaurant in Atlanta and it wasn't doing so hot?"

I nodded, not wanting to remember, not wanting to be back in that moment where Jack had told me that, wanting to keep myself in the present and out of the past. "Yeah."

"I opened one in Athens, and it did great. So then I opened one in Chapel Hill. It did even better. And one in Columbia. It was the best of all."

"Ah," I said, getting the drift. "So what worked in one college town worked in all the others?"

He nodded, holding a sip of wine in his mouth. "Not all of them, but for the most part. So that one little hot dog joint turned into one hundred and eighty-five hot dog joints." He shrugged. "And then I sold out."

"Now that's the American Dream," I said. "Starting with something small, working your way up."

He smiled. "Yeah." I could tell that he was starting to feel more comfortable with me as well. "Just think. A few hot dogs led to all of this." He swept his arm majestically around the dilapidated boat, and we both laughed so hard I thought wine would come out of my nose.

This was nice, actually, reconnecting with an old friend. It wasn't so scary after all. It would be fun to work with him for a few weeks.

"I was really sorry to hear about Carter," Jack said.

"Thanks." I took a sip of wine.

"I wanted to reach out but . . ."

He trailed off, and I picked up. "No. That's all right. I understand. I understood then, too."

"So work is good with you?"

I looked out over the water, the sun now a bright, fiery red before its final descent. "It really is. I was scared, you know? I hadn't worked in all those years. But I had nowhere to turn. And I made it."

Jack smirked, but he didn't say anything. And he didn't have to open his mouth for me to know that he was rolling the phrase "nowhere to turn" around in his brain.

"You?" I said. "Wife? Kids?"

"Ex-wife," he said, turning toward me. By the look in his eyes I could tell that he wasn't drunk, but he was almost to that point where the wine was going to make those lips a little too loose. I almost said I needed to go. But, really, I had to hear about the ex-wife.

"Sorry," I said.

"Yeah. She left me when she saw the boat."

We both laughed and Jack looked me in the eye for the first time that night. "Your laugh is exactly the same."

I looked down into my wineglass, and he asked, with something like sadness in his voice, "Do you remember the night we met?"

And, there we were. The loose lips. That was my cue to go. I started to stand, but I made the mistake of looking at him again, of remembering the Jack and Ansley we used to be.

He wasn't handsome then. Not like he is now. He was a scrawny sixteen-year-old kid, a line of sweat around his buzz cut. Nope. Not a thing handsome about that kid. But he had something. Swagger. That's what they would call it now. Back then, we would have said confidence. But either way, I couldn't possibly forget. He still had it. It was a quality you could see clearly, as though you could reach out and touch it. It was a quality you couldn't help but be drawn to.

"Of course," I said softly.

I didn't want to remember. But I was a tad tipsy, and it felt so good. I knew already, even then, that it couldn't keep feeling this good. It wasn't possible. But for the moment, I was riding the wave. After all of the pain of the past decade and a half or so, losing Carter, my daughters hating me, hiding Carter's secrets, hiding my own . . . It felt good to drink wine and smile and remember.

That night I met Jack had been the first sandbar party of the year. In between Peachtree Bluff and Pecan Beach, which was right across the bridge and was where my girls built many a sand castle, lies the sandbar, the one where Jack and I had run into each other a few days earlier. If you don't know the area, it's treacherous, because your boat is sure to get stuck there, as it's completely hidden during high tide. But when the tide is low, the sandbar makes its appearance, barely popping up out of the water. It's as long as a football field and about half as wide. Only the most seasoned boaters know how to weave among the marsh grass without getting stuck. To the right, the coastline was dotted with what we called the mermansions, huge cedar-shake houses with boat docks and breathtaking views. To the left were smaller, simpler houses with views made even lovelier by the fact that the mermansions were in their line of sight. Every summer, at least three or four times, we would all anchor our boats around that little patch of sand.

This first party began as a family picnic. Everyone pitched in, setting up tables and portable grills on the sand, and then we all stood around with plates of cold fried chicken and barbecue or hot dogs and hamburgers, sipping sweet tea and beer, the kids sneaking another one of Mrs. Bennett's famous brownies. It was almost Memorial Day and just cool enough. The entire summer lay ahead, ripe with promise, teeming with possibility, a flower right on the verge of blooming. You could taste the energy of that night as clearly as the potato salad, as if everyone was leaving behind the stress of the year, sending it out to sea, letting it go to fully enjoy this, one of the most special places on the planet.

It was there, on that sandbar, over a plate of Mrs. Bennett's brownies, that Jack's hand brushed mine for the first time as we both reached for the biggest one on the top.

"I remember, too," Jack said now, interrupting my thoughts. "Those cutoff jean shorts. That yellow-and-white-striped bikini top. Those big hoop earrings. The way you tasted like bubble gum when I kissed you."

I was close enough that I could swat his leg with my hand. He grabbed it. "Do you still taste like bubble gum?"

"Stop it," I said. "Stop it now, or I'm going home." I pulled my hand away and sat up straighter.

Truth be told, I hadn't been alone with a man since Carter died. Plenty had asked. Occasionally, I had been tempted. I was only forty-two when he died, after all. But I couldn't imagine trying to start over with anyone else. No one else could possibly understand the life we had lived.

"So tell me about this wife of yours," I said.

"Ah, yes," Jack said. "The wife." He paused. "She was entirely too young for me. Thirty-five."

I laughed. "Thirty-five. For heaven's sake, Jack. That's practically Caroline's age."

He looked at me, and I looked back. It wasn't fair not to face him.

"I'm sorry," I said.

"There's nothing to be sorry for, Ans. It is as we always said it would be."

"Well, I'm sorry your marriage didn't work out." I was. Kind of. But really, Jack was mine. He had always been mine. He would always be mine. And that was how I had seen it from that very first night on that sandbar. Not that I was interested in him in that way now. But still. It was the principle.

As the tide began to rise, the parents had fled, leaving just the teenagers splashing around. That was when the sandbar was the most magical, if you asked me. You couldn't see the ground we were standing on, and all around us was deep, dark water. I imagined from the mermansions it must have looked as though we could walk on it. It made me feel timeless, weightless, fearless. The lukewarm beer we sipped out of Solo cups didn't hurt, either. I remember the way Jack flirted with me that night, the way I knew already that he wasn't scared of anything, not like I was. But it was more than that. The molecules in the air rearranged themselves when Jack and I were together. Anyone around us could feel it, knew from that first night that no matter what the future held, in some small way, the stars aligned for us, the moon rose for us, pulling the tide higher and higher until we were forced back onto our boats. Jack kissed me that night, standing in his fifteen-foot Boston Whaler, our hearts thumping in time, the mosquitoes circling around our bug-bitten ankles under the sweet, sweet full moon of summer.

"Want to tell me why your marriage didn't work?" I asked him.

He gestured around with his beer bottle. "I told you already. The boat."

I rolled my eyes. "It was not the boat."

He nodded. "Before we got married, she didn't want children. After we got married, she decided she did."

"And you didn't?" I said. But I already knew the answer. Jack had never wanted children. And it had broken my heart. Because as much as I had loved him, I knew I was meant to be a mother.

"It seemed . . ." He trailed off, fiddling with his beer bottle. "Complicated."

I swallowed a lump in my throat. "Yeah." I paused. My phone beeped. Caroline. I held it up. "Kids complicate things. That's for sure."

"Actually, by then, I realized that I would kind of like to have kids." He cleared his throat and looked out over the water. "And I loved her and she made me happy in a lot of ways. But I also knew that she wasn't who I wanted to have children with." He smiled, but I could see the sadness behind his eyes. That's how it is with people you've known since you were teenagers at the sandbar party. "I've never admitted that before, not even to myself."

He finally looked at me again, and I looked back. I didn't say anything, but he could read my face.

"It's not your fault, Ans." He said it, but as the words tumbled out, there was an edge to his tone. One that made me uneasy. One that made me know that despite how cool he seemed, despite how nonchalant he was trying to be, he thought a lot of things were my fault.

I looked down into my wine. He couldn't have blamed me for his unhappiness any more than I blamed myself. I always felt that if I had compromised, if we had been together, his life would have been better. But mine, I knew, would have been unspeakably incomplete.

He reached over and lifted my chin toward him, softening. "I'm sorry," he said. "I really mean that. It's not your fault."

I could feel the tears in my eyes. I was suddenly aware that I'd had too much wine and too much heat for one day. I wiped my cheeks quickly. "I need to go home," I said.

"Want some company?" he asked. And he was back to normal, back to the easy Jack I knew.

Everything inside me wanted to say yes. Everything inside me wanted not to be alone. I wanted to pretend that we were teenagers again. That the world was fresh and new. That we were standing on the edge of everything, that life was out there waiting for us to grab it. But we weren't. And it wasn't.

And he knew it, too. That's how he knew I meant it when I said, "No."

TEN

fairy stones

caroline

Everyone used to call Sloane and me either two peas in a pod or trouble. Both were equally accurate. When we were younger, Sloane was fearless. As free-spirited and wide open as she was, her big sister was the complete opposite. I've always been by-the-book, structured, regimented. I knew from the time I was small that I wanted to grow up and marry New York City royalty, have his babies, raise them, volunteer, and maybe get invited to the Met Ball one day. That was really it. I mean, yeah, I went to college because that's what you did. But I was there to meet a man, plain and simple. If that didn't work out, I'd have some cool job in the meantime.

The weird thing was that when our dad died, Sloane and I sort of flipped. Where I had been so uptight, I suddenly realized that today was all we had and that I had to take every chance while the chances were around for the taking. She, on the other hand, became more fearful. It evened the score for us a bit, his death.

I begged Sloane to come to NYU. But she said she didn't think she'd ever be able to go back to Manhattan. True to her word, she hadn't. Since she'd set foot on Georgia soil, the only relocating she'd done was to North Carolina, where Adam was stationed. And let's face it, it's the same place.

It made me sort of sad that our lives had diverged on such different paths. We weren't as close as we once were. I mean, we were still sisters, sure. But in a lot of ways, we simply could not relate to each other.

Like when she pulled into the back driveway in her—wait for it—minivan. I about fell over. Because, you see, although I concede that they are quite convenient, I would never be caught dead in a minivan. But Sloane doesn't think like that. She thinks about what is economical and what is practical. And yeah, sometimes I envy her that.

When she pulled into her spot beside Mom's car in the driveway, we all made a mad dash for the van. The doors automatically opened to reveal my two nephews in their car seats, Goldfish crumbs everywhere, TVs in the headrests playing *PAW Patrol*. The interior smelled vaguely of sour milk.

That was the moment it really sank in. These vermin were going to have their mitts all over my fresh, pure, un-germed baby. My throat constricted.

But then Adam said, "Carowine," with those sticky hands reached out to me, and he couldn't help but melt your heart. He had Sloane's big brown eyes, but everything else was Adam's. It made complete sense for him to be Adam's namesake, because he could have spit him out.

I reached in and pulled him out of the car seat, resting him above my protruding belly.

Sloane got out and said, "Caroline! He's too big for you to hold now!"

I tried not to let my disapproval of her outfit choice show on my face. She had on these dumpy, flare-legged, faded black yoga crops that no one should ever wear and a too-tight T-shirt that made it very evident she hadn't lost the last ten pounds of baby weight.

"Sorry for the outfit," she said, as if she knew what I was thinking. "Taylor peed on me at about mile three-fifty."

Gross. I had forgotten about all of that. Maybe this baby wouldn't do that.

Mom was bouncing Taylor on her hip, and he was cooing delightedly.

Emerson hugged Sloane, and Vivi held her arms out to Adam, which was comical, because he was probably half her size. But he went to her.

"Wow," I said, hugging Sloane. "These are some amazingly well-adjusted kids. Vivi never would have done that."

Vivi shot me a look. "Thanks, Mom."

I laughed. "It wasn't a bad thing. Just a difference in personality."

"So what have I missed?" Sloane asked. "You know how much I hate it when y'all are here together without me."

I cringed. They had her now. It was official. Once you go "y'all," you never go back.

I winked at Emerson, whose hair was piled up on her head, making her cheekbones even more severe. I put my arm around Sloane and led her to the back door. "How about I fill you in on everything while Emerson whips you up some . . ."

I looked toward Emerson, who looked down at her watch. "Celery juice!" she exclaimed. "Sixteen whole ounces if you want."

Sloane looked disgusted, her nostrils flaring. "I think Taylor peeing on me might end up being one of the more pleasurable parts of the day."

"What if I get these guys into the bath?" Mom asked.

"I'll help!" Vivi called behind her, struggling to carry Adam up the steps.

And then there were three. Three sisters, standing around the kitchen island, Emerson pulling two bunches of celery out of the refrigerator while I removed the juicer from the cabinet under the microwave drawer. It wasn't that I was naturally helpful or caring. It was simply that she was so thin I wasn't sure she would be able to handle the weight of the machine.

I pulled one of the stalks off of Emerson's cutting board and crunched. "So," I said, "the rumor around town is that Emerson has already slept with a guy named Kyle."

Sloane's eyes got wide. "Wait. You mean Coffee Kyle?"

"The very one," I said, chewing.

Emerson laughed. "It's not true, of course."

"If there's going to be a rumor, which, duh, there is, at least it was someone hot," Sloane said.

This was the good stuff right here, three sisters sitting around talking and laughing like old times. I missed these girls so much. Being home for a while might not be that bad after all.

Emerson handed us each a wineglass full of green, pulpy stuff. Sloane and I looked at each other skeptically.

"You're going to drink it, and you're going to like it," Emerson said sternly.

She walked out of the kitchen, and we followed her through the dining room and the family room out onto the wide front porch.

My phone buzzed in my pocket, and my stomach clenched. Before I even saw it, I knew it was James. Could I please talk to Vivi? I want to explain before tonight happens. Please don't keep me away from her.

I laughed.

"What?" Sloane asked.

"Oh, nothing," I said, continuing to walk toward my seat. I read in an article that more injuries occurred while texting and walking than while texting and driving, so I stopped. For the baby's sake.

I am not keeping Vivi away from you. I can't MAKE her talk to you. We are going to Peachtree. Need to get her out of the city.

The phone beeped again. You can't take my kid away. What about school?

I typed back: I'm not keeping her from you. You need to give her some time to cool down. I couldn't help it. I added: Best of luck on your TV debut tonight. I hope it's everything you dreamed.

Then I turned the phone off, partly because I didn't care what else he had to say, mostly because I didn't want him to ask me the school question again. If I could hide it for a little longer, maybe I could make him see that keeping her in Peachtree this semester, while the show was airing, was a good idea. Which reminded me that I really did need to call a lawyer now.

Emerson and Sloane were chatting, but I was so distracted I couldn't focus on what they were saying. I looked out over the porch railing. The views were by far the best part of this beautiful home. It seemed you could see forever from this front porch. Across the water, three wild horses roamed amid the sea oats, their hooves splashing in the tide. It couldn't help but make me think of Emerson, Sloane, and me. When we were younger, our weeks at this house with our grandparents and great-grandparents felt like paradise.

The summer when Emerson was born is the first one that really sticks out in my mind, that I remember in detail. Our grandparents took Sloane and me over to Starlite Island almost every day while Emerson was napping. It was our special time to be with them. It brought us so much closer together.

That summer, Sloane and I spent hours exploring that island, wending our way through the trees and the marsh grass, occasionally coming upon a wild horse. We were always hunting for shells, and I'll never forget the day I found one that I had never seen before. I was digging in the sand with Sloane, plotting how we would make our way to China. When I hit something hard with my plastic shovel, I pulled it out. It was a smooth, white rock with flecks of black, shiny spots. But the strangest thing was that on the top was a dark formation that looked like an X. I pulled it out, added it to the pile, and kept digging. Throughout the course of the day, I found two more of those stones. One for me, one for Sloane, and one for baby Emerson.

"Grandpop," I asked later. "What is this?"

He pulled me onto his lap and, eyes big, said, "Why, Caroline. Where did you find those?"

"In the sand."

"That is amazing," he said.

Grammy came over to have a look, too. "Caroline!" she exclaimed. "Those are fairy stones!"

I didn't know what that meant, but I liked the sound of it. "Fairy stones?"

"Yes," Grandpop chimed in. "They're fairy stones. Their real name is staurolite. The island is named for them. They used to be everywhere over there, though no one can figure out why. They're normally found in the mountains."

"Legend has it," Grammy said, "the fairies who live on the island bring the fairy stones." She paused. "Only very special little girls and boys get to find those, so you should feel honored."

I was right at that age where the idea of fairies was still exciting, but I was also a bit skeptical.

"Keep it in your pocket," Grandpop said. "It will keep you safe."

"Keep me safe," I repeated. "I got ones for Sloane and Emmy, so they'll be safe, too."

"That's so nice," Grammy said. "You can be the Starlite Sisters. These can be your special rocks, and Starlite Island will always be your special place."

Sloane had been sitting on the floor, hanging on to every word. "Can we be fairies, too?" she asked.

I wasn't sure that I wanted to be a fairy, although anyone could see that being able to fly would be nice.

Grandpop said, "Girls, you can be anything you want."

Now I wondered, sitting on Mom's porch that day, if maybe we hadn't become exactly who we wanted to be, at least in some ways. Just the thought made me hope that I wasn't going to have to go back to work after this baby was born. I assumed that James would be fair to me and that our lawyers could reach an agreement—once the divorce papers were filed, of course—but who really knew? I'd heard horror stories about how these things went down. Thank God I hadn't signed that prenup. And at least there was still the money from my dad. I made a mental note to talk to Mom about it later on.

I took a sip of celery juice and mirrored the face my sister was making. "Emerson," I said, "this is positively vile. I do not know how you do it."

She shrugged. "I kind of like it."

"Blech," Sloane said. "Can't you mix some lemon or something with it?"

Emerson looked at the glass. "No. Too much sugar. You can only have one lemon per day, and I have to have it to balance out the kale."

Sloane raised her eyebrow at me.

"I know," I said.

"It's for a *role*," Emerson said. "Why doesn't anyone get this? I've been acting since forever, remember? You always have to come to my D-list stuff?"

"Speaking of," I said, "what is the role, anyway? You've been awfully cagey about the whole thing."

She waved her hand. "That's work. It's boring. Let's talk about something more fun."

"Like what?" I asked.

"Like Mom," Sloane chimed in. "How does she seem?"

I looked out over the water again. It was so hard to read my mom sometimes. Ever since our dad died, she had made it her life's mission to be perpetually fine. "She seems good," I said. "She looks fantastic."

"Doesn't she?" Emerson said. "Did you see her arms?"

"I know," Sloane said. "It's bad when you're jealous of your fifty-eight-year-old mother's body."

I didn't say it, because I'd been working on the whole brain-to-mouth filtration situation. But Mom definitely looked better than Sloane. So I politely said, "If anyone would like a copy, I'm happy to forward you the workout regimen I have Mom on."

They both burst out laughing. They could laugh all they wanted, but Sloane would be receiving an e-mail. And Emerson would be receiving one about how being too thin ages your face more quickly. My therapist said my weight obsession was a control issue, a response to my father's death. But, even if she was right, I couldn't *control* my control issue, ironically. Besides, she didn't get it. I did these things out of love. I was very misunderstood.

"Oh, my gosh!" Sloane said.

"What?" I asked.

"Do you think Mom has a man, and that's why she looks so good?"

Emerson shook her head. "No way. I grilled Kyle about it, and he said there is no action at the Murphy house." She paused. "But honestly, if you ask me, it's about time. I mean, no, I don't want to have to call anyone Daddy, but the woman can't be alone forever. It has been sixteen years."

We all got quiet. It might have been sixteen years, but it still felt fresh every single time it was brought up.

"I think we should make it our mission while we're home to find Mom a man," I said.

Sloane nodded. "I agree wholeheartedly. Can you imagine how lonely she gets around here in this big old house, rambling around alone?"

Emerson shook her head.

I heard the door creak open at the neighbor's house. "Hi, Mr. Solomon," I called loudly, waving.

He muttered something under his breath and walked back inside.

I accidentally took another sip of that vile celery concoction and said, "I think he's warming to me. What do you think?"

We all laughed. I wrapped my thin sweater around myself.

Emerson said, "Who wants to go for a nice long walk?"

Sloane nodded. "I have nine pounds to lose. I'm going to be in the best shape of my life when Adam gets home."

Whew. That was going to save me so much e-mail.

"You look great," Emerson said, smiling and looping her arm around her sister's.

"She's lying," I said, also smiling.

Sloane looped her other arm around mine. "I know she's lying," she said. "But sometimes it's nice to hear something nice. You know?"

"Oh," I said. "OK. Your kids are adorable. That's the truth, and it's nice. Aren't you proud of me?"

"Growth," Sloane said.

"Absolutely," Emerson said. "We'll get a little Southerner in you yet."

I doubted that very highly, but it was such a nice day I didn't argue. Walking down the street with my two sisters, I felt like life was going to go on—yet again. It might have been slightly south of simple. But like we always did, we'd figure it out together.

ELEVEN

work for it

ansley

One Saturday night before my senior year of college, my brother Scott and I were in Peachtree, out with a big group of friends, the same ones we had been cultivating since our childhood, when a man caught my eye.

Not a boy, mind you. A *man.* He was wearing pressed khaki pants, a starched blue shirt, and a neatly knotted navy and white bow tie. I must have caught his eye, too, because he came over to me, ordered two beers, and said, "Hi, I'm Carter Murphy. I'm Eunice Murphy's grandson. We've met a couple of times at your grandmother's Fourth of July barbecues."

"Barbecue" was a loose term. It was more like a five-star affair, with tents in the backyard, a fabulous caterer, a combo band, fireworks, and dancing until midnight.

When Carter introduced himself, I suddenly felt the night take a turn. I could have sworn there was a moment between us. But there couldn't have been. He was much older than I was. So he was definitely not interested in me in that way.

We moved to a high-top bar table to get away from the noise. "So what's going on with you?" I asked.

He shrugged. "Trying to make a name for myself on Wall Street."

I tipped my beer to him. "Oh, isn't everyone?"

He laughed. "Maybe so. But between you and me, if you don't have to work for it a little, it doesn't mean a damn thing once you get it."

I smiled. "I will remember that."

"What about you? What's going on in your life?"

I realized I was a tad tipsy. Emily and Sandra were making kissy faces at me from across the bar. There wasn't any discreet way for me to signal that it wasn't like that. So I let it go.

"I have one more year of college, and then it's out into the cold, cruel world."

He winked at me. "Manhattan is a great place for young up-and-coming decorators."

I had assumed that Atlanta was going to become my new home, at least temporarily. I had never imagined leaving Georgia. Even Atlanta, where I had spent a lot of time, felt scary and new.

It didn't occur to me yet that Carter was flirting with me when he said that. "So," I asked, "you settling down? Making an honest woman of someone? Making your grandmother proud?"

That was when I realized that I was flirting with him, even though I knew it was completely inappropriate.

He laughed. "I date, but I haven't found the right one. You know?"

I knew very, very well. "Oh, yeah," I said. "I just broke up with my boyfriend before we left for the summer. He's nice and everything, but I want real love. I want something like what my grandparents have."

He smiled at me. "I agree. Something that stands the test of time."

I looked down at my watch. "Oh!" I said, realizing it was almost one in the morning. No one would be waiting up for me, but Grandmother would expect me to be down for breakfast at eight. "I need to get home." I reached my hand out to Carter. "It was so nice to see you again."

"I'm not going to let you walk home alone," he said.

"It's only a couple of blocks away. I'm sure I'll be fine."

He got up. "I could use some air. This is my favorite time on the boardwalk anyway."

We walked out into the crisp darkness. Summer in Peachtree Bluff was heaven. The days were warm and breezy, and the nights were cool and refreshing.

"So this is your favorite time of night? Are you up this late often?"

He laughed. "No, actually. I usually go to bed early so I can get up by five to fish."

I groaned. "I can't imagine ever having a hobby that required waking up at five a.m."

He laughed, putting his hands in his pockets. Our feet tapped on the boardwalk, and I suddenly realized that I wasn't all that anxious to get home anymore. I scolded myself for being so silly. He was unreasonably too old for me.

"It's not that much of a hobby since I only get to do it like three times a year."

"Do you miss the South?" I said. "Will you ever come back home?"

"I don't think I will," he said. "I'm pretty firmly entrenched there in my job and everything. My dad's family is from New York, so it was pretty easy to slide right in."

"I can't imagine leaving the South. It would be so different anywhere else. I like the slow pace and the nice manners, the food . . ."

Carter laughed. "It's not another country, Ansley."

I stopped and leaned over the boardwalk railing, suddenly not wanting the night to be over so soon. "Isn't it, though?"

Carter leaned beside me, his grin now close to mine. "I think you'd like it. You never know until you try. It's different there. The people, the energy. It's electrifying."

All of a sudden, I realized that maybe I would like New York because that was where Carter was. I scolded myself again. I was sure he would think I was nothing more than a silly girl for imagining such a thing.

"You should come visit me there sometime," he said. I felt the blush coming to my cheeks. I was sure he meant as friends.

I was staring out over the water at the moon painting a luminescent trail from Starlite Island right up to what looked like Grandmother's front door. But the alcohol had made me brave, and I turned to look at him. You could feel this heat between us, something almost palpable in the air.

"Where would you take me?" I asked demurely.

He inched slightly closer. "Everywhere," he said.

When his lips met mine, I wasn't quite sure that it was happening. It was strange and exciting and surreal all at the same time.

He pulled away and smiled at me. "How about this?" he said. "I'd like to take you to dinner tomorrow night before I leave."

My turn to smile. "I think I'd like that."

It was the first of many wonderful dates. And it wasn't until much later that I confirmed that he was thirty-seven. No matter how you sliced it, sixteen years was a big age difference.

But being wanted by Carter was something akin to being the prize diamond at a Sotheby's auction. You were suddenly treasured, admired, sought after. You were important, unique. There were no games. There was never a day in my life with him that I didn't know exactly where we stood, precisely how much I meant to him. That being said, I remembered what he told me that first night. And I most definitely made him work to win me over.

My parents were less than thrilled. Yes, he was sixteen years older than I was, only six years younger than my own mother. They worried about the big New York City Wall Street man taking advantage of their baby girl, stealing her virtue, which, unbeknownst to them, had been stolen long before.

In fact, one night, sitting around the dining-room table,

Mom asked, "Whatever happened to that sweet Jack? I always thought you two might end up together."

It was like being punched in the gut. I spent so much time consciously not thinking of Jack. In fact, Carter was the first man who really was able to make me forget. But I kept my cool.

"Jack and I want different things, Mom. We've been through this."

I remember her shaking her head at me like I was a silly little girl. But she was the one who was silly. I knew that then, and I know it now.

"He's a child, Ansley. He's twenty-one years old. How does he know he doesn't want children? Surely he'll change his mind."

I looked at my daddy when I said, "Mother, men do not change their minds. Women try to change men. Sometimes they get them to act a certain way, think a certain way. But you cannot change a man, and I will not be a woman who tries to trick one into having a life he never wanted."

I'll never forget what happened next. Daddy, who was chewing his steak, took a sip of water from the crystal goblet in front of him on the table and said, "That's a wise decision." Then he paused and added, "I quite like Carter. You need a man who can take care of you."

The last of my worry about Carter fell away. I don't know if I was so sure about us because I was young or because I was that assured of his affections toward me.

Carter made clear what to expect in our life together. He did well, but he was not rich—not by Manhattan standards, anyway. He had a nice family name but few of the assets that came along with that. We could rent a house in the Hamptons; we would likely never buy. Because, as optimistic as he was, the man was a realist. And that was one of the things I loved the very most about him. Because I always, always knew what to expect.

He knew how to grill a steak, fix a sink, kill a deer, and give you a kiss so sweet that you forgot your own name. He was needlessly thoughtful, unfailingly generous, and could accurately predict the vintage of a wine down to the year.

But none of that mattered to me. I, quite simply, was in love with him. Every day. All day. There was no explanation for how or why. And I think that's how I knew it was true. Because I didn't care what my parents thought. His job didn't matter. His money didn't matter. If he told me he was quitting everything to move to a hut in Uruguay and minister to the sick, I would have packed my bag and bought a Bible.

And so, where I always thought that one day I'd be leaving on that midnight train to Georgia, instead, I graduated from college and left on a red-eye flight to JFK. Didn't matter where it was. All I knew was that, like Gladys Knight before me, I'd rather live in his world than live without him in mine.

inhumane

caroline

The worst part about your husband leaving you when you're pregnant is that there is no alcohol of any kind involved. I mean, how are you supposed to heal when you can't drink your troubles away? It's really quite inhumane, if you ask me. I had just put Vivi to bed and was in the kitchen making a sparkling water with a splash of pineapple juice for myself and plain sparkling water for Emerson to take back out onto the front porch to enjoy the crisp evening and bright stars with my sisters. As you can imagine, wine was not part of Emerson's cleanse. If it had been, she would have been incoherent after three sips.

My phone beeped on the counter, which is when I realized it was 9:08. *Ladies Who Lunch* had officially premiered for the season. The text was from James.

I'm sorry, Car. I really, truly am. Can you ever forgive me?

I didn't respond, because I was pretty sure I couldn't.

My friend Lucinda texted: Hang in there, lady. I've got your back.

Then Sarah Peters: Love you! It's not that bad. It's really not. They look ridiculous, don't you think?

I could feel that queasiness developing in the pit of my ever-protruding belly. I wasn't sure which was worse, not watching or just watching and getting it over with. Fortunately for me, Mom's lack of a TV made it a choice I didn't get to make.

My phone chimed. Jenna Franklin. Gag. You hold your head up high, Caroline. She may be a supermodel, but she doesn't have your class.

Jenna was the queen of the backhanded compliment. I was glad she reminded me that Edie was a supermodel, lest I forget for a mere moment.

I screwed the top back onto the fresh pineapple juice that Emerson had made for me. So this was it. The secret was out. The last few people in the United States who didn't know that my husband was screwing a supermodel and not his pregnant wife now knew it for a fact. I leaned over on the counter for a second, feeling like I couldn't breathe.

The phone dinged again. James. Again. Can we talk?

I laughed out loud. No. No, we could not *talk*. I liked giving him the silent treatment, because I knew the uncertainty of it all would drive him bananas. But I couldn't help texting back: You have Edie to talk to now. You don't need me.

Don't be like that.

Was he serious? Wow. That was just like a man. While he is

smearing you all over the papers and TV and Internet making you look like a fool, making the entire life you led look like nothing more than a farce, he wants you to call him and reassure him that it's OK.

"Well, guess what?" I said out loud. "It's not OK."

I heard footsteps and turned to see Mom walking into the kitchen, clad in the robe and slippers we had sent her for Christmas. I had felt terrible about not coming home. We all had. But I think it was fair to say that we were making up for it now with this visit.

"You talking to yourself?" Mom asked. She smiled and rubbed her hand up and down my back. "How you holding up?"

I dropped my chin to my chest, trying to stretch my neck, which always got very tight when I was stressed. "My husband is currently canoodling with a supermodel, and millions of people are watching it." I took a sip of my mocktail. "But, you know, considering the circumstances, it could be worse."

And it *could* be worse. I'd lived through worse. We both had. In some ways, we still lived through it every day.

"Let's go on the porch," I said.

Mom nodded. "Let's. It's such a beautiful night." She handed me a throw from the back of a club chair on the way out. "Just in case."

I opened the door, but Sloane and Emmy were nowhere to be found. The sky took my breath away. What seemed like millions of stars twinkled over the water. I didn't know if it was the lights or the buildings, but star sightings in Manhattan were not quite as brilliant.

"Where did they go?" I asked.

Mom shrugged. "I don't know. Let's get comfy and wait for them to come back."

I cut my eyes at her. "Where are they, Mom?"

She was the world's worst liar. She took a sip of her real wine, which was another tip-off, because Mom basically never drank unless it was someone's wedding.

"Moooommmm," I said.

"Sit down," she said. "Let's talk about baby names."

I opened the door again and walked upstairs.

"Caroline," she hissed, so as not to wake the children. "Get back down here this instant."

Of course, all that did was make me walk faster. Now I knew for sure that they were up to something. I poked my head into Sloane's room. Lights off. Beds made. Empty. I knew the boys were asleep in the room next to hers. So I went to the end of the hall to the guest room, flung the door open, and there were Emerson and Sloane sitting on the bed. Emerson slammed her laptop shut.

I crossed my arms. "My own two sisters. Seriously? You are such traitors. Could you not even wait until I went back to the guesthouse?"

Emerson looked sheepish. "Honestly, no."

"We were coming from a good place," Sloane said. "We thought we could be like the pass-through. You wouldn't have to actually watch it, but we could tell you what you need to know."

I was seething. "How could you do this to me? Tonight of

all nights? I'm down here with my phone about to vibrate off the kitchen island from all the *Ladies Who Lunch* texts, and I need my sisters to sit on the porch with me and talk about old times. Instead, you're up here reveling in my disgrace."

"Caroline," Sloane said pleadingly.

I thought about dramatically stomping out and slamming the door. But, even as worked up as I was, I wasn't going to wake Sloane's kids like that. That was like a whole other level of meanness.

And yeah, that was dramatic. None of this was about my sisters, in reality. It was about James and the show and my feeling like my life was a volcano that wouldn't quit erupting. I knew they weren't reveling in my disgrace. Although I wondered if maybe they weren't a tiny bit happy that I had finally gotten what was coming to me. Because I had, hadn't I? I always thought in the back of my mind that it had all gone too well for me. The life I wanted had fallen into place a little too easily. It had to blow up sometime, didn't it?

It had blown up badly. And I didn't have the courage to face it head-on. Instead, I had run away to my mom's house, had kidnapped my daughter, of all things, and hadn't even had the nerve to tell my cheating husband that we were moving, she was finishing the school year here, and that was on *him*.

Mom appeared in the doorway and whispered, "They meant well."

"We really were trying to help," Sloane said.

"And?"

Emerson grimaced. The look on her face said it all. It was

as bad in real life as it was in my head. "But we absolutely were not reveling in your sadness," she said. "We were trying to protect you in some weird way."

I nodded. "I know that. I need someone to yell at, and I'm not ready to yell at James quite yet. So I yelled at you instead."

"You can yell at me anytime," Sloane said, squeezing my hand.

"Not me," Emmy said. "Get it together."

We all laughed.

"Do you ever wish you could do it all differently?" I asked. "I mean, do you ever wish that you could rewind and take so many things back and add so many others in their place? I keep replaying it." I paused. "I mean, obviously, I wouldn't take back meeting James, because then I wouldn't have Vivi." I looked down at my stomach. "And this little one. But I question every move I've ever made."

Everyone was silent. Emerson and Sloane didn't say anything, but we all looked at Mom. And you didn't have to know her as well as we did to realize that she was thinking about all the things she would change if she could.

THIRTEEN

the high priestess of teak stain

ansley

It was a hallowed morning in Peachtree Bluff. Peachtree High had just won the football game against its major rival. And that could only mean one thing: A parade!

Peachtree has a parade for every occasion. *Every* occasion. Of course, there are the usuals: Thanksgiving, Christmas, and Fourth of July. We also celebrate Arbor Day, Biker Week, Teacher Appreciation Day, every mayor in history's inauguration anniversary, Pirate Invasion. (Yes, pirates invade. And they camp out in authentic pirate-era tents and eat food off fires and drink grog.) Oh, and Dr. Seuss's birthday—that one is actually my favorite. Anyway, you get the idea.

After the parade, every dock owner in town has to have fireworks on his or her dock. I am terrified of fireworks, so Hal sees to it that my dock is appropriately lit—in more ways than one, I can assure you.

And today we would get to do all of that. I knew the kids were going to love the parade, and I was excited for the opportunity to show off my family. The entire town attends every parade, of course. You would think it was mandatory, considering how many of us show up. As I looked in the mirror, applying my mascara, I briefly wondered if Jack would be there. But I pushed the thought away. It was one of many, many thoughts about Jack I had pushed away ever since that night on his boat.

"Good morning, good morning," I sang as I walked down the steps. It was certainly nice to have this house filled with little voices and even smaller feet. So sure, there were wet towels on the floors and toothpaste stuck to the sinks and diapers filling the garbage and crumbs everywhere. But it was wonderful all the same. Taylor and Adam were chasing each other around the kitchen island, giggling. I couldn't wait to watch their towheads get even whiter in the summer, just like Emerson's hair had. Emerson was throwing a bunch of inedible-looking plants into the blender. I was glad to see that she was blending whole foods this morning, not extracting their juice. This was progress, sadly.

Caroline was texting, brow furrowed.

"Where's Vivi?" I asked.

"Sleeping." Caroline smiled, but I could tell it was fake.

"Don't torture yourself."

"Oh, I'm not." She looked back down. "Well, I mean, I am. But I'm torturing myself because I have to do my hospital tour."

Caroline was a bit of a germophobe. Maybe not a bit. More like someone should medicate that child. I was hoping that her midwife would calm her. I didn't want to add fuel to the fire but figured giving her something else to think about would help.

"Have you given any thought to whether James will be there for the delivery?"

She scrunched her nose. "I may not have told him that Vivi's going to school here yet."

My eyes widened. I couldn't imagine that she still hadn't told him. But my job here was to keep my daughter as calm as possible. "Well, darling, I am sure he will understand."

He most definitely would *not* understand.

"All right, crew," I said. "I'm heading down to the store. If anyone needs anything, holler. Or send a carrier pigeon." I don't know why I thought that was funny, but I laughed. No one else did. Just like old times.

Sloane hugged me. "Thanks so much for letting us stay, Mom."

I patted her back, wondering if Caroline was going to mention that she was spreading cream cheese on a bagel.

As I turned to walk out the front door, I heard Caroline say, "Oh, my gosh. That's so funny. I had forgotten that people even ate gluten."

Yup. There it was.

As my feet hit the sidewalk, I looked back and forth between the rolling water on the right and the white clapboard homes on the left. As I was beginning to feel calm and free and meditative, my phone rang. I rolled my eyes. I wasn't going to answer it. But it was Scott. And he never called. We were rarely in the same time zone.

"Scott!" I said.

"Ans!" he said back.

Every time I heard his voice, I wished I talked to him more.

"Where in the world are you?"

"Well," he said, "I'm actually hopping on a plane to Florida."

"Oh, please go see Mom," I said. I waved to a couple of people on the street.

"That's what I'm doing," he said. "I haven't seen her in a few weeks, so I thought I'd go check things out." He paused, and my stomach sank. "Do you think she's doing OK?" he asked.

I thought back. She had seemed like her usual self to me. Although truth be told, I'd been so preoccupied with the girls lately, I hadn't talked to her as much. When I did, she always seemed to be flitting off to one place or another. She and Scott had always been closer. "I haven't noticed anything off, but I haven't seen her in six months. She seems happy and busy to me. What's up?"

"Maybe nothing," he said. "I'm probably overreacting. She has seemed confused to me sometimes lately."

I laughed. "Well, Scott. She's eighty-three. Some confusion might begin to set in at some point."

"I guess," he said. "How are four of my five favorite girls?"

"Is that like the four out of five dentists that prefer Trident?" I smiled. "Well, your favorite sister is doing really well. She is ecstatic to have all her grandchildren home at once. And your nieces are hanging in there."

"Do you know what's cool?" Scott asked.

"What's cool?"

"How it used to drive me nuts when we were kids that you had to be my favorite sister but I wasn't necessarily your favorite brother, but now . . ."

I laughed. "Scott! You should be ashamed of yourself!"

"Oh, I knew this whole time that if I just waited long enough John would screw it up, and favorite-brother status would be mine." He laughed a villain-in-a-superhero-movie laugh.

We said our good-byes, and I was still smiling as I entered the store.

But the light feeling floated away, and I began feeling heavy. And stressed. I had no idea what we would do when we got to the point where Mom needed help. But you didn't have to be a genius to realize that it would fall to me. It was a Southern daughter's life purpose to care for her mother. Which was the highest form of irony, since she hadn't helped me one bit when I needed her the most. As Mom (and Scarlett O'Hara) would say, I'd think about that tomorrow.

When I got to the front door of the store, Kimmy was waiting for me. She had a huge basket filled with delicious-looking produce.

"Oh, thanks, Kimmy," I said, as I slid the key into the lock. I pushed harder than usual. It had rained late the night before, and rain always made the door swell.

"Word on the street is that you're feeding more than one these days."

I laughed gleefully, realizing that I truly felt as happy as I sounded—today, anyway. "I am, indeed," I said. "In fact, could you head down to the house? Emerson consumes the amount of produce in that basket hourly, and I'm sure she'd be glad to see you."

Kimmy's eyes lit up, a bit of a rare sight. "Sounds great."

I reached into my bag and handed her a hundred-dollar bill. "Just keep a tab going, if you don't mind."

"Kale yeah, I will."

We both laughed. I elbowed her lightly. "Maybe we could make you 'Kale Yeah Kimmy.'"

She rolled her eyes. And I had enough of that to deal with, didn't I?

The door had barely closed behind me when the bell tinkled its happy sound. "She's an odd bird, isn't she?"

I couldn't help but smile, and I so hoped I wasn't blushing. But he had that effect on me. "She is that."

I turned to smile at him, and he smiled right back. Jack motioned with his head toward the waterfront. "Some guys are here today replacing the teak on the deck. Would you mind giving me a hand with the stain color?"

I looked down at my watch. "Now?"

I was a little disappointed. This wasn't a social call.

Just then, Leah breezed in. "I'm here. All is right with the world. I'm going to finish putting together the mood boards for Jack's boat today. And then I'll sort that new shipment of accessories from Barbara Cosgrove and arrange them—so that you can rearrange them."

"Well, then," Jack said. "Seems like you're nothing more than a fixture in this store." He pointed up. "Like the pretty light. How much is that?"

I pulled his hand down and shook my head. "You can't afford it."

He laughed and held his arm out to me, and I took it. "A beautiful fixture," he whispered, as we crossed the threshold, making me blush in earnest now.

I wondered what my daughters would think if they saw me on the arm of a very handsome man—who wasn't the one who raised them. But a few minutes of pretending wasn't going to hurt anyone. Nope. Not a bit.

"Thanks for coming by the other night," Jack said. "Sorry if I was a downer."

I smiled. "A downer? No, not at all. You were wonderful."

"Good. How is life at the Murphy mansion?" Jack quipped.

"It is hectic and lovely." I smiled at him.

It was such a beautiful morning. The sun was shining, and the trees were blowing in the breeze. My dress and light sweater were perfect. There was no doubt about it, spring was around the corner. But I couldn't focus on any of it, because all I could think about was my arm and Jack's arm and his eyes and those dimples and the way he made my stomach feel like it was flip-flopping around in my insides. I was too old to be acting and feeling this way. And he would be gone in a matter of weeks when his boat was seaworthy again. But maybe that was what made it so good. I didn't have to feel that urge to run away, because it couldn't go anywhere.

I let go of Jack's arm reluctantly, knowing that I would only put mine back around his if he offered and not knowing whether he would. It was like being a teenager again in a lot of ways. You weren't even considering sex. Not even kissing, really. Just flirting a little, testing the waters, wondering when your hand would brush his again. When he would say that thing that made you feel special and beautiful all at once. And hoping it wouldn't be too long.

"I would love to meet your girls," Jack said. "And I made a gift for little Adam."

Despite my happy feelings, the warning bells rang in my mind. I had realized decades earlier that a part of me would always love Jack. But my love for him couldn't begin to touch my love for my girls. Yes, they were encouraging me to date. But my motherly instinct told me that this wasn't the right time to bring someone new into their lives. They had enough turmoil. Plus, I couldn't be sure since I'd never been through this, but I felt pretty certain that you didn't introduce a man to your children until you were very serious. Jack and I hadn't even been on a date.

"Jack," I said softly. "Would it be OK if I waited awhile before I introduced you to the girls?"

He stopped walking and was looking at me. "Oh, yes. Of course. Sorry." He shook his head. "I'm getting ahead of myself. It's just that it has always felt so easy to be with you."

I nodded. It had. It was natural, like sliding back into a great-fitting pair of sunglasses that you had lost and then found again.

As I approached the hunk of junk that was supposed to be a boat one day, my stomach turned again, for a different reason. I had vision, but honestly, I wasn't sure about this one.

"Ansley!"

"Sheldon!" He was sanding the front of the boat.

He embraced me in a big, sweaty hug that, frankly, I could have done without. "So are you the high priestess of teak stain? That's what I'm told."

I laughed and looked at Jack. "Why, thank you, sir."

He tipped a fake hat at me.

I reached my leg over the side of the boat, my patent-leather-wedge-clad foot tapping the deck.

"Ma'am," Sheldon said. "I'm not sure about your footwear."

I lifted my foot. "See? Rubber soles."

"That's a real woman," Sheldon said, handing me three pieces of teak. I pretended to study them, but in reality, I made up my mind the moment I saw them. I handed him back the one in the middle.

"Wow," Jack said. "I looked at those for like forty-five minutes before I came to get you. What do I owe you?"

I shook my head and looked at him. "You've given me enough, Jack."

I turned to walk back to the store, and he followed me, matching my pace, our legs moving in sync. "Can I take you to lunch?" he asked.

I had so much to do. It pained me to say, "I need to get back to work."

His face fell, and I couldn't stand that I had been the one to make it do that. So I said, "Well, maybe we could grab a quick bite."

He smiled and offered his arm to me again, and, just like that, I was giddy and carefree.

"I'll have your mood boards ready tomorrow," I said. "I'll get a feel for what you want, and then we'll go from there."

He stopped walking and said, "I want whatever you want, Ansley."

And I knew right then and there, despite my fear, despite my hesitation, despite the queasy feeling in my stomach, that I wanted much, much more.

FOURTEEN

short straw

caroline

I used every trick I had to try to get Emerson to move to Manhattan instead of LA. I mean, sure, anyone could see that if you wanted to be on TV, LA was probably the spot. But there was Broadway. And off Broadway. And way, way off Broadway.

I always said things like "You can get Chinese food at two a.m.!" But when had I ever gotten Chinese food at two a.m.? I didn't like Chinese food. I did, however, like the energy. It felt like everyone was on a mission, had a purpose. Here, it was kind of like people were meandering around until they died. I mean, yeah, they had to walk their dog or whatever. Catch some fish for dinner. But that was about it. Usually, this would have driven me insane. Now, though, I was nesting. So it was actually kind of appealing.

I was in the guesthouse by myself. Vivi was in the main house playing with Adam and Taylor, which made me very happy. You wonder how your kid is going to adapt after being an only child for so long. Seeing how much she loved her cousins, I got the feeling that my girl was going to be all right.

What was not going to be all right was this crib. One, I was gigantic. Two, I had never used a tool in my life. Three, all I could think about was the fact that my husband had just appeared on TV with another woman, and the entire country, it felt like, was talking about what an idiot I was, knocked up and hiding out while my husband was gallivanting around. It felt like he had won. And I hated losing. Hated it. I finally threw the directions into the air and marched down the stairs, over to the main house.

"I am not suited for crib construction," I said very dramatically, before thrusting myself onto a chaise, hand over forehead.

It wasn't until afterward that I realized Kimmy and Kyle were standing in the living room.

I sat up sheepishly. "Sorry," I said.

Kyle said, "Perfect timing. This is a decaf, low-sugar, dairy-free creation for the mother-to-be. It has rooibos tea, which I read Indian women drink to keep their iron levels up during pregnancy."

I took a sip and gasped. "Kyle! You have outdone yourself! This is heaven in a cup."

He grinned. God, he was good-looking. I winked at Emerson, who grinned back at me. For a split second, I considered that maybe I could have a little rebound fling with Kyle. It was probably the pregnancy hormones talking. Probably.

"Let me get a pic," Emerson said. "We need to commemorate the moment that my sister realized there was life—and coffee—outside of New York City."

I motioned to her. "Come get in, too!"

"OK," Kimmy said, annoyance lacing her voice. "I suppose I'll take the picture, then."

"Take a few," I said, twisting this way and that like a belly dancer to see which angle made me look thinnest.

"OK," Em said. "Last one! Double kisses!"

I threw my arms around Kyle's neck and planted a kiss on his cheek. Emmy much more demurely pecked his other cheek.

"Thanks, Kyle," I said. "This has really brightened my day. Now, if I could find a way to get *Ladies Who Lunch* off the air, that would really cap it off."

"Yeah, that sucks," Kyle said. "What idiot would leave *you*?"

"Evidently, *you* would," I said.

He furrowed his brow but continued to smile.

I pointed to my stomach. "The rumor around town is that my baby could potentially be yours, and Emmy and I are in a family feud because you dumped me for her."

"Wow," Kyle said. "I am the man."

Sloane walked through the front door with some other hottie. I mean, Kyle was a young hottie. This guy was kind of old. Like Mom's age. I had to investigate.

"Hi," I said, reaching out my hand. "I'm Caroline."

He had deep brown eyes, distinguished-looking eyebrows, and a nose that was appropriately large for making him look very masculine. And he was wearing shorts, so you could tell that his legs were tan and muscular. But I got this weird feeling like I knew him. Which, of course, I probably did from when we lived in Peachtree before.

He smiled, those eyes dazzling me. "You must be the actress," he said, laughing.

It took me a moment to figure out why that was funny. "Oh, I get it," I said. "As opposed to the pregnant one. Nope, I'm definitely the pregnant one."

"Jack is looking for Mom," Sloane said.

"I just wanted to drop off her sweater. She left it on my boat."

I guess I didn't hide my shock that my mother had left her clothing on some strange man's boat. And, obviously, he was a man that she knew well enough to tell him all about us.

He laughed again. "Your mom's my decorator. She came by the boat this morning to pick out a stain."

Still. Mom should really explore that. Sloane had obviously had the same thought, because it was clear she had trapped him here. This guy looked like he wanted to get the hell away. And fast. I was pretty sure he wouldn't be standing in our kitchen if Sloane hadn't sweet-talked him in some way.

I did a quick hand check. No ring. And I liked him right away, which is really saying something, because I generally like no one. I looked at him intently. "Are you married?"

"No."

"Dating anyone serious?" Sloane chimed in.

He looked back and forth between us. "Am I on some sort of trial here?"

"Yes, you are," Sloane said seriously.

He pointed to the door. "Maybe I should be wearing a tie for this."

Emerson caught my attention. She was chomping on something, thank God. Maybe she would live until next week when the movie started filming.

That gave me an idea. "So our little Emmy is starting her new movie, and Sloane and I are having a dinner party to celebrate."

"We are?" Sloane said. I gave her my sternest look. She caught on. "Oh," she said. "I mean, we are. Yes. And we'd love it if you would come."

"Oh," he said. "Shouldn't you ask your mother?"

"Our mother is not capable of deciding what is good for her," Emerson said. "So we are stepping in."

"Yeah, it's kind of like an intervention," I said.

He smiled and looked very pleased by all of this. "I will come if you promise you'll ask your mother if it's OK first."

"Oh, sure, sure," I lied. Which was when I had my brilliant idea. "Actually, though, we have one more hurdle for you to jump before you are officially invited."

He crossed his arms, looking less terrified and more amused now. He had these great dimples. I know great dimples, because I have them. His weren't quite as good as mine but pretty good. "I'm up for it. I am certain."

I took his arm and began leading him through the house. "How are you at crib assembly?"

He put his arm around me in a way that should have been entirely too friendly for someone I had met three minutes before in the foyer. But he squeezed me to his side and said, "Caroline, for you, I'll even put a crib together."

He did. And there weren't even any pieces left over, which was comforting. That was when I knew for sure that Mom had better not screw this one up.

———————

WE ALL GOT A little messed up when Dad died. Mom made us go to therapy, even though she wouldn't ever go, which I thought was incredibly unfair. Anyone could see that she was drowning. Sloane was terrified even to come out of her room. Emerson was crying in her sleep. But me? I was OK. Super sad, obviously. But not totally unglued like the others.

At the time, the fact that I developed this intense germophobia right after 9/11 didn't seem related. I couldn't ride the subway and held on with antibacterial wipes if I had to. I would only get into a cab if I was wearing pants. I wouldn't shake anyone's hand and got jittery in crowds. It honestly took me years to realize that perhaps this was somehow related to Dad's death.

But now I think it's too late. Being outside in the truly fresh air of Peachtree Bluff helped ease my panic, but I wasn't cured or anything. And Mom definitely drew the short straw that day. I could feel my palms starting to sweat as we got into the car that afternoon. She cranked the ignition, and as we were getting ready to pull out, the back door flung open. "I'm coming, too!" Emerson said.

I looked back at her. "You're leaving Sloane with all the kids?"

She raised her eyebrows, as if to say *They're not my kids*. "Vivi is holding a sidewalk chalk workshop, and Sloane is catching a few rays. I'm pretty sure they're covered."

"You must be hard up if you're willing to come tour the hospital with us instead." I paused. "By the way, any new men in your life?" I looked at her pointedly.

Mom glanced over her shoulder to back out of the driveway and said, "I swear, you girls are going to be the absolute death of me."

Emerson laughed. "Sorry, Mom. But there are no guys. I don't have time for guys. I feel like with this movie, I'm finally going to gain some ground."

"You've already gained ground," I said. "I think sometimes you're so busy looking toward the top of the ladder you forget how many rungs you have already climbed."

"That's true," Mom chimed in. "Emerson, you're supporting yourself as an actress. You have steady work. Do you know how amazing that is?"

She smiled happily. "Yeah. That is pretty cool. But I just feel like in a couple more years, my career will be on stable ground, and then I can worry about love and all that."

"Speaking of," I said. "Mom, we have all agreed that you should marry Jack immediately if not sooner."

Her face went kind of white at the mention of his name, which was a weird reaction, if you asked me. Knowing her, I would have guessed that an on-trend shade of plum would be more fitting.

"Where did you meet *him*?"

I thought she was just embarrassed, but then I realized she was something more like mad.

I reached into my bag to get a Preggie Pop. I didn't have morning sickness anymore, but I was kind of addicted to the things. I handed Mom one, too. She looked sort of morning sick. Much to my surprise, she pulled the wrapper off and put it in her mouth.

"He came by earlier," Emmy said. "He brought your sweater."

"He may or may not have put together the baby's crib."

"He came to our *house*?" Mom asked.

Now I realized she wasn't mad, exactly. Maybe more like confused. Incredulous, even. Fortunately, I was so distracted that I had barely realized we were pulling into the hospital parking lot. But when I did, my entire body went cold.

Mom put the car in park, and I saw the look she gave Emerson. "Let's get out of the car."

"And while we're walking in, you'll tell us all about Jack?" I asked.

"Wait," Emmy said. "So there's a story?"

There's always a story, I thought. But I couldn't say it.

Now I was hot. I pulled my maternity dress in and out a few times. Maternity dresses really were tragic. They were probably all designed by men to make you look like an absolute cow.

Emerson opened the car door and took my sweaty hand. "You know what?" I said. "I'm fine. I don't need to see the hospital."

Mom was now beside Emerson, coaxing me. "Sweetie, you

are going to feel more anxious if you haven't seen where you're giving birth. Let's take a quick peek at the room, and then we'll get out of here." She smiled. "And I'll tell you all about how Jack and I dated a couple of summers during high school."

I perked up at that. "Really? Was he your first love?" First love stories are my favorite. I gave her a withering look. "Are you just saying this to get me to go in there?"

"No." She waved her hand at me.

I leaned over and started breathing heavily.

"OK, OK," she said. "Yes. He was my first love."

I got out of the car.

"We met in Peachtree, actually," she said. "He was sixteen, and I was fifteen."

"Was he your first kiss?" Emerson asked.

Mom put her hand on the small of my back and led me through the automatic doors. It was as though I could feel the millions of germs leap onto my body. I needed to go home and get into the shower. Oh, God, I had worn my new wedges. Now they were ruined. Everyone knew that once you wore shoes in a hospital, you had to throw them away.

"He was my first kiss," she said, while Emerson grabbed a nurse and spoke to her tersely.

The nurse jumped in and said, "Ms. Caroline, we are so glad to have you here." You could tell that she started to put out her hand and then withdrew it. She had obviously been told that I had no doubt she was highly infected with something disgusting. Probably hospital-acquired pneumonia. Yup. That's what it looked like to me.

"This is our brand-new, state-of-the-art facility, and the good news is that you will likely be only the third or fourth person ever to give birth in this room."

My breath was getting shorter.

"Relax, Caroline," my mom said.

Have you ever noticed how someone telling you to relax makes you more uptight?

Emerson appeared beside me and handed me a cup of water.

"Have you completely lost your mind? Do you honestly think that I would drink *hospital* water?"

"OK," the nurse said. "Here it is. Your big, beautiful birthing suite."

There was a curtain. I looked at my mom. I didn't have to say another word. "Ma'am," she said, "is it possible to get that curtain taken down when Caroline is here?"

She scrunched up her face. "It's here to give Ms. Caroline some privacy."

I felt my strength returning. "No, that's a great idea," I said. "So my doctor washes his hands over here, touches this MRSA-infected curtain, and then comes and delivers my baby, transmitting deadly bacteria not only to the baby but also to me. That sounds like a swell idea. Has anyone in this hospital ever seen an OSHA report?"

"Oooo-K," Emerson said. "Mom, I'm going to take Caroline to the car now." She made a face at the nurse like she was sorry, but they should be sorry. Imbeciles, every last one. No wonder people came into the hospital and didn't make it out.

"I'm going to have a home birth," I said. "My midwife,

Hummus, is coming anyway, and we can get one of those big birthing tubs and put it in the living room. It will be great. Everyone can help." (Yes, my midwife was named Hummus.)

Emerson led me back through the double doors, and I started to relax immediately. I knew already that by the time I came to this hospital again, I wouldn't feel like this. I would be in intense labor, and I wouldn't care if I lay down in the parking lot to give birth.

"But, honey," Emerson said, "then you won't be able to have an epidural."

Good call. I realized that my phone was ringing in my pocket, and I silently prayed it wasn't James. I couldn't take one more thing today. Nope. My friend Lucinda.

"Hi there," I said. I knew I sounded weird and winded.

"Are you OK?" she asked.

"Just did my hospital tour."

"Ah," she said. "And you didn't pass out?"

"Nope. Just almost."

"Good for you, lady. That's major growth."

"It really is."

Emerson opened the car door, and even though it was hot inside, it still felt good to be out of there.

"So what's up?"

"I know you're not doing the social media thing," Lucinda said, "but all our friends are dying to know who the Instagram hottie is."

"Em, did you Instagram the pic of you and me and Kyle this morning?"

"Yeah," she said absentmindedly. I could tell she was check-ing her e-mail.

"Well, I owe you. Lucinda says people are talking about it, and surely it will get back to James."

"Oh, I'll make sure it gets back to James," Lucinda said.

I smiled. There was a bit of commotion from Lucinda's end, and she said, "Got to go!" before hanging up.

"What?" Mom said, as she opened the car door. "What did I miss?"

I handed her the phone with the Instagram post open.

She gasped. "No! Caroline, you can't catch a break."

"Can't catch a break?" I said. "That's the best thing that's happened to me in a long time."

I read the first few comments. "Wait," I said. "Is Kyle an actor?"

"Well . . ." Emerson said. "He isn't an actor per se, but he's going to have a one-line part in my movie. When somebody asked what he did in a comment, I didn't think 'barista' sounded quite as revenge-ish."

I turned to her as Mom started toward home. "You're the best sister in the whole world!"

I was so excited by this turn of events I decided I wouldn't even throw my new shoes away. Nope. After my shower and dropping my white dress into some Clorox, I would have some-one thoroughly Lysol them. And then I'd give them to Emerson as a thank-you.

As we pulled into the driveway, I said, "OK, Mom. More info about Jack."

"Nah. That was more like a hospital bribe. Now the moment's over."

"Noooooo!" Emerson cried, as Mom grabbed her purse and shut the door.

"Well, damn," I said.

"It's OK," Emerson said. "I don't need another piece of information to be totally sure that she's in love with him."

"You think?" I said.

But she didn't need to answer for me to know that it was probably true. First loves never completely go away, after all. He seemed like a great guy, and I wanted to share in my sister's excitement. But I couldn't shake the feeling that there was something we didn't know about Jack.

FIFTEEN

ulterior motive

ansley

Whether he was near the calming waters of Peachtree or in the hustle and bustle of Manhattan, whether it was the best day of his life or the worst, Carter was an eternal optimist. Which is probably why it took me so long to understand how it was possible that he could have been killed in our country's worst tragedy. Those things happened to other people. Not me. And certainly not Carter. He was one of the good guys.

In fact, for weeks after the attacks, I kept expecting him to walk through the door. It would be a sort of joke. "Oh, honey. You poor thing. You forgot I was in Hong Kong? I couldn't get home because the airports were shut down."

Something like that. Only he didn't come home. We stayed in Manhattan for ninety-nine days. It took ninety-nine days for the fires to go out, and it was then and only then that I felt I could leave. I knew I would never see my husband again. I knew he was gone. I hoped he hadn't suffered, but if he had, I wanted to know that I had been there with him the entire time. I had never left his side. I had been his wife until I was sure it was the bitter end. There was nothing more for me to do.

Then I packed my girls up and got the hell out of there. I had to. It was the only way.

I don't know why Caroline became so afraid of hospitals and germs after that. It was so strange. Carter wasn't in a hospital, although I assure you, we most certainly wished he had been. I kept hoping and praying that maybe he was there, maybe he had been rescued after all, maybe he had gotten a head injury, maybe he was in a coma and it would take a while to discover who he was. Then they would find us. It would be our miracle, the miracle that brought our family back together.

My miracle never came. It had always been Carter who believed in miracles. After we were married, after we had found out the two of us were never going to have a baby, he had still hoped.

But after another year or so, even my miracle-believing husband had become weary. "I'm forty-two," he had said. "At this rate, I'll be sixty-three before the first one gets out of college."

"So let's adopt," I said. "Let's get on some lists."

Carter didn't like the idea of that. "Just because we can't have my baby, that doesn't mean we can't have yours." I'll never forget his saying that, the way he looked at me like I was this perfect specimen whose legacy needed to be maintained.

Truth be told, adoption wasn't my first choice, either. I would have done it in a heartbeat if that were the only way. But

I longed to carry a baby, to feel it inside me, to know it before it was born. I had seen my friends, that glow they got, the way I knew they must feel, like the most important people in the world. I wanted to feel important. I wanted people to ask me when I was due, to ask if I knew what I was having. I wanted all of that. Carter did, too.

I hated the term "artificial insemination." It sounded like a sci-fi movie, like my baby was going to come from an alien life force. But it was fairly common.

Now, as I was lost in the past, lost in my thoughts about my husband, Caroline walked through the kitchen door, head wet, robe on.

"All clean?" I asked.

"All clean."

"Why are you so terrorized by hospitals now, my love?"

She shrugged. "I don't know. Too much *Sixty Minutes*, I guess. Sometimes you wish you didn't know things. You know what I mean?"

I knew exactly what she meant. More than she could possibly imagine.

Sloane had stepped up for Caroline's second hospital visit in as many days. Sloane was nothing if not a calming influence.

Evidently, the major part of the hospital tour was filling out the paperwork, something that Caroline had failed to do in her panicked rush to get out of there the day before. I thought I would throw up when I heard the message. So I had done what any good mother would do. I'd tapped on Sloane's door. "Hi, darling," I had said.

"Hi, Mom."

"I would love to keep the kids in the morning. It's story time at the library, and it's so adorable. They'll love it. I'll take them for a stroll afterward and maybe to lunch. We can go to the club, where they can run around outside, not have to be stuck in high chairs."

Sloane had smiled at me warily. "That sounds great, and I'm not questioning your status as a terrific grandmother, but I feel like there's an ulterior motive here."

I had shot her my best wide-eyed, insulted look. "I have no idea what you mean. Of course, if you wanted to go with Caroline to the hospital to fill out her paperwork, I wouldn't stop you . . ."

Sloane had laughed. "I'll go with her. You and Emerson had to do it yesterday."

Emerson had popped her head in. "Never again," she'd said.

Now I asked Caroline, "You feeling OK about everything? Are you sure you want to have the baby here? Because you won't be able to fly back to New York soon."

She nodded. "I know." She raised her lip. "I guess I have to call James and tell him we're staying here. Do I have to let him come for the delivery?"

I couldn't imagine having that man in the room to deliver our baby, when he was running all over television with some tramp who, if you asked me, wasn't nearly as beautiful as my Caroline. Edie Fitzgerald was one of those girls who photographed really well but looked kind of strange otherwise.

Vivi flew into the kitchen. "Mom! Mom!"

I was happy to see her this excited. She seemed to be adjusting shockingly well. But I had a feeling that being in Peachtree was a vacation, simply prolonging the true agony. When they got back home, that was when things were going to get dicey.

Caroline held her arm out for her daughter to get under. "Can I go to the set with Emerson? Please, please, please!" Vivi begged.

She laughed. "Honey, I don't know. Did she ask you?"

"I did," Emerson said, appearing from around the corner. "I thought it might be fun for her to come with me." She paused. "And, well, when they see how fabulous she is, I'm sure they'll have to come up with a part for her."

Caroline gave her sister the evil eye, and Emerson smiled triumphantly. Caroline couldn't say no now, after Emerson had asked in front of Vivi. It was wrong on so many levels, but Emerson obviously knew that.

I, for one, was relieved that the filming was starting so my child could eat again in the near future. It was worrisome.

As Emerson and Vivi left, Sloane, Taylor, and Adam came in. Adam rushed to the toy workbench in the corner that I had gotten for him. Much to my delight, Taylor reached his arms out to me. I smiled triumphantly.

"Hi there, Taylor," I said, kissing my grandson's cheek. "A little Southern gentleman, just the way I like them."

Caroline rolled her eyes. "Yeah, I probably should have listened to you on that one. Why did I have to rush off to New York? I could have gone to college in South Carolina or somewhere and met a guy there. Then I wouldn't have to deal with all this right now."

We all laughed. The mere idea of Caroline living anywhere but New York was like the idea of a fish suddenly growing legs and walking on the land.

My phone buzzed in my pocket. It was a text from my brother Scott. I held my breath. Mom seems fine. Kind of moody sometimes. But fine. Overreacted.

Thank the Lord.

The phone buzzed again. Love, Your FAVORITE brother.

I smiled.

The doorbell rang, and Taylor looked at me disconcertedly. "It's OK," I said. "It's just the doorbell. Let's go see who it is," I practically sang.

When I first saw the outline of a young man's body through the paned glass, I thought it was Kyle with some new concoction. But as I got closer, I realized it wasn't Kyle at all. And I knew, without question, that our quiet girls' day was coming to an end.

I've always been that woman who thinks of the right thing to say after the fact. In the moment, I'm tongue-tied and stupid, but afterward, I discover the perfect words.

Not this time. Nope. I had played it out plenty in my head. And I wasn't letting the moment pass.

"I'm sorry" was the first thing James said. Not the best opening argument I've ever heard from a lawyer, but maybe not the worst, either.

I laughed. I hoped it sounded malicious.

"I am, Ansley," he said. He was all New York City–slick in

his suit and tie and fancy shoes. The men around here would have eaten him for lunch. I bet he'd never even cut his own grass. "I don't know what I was thinking or what I was doing, but I've loved Caroline from the moment I saw her."

I crossed my arms. I hoped he'd noticed that I had yet to invite him in. "You have a funny way of showing it," I said.

He looked down at his feet. "I think I must have lost my mind or something."

I nodded. "Lost your wife, too, so I hope it was worth it."

He looked shocked. "Do you really think I've lost her?"

I was incredulous. "Are you serious? Have you met her?" I still hadn't invited him in.

"I just want a chance to explain."

This was where it got good. This was where I made up for all those times I didn't say what I meant. "I'd like a chance to explain, too," I said. "I'd like to explain that you have never been good enough for my daughter. I have never thought you were. I've always thought you were untrustworthy and slimy and that you tried to buy her love. She always has been and always will be too good for you. I can't imagine that she would even think about taking you back, but if she asked my opinion, I'd tell her not to."

It might have been the first time I'd seen James stunned speechless. I opened the door wider and motioned with my arm to let him through.

I waited for that feeling to set in, the one where I felt bad about what I said, where I wished I could take it back somehow. But that feeling never came.

pregnancy fetish

caroline

I was almost eighteen by the time we moved to Peachtree. I had already been accepted into NYU summer school and was actively searching for summer jobs or internships in the city. When Mom kidnapped us, forcibly removed us from the center of the universe, and relocated us to the seventh circle of hell, as it seemed to me at the time, I knew I was going to be living there for only a few months. There was no point in getting a license or learning to drive. I was raised having a driver, and I knew the subway system like the back of my hand. That was the beauty of living in Manhattan. It was a pedestrian city.

I was still in the kitchen talking to Sloane and Emerson that day when Mom went to answer the door. I filled them in on the tiny tidbits I'd gained from Mom about Jack. I opened the refrigerator door to look for my coconut yogurt. We were out.

"Hey," I said, turning back around. "Could one of you take me to the grocery store tomorrow?"

"Caroline, for God's sake," Emerson said. "We're sick of driving you around. You have to get a license."

"I don't need a license. You two can take me everywhere."

Emerson and Sloane looked at each other wearily.

"Can you even imagine that I came to this brand-new world with no Uber? I'm in shock enough, and now you want me to get a driver's license?"

"Honey, it's a normal thing. We're not asking for something crazy here." Emerson paused. "Plus, I'm pretty sure you won't want to haul a car seat in and out every time you have to go somewhere."

Oh, my God. I looked down at my belly. I wasn't delusional. I knew this baby was coming. I had simply forgotten about all of that. The car seats and the breastfeeding and the sleepless nights. I could feel my heart racing in my chest. I was going to be a single mother. A *single mother*. It sounded so blue-collar.

I barely got through having Vivi, and James was like Super Dad. How in the hell was I going to do this alone?

Earlier, James had texted me: Hey, Car. I know you're pissed, but I really want to see Vivi. I'm going to stop by the apartment tonight.

I typed back, rapid-fire: We're already in Peachtree.

I get the feeling you're avoiding me.

How astute.

I miss my kid, he typed. You're coming back by Friday to get ready for school to start, right?

Hmmm . . . Keeping him from getting suspicious was going to be tricky.

I'll call you tomorrow.

I knew I couldn't hold him off forever. But if I could make it another week or so . . . I still hadn't decided whether it would be better to go ahead and tell him now that we were moving for the semester, giving him time for it to soak in, or to spring it on him later. We all knew it was easier to ask forgiveness than permission—unless it negatively affected your upcoming custody case. Then that was a different matter. Part of me wanted to have Vivi tell him, but I knew that was not a good parenting move. I needed to buy more time.

"Yeah, Caroline," Sloane said. "You might meet the new love of your life if you get your driver's license."

I raised an eyebrow. But yeah, the girl knew how to get to me. I was intrigued. "How's that?"

"Oh, I know," Emerson said. "Remember how Sloane was always getting speeding tickets when we were younger?"

I shrugged. "Yeah. I guess."

Poor Mom.

"You could get pulled over," Sloane said. "You're reaching for your license and registration as the sexy cop saunters up to the car and lowers his aviators at you."

"He has that three-day beard you love," Emerson said. She paused and added, "And a pregnancy fetish."

We all laughed. "And you say, 'Here's my license and registration, Officer,' " Sloane said.

Emerson chimed in, "And he says, 'All I need is your number, little lady.' "

"And then he takes you out to a beautiful dinner with white tablecloths."

Emerson scrunched her nose. "No, Sloane. Then he makes out with her on the hood of the cop car."

Sloane's turn to scrunch her nose. "Ew, Em. No. Nice dinner."

They both looked at me as though they were waiting to hear my choice. I smiled. Then I grabbed the laminated sheet out of Emerson's hand with pictures of all the road signs on it.

"Fine." I sighed. "I guess I can get my driver's license."

"Yay!" Sloane said.

I rolled my eyes. It wasn't like I was getting my PhD.

I heard Mom call, "Caroline!"

I reached up over my head. I was at that point in my pregnancy when my skin wasn't stretching quickly enough to keep up with my expanding belly, and it felt tight and itchy. *Oh, my God*, I thought, as I walked through the dining room. *What if I get stretch marks*? I had been very young when I had Vivi, after all.

Between the dining room and the living room, I stopped dead in my tracks. I hadn't expected to be caught so off guard. I hadn't had time to formulate my story, to be charming, to try to finagle my way out of this thing that I had done that was very, very wrong. I had brought Vivi for vacation. That was my story, and I was sticking to it.

"What are you doing here, James?"

He had on my favorite suit, with the loafers I had gotten him for Christmas. Why did he have to look so handsome? It was horrible, adding insult to injury. At least if he had let himself go a little . . . Although if he'd let himself go a little, we wouldn't be in this mess, because what in the world would Edie Fitzgerald have wanted with him?

He walked up to me, his jaw steeled, that anger he stored between his eyebrows creating parallel lines above his nose. But I think I could argue that I had more right to be mad than he did.

Instead of answering, James practically spit out, "Who is he?"

I looked around, confused. I hadn't seen my husband in weeks. I had just lied to him repeatedly via text message, and he obviously knew it. This seemed like an odd first question. *Like maybe you'd be mad I stole your daughter?* But this was good. Whatever was making him so angry was something I might want to go with. It might keep me off the hook a little longer.

"Who is who?" I asked nonchalantly, crossing my arms over my belly.

He thrust his phone into my hand and pushed past me, looking around, as though this were my love nest and I had some man sequestered away here, not that it was my mother's house that I was sharing with my entire family.

I almost laughed out loud. There it was. That picture of me kissing Kyle on the cheek.

If it were possible, Kyle looked even hotter online than he did in real life. Way to go, Coffee Kyle. Giving me my street cred back. And there I was, pregnant belly in all its glory, as I was turned to the side. But my cheekbones looked very high. Mom and Emerson high. My facial skin must be stretching with the pregnancy. Or Emerson had used the Photo Plastic app before posting the picture on Instagram. I was going to go with that being what I actually looked like.

I smirked. "So what, James? Did you expect me to sit around here and mope and mourn forever?" *Like I actually have been doing . . .*

"Gee," he said sarcastically. "I don't know, Caroline. I guess maybe I thought that you would wait longer than a few weeks to be out gallivanting."

I laughed ironically. "Is that a joke? Are you serious right now? You've been screwing Edie Fitzgerald for months, while we are married, while I am pregnant with your child, and you're worried about *me* moving on." I stomped to the front door, flung it open, and said, "Get out."

He stopped in his tracks, a stunned look taking over his face. "Wait," he said. "I got off to a bad start here. This isn't how this was supposed to go. I got so worked up on the plane that I couldn't do this right."

I crossed my arms. "James, get the hell out of the house. I will call the police chief, and let me tell you, this is a small town. We are friends, and he won't give a shit about you and your slicked-back hair and your tight suits. Understand me?" Oh, that suit . . . He did this on purpose. He knew I couldn't resist that suit. It was cruel.

He looked around. "Where is Vivi?"

"She's on set with Emerson."

"Set?" he said, his nostrils flaring. "Is she with *Kyle*? Are they bonding? Getting tight? Is he moving in on my wife *and* my child?"

"James, I'm only your wife on paper. I would think you would know that better than anyone."

He smiled at me with something like nostalgia on his face. It was so odd. James took two steps closer to me and reached out to take my hand.

I slapped his away. "Do not touch me ever again. Do you understand? I do not want your nasty supermodel hand on me. God only knows where she's been."

"Caroline," he said softly. "I came all the way out here to tell you that I miss you, to tell you that I made a huge mistake. I want our family back."

They weren't bad words to hear. They really weren't. They almost brought tears to my eyes, despite how angry I was. Because no matter how I acted, all I'd ever wanted was a family. But I knew better than this.

I narrowed my eyes at him. "James Beaumont, if you think I'm going to take you back and then you won't have to pay me, you've got another think coming. I suggest you get the hell off my property." I realized I sounded downright Southern when I said it. A few weeks here, and I was totally ruined—or saved. It was hard to tell.

He smiled calmly. "That's fine, Caroline," he said. "Have it your way. But I'm not leaving until you give me another chance."

I crossed my arms. "Then you'd better head over to the graveyard and pick out a burial plot, James Beaumont. Because I will never, ever take you back on this side of hell."

I picked up my phone and showed it to him. "I will ask you

one more time. And then I will call the cops. They have nothing else to do."

James smiled and put his hands up in surrender. "Fine," he said. "But I'll be back tomorrow." He stopped on the first step and turned to look at me. "And Caroline, so you know, the only reason I'm not suing the shit out of you right now for kidnapping my daughter is that I love you so much and I want to work this out. But don't think that I don't know what you're up to. Got it?"

And it made me think there was a chance, a small one, that James might actually want me back for real.

I WAS INCREDIBLY SUPPORTIVE of Emerson's acting dreams, sure. But that didn't mean I understood where she was coming from. Obviously, I had gone through a stage where I wanted to be Cinderella, like any other self-respecting American girl. But once I outgrew that, I never dreamed of my name in lights.

I hoped against hope that Vivi's overwhelming enthusiasm about being in this movie wasn't a sign that she would want to act. I sat in the passenger seat and looked out the window while Mom drove. Sloane had stayed behind to start working on dinner. That was a good thing, because I certainly couldn't cook.

I wasn't sure how I could do anything except think about what had happened a few days ago with James, but we had promised Vivi that we would come watch her film. Emmy had acted liked she didn't want us to come, but Mom and I reasoned that she was simply being shy about her accomplishment. It was kind of charming. So we were excited to surprise her.

Today's scenes were on the beach, which I thought was particularly fabulous—and particularly close. The best way to get the real feel of the Georgia coast was to film on the Georgia coast, after all. I hadn't gotten to see Emmy in action in quite some time, and I couldn't wait to find out more about this secretive project she was working on.

When we got there, Vivi ran to me, amid the cameras and lights and throngs of people milling about. There were clothes racks and sun reflectors, hair and makeup people, sound crews. This was the real deal.

"Mom!" she said. "I get a whole line! I'm going to say, 'I want to be exactly like her when I grow up.'"

"Wow!" I said. "That is so amazing, sweets. You'll be in the credits and everything. First step toward stardom." I winked at her, and she ran back over to Emerson, while I silently hoped that she would realize this life wasn't as glamorous as it seemed.

Mom said, "Wow. Can you imagine getting all of this together here?"

I shook my head. "No. But it will be authentic."

I snapped a few photos and sent them to Sloane. She had a Skype date with Adam later, and I thought he might like to see. Sloane always seemed so calm, so composed. It was such a one-eighty from how she had been after Dad died. She had carried so much anxiety for so many years. I knew there had to be some major fears lurking underneath that sparkly "this is the life I chose" façade. But she never let it show. A few days earlier, I had peeked into her room to ask if she wanted to go for a walk. I didn't know she was on Skype with Adam, and I was not trying to snoop. But it actually made me feel better that she was crying, that I heard her say, "Adam, I just don't think I can do this anymore. Please don't do this anymore. You could retire. This could be your last tour if you wanted it to be."

I know it sounds crazy, and it's not like I was relishing my sister's pain. Not at all. But her lack of emotion always scared me a little. It made me worried for her, for what she was keeping inside. I wished that she would let Emerson and me in a little bit, that she would give us some of that burden to carry. But she didn't. I couldn't imagine the uncertainty of that life.

Although as my heart raced thinking of my encounter with James a few days earlier, I realized I was living with uncertainty of my own. I was furious, sure. But I also wanted things for myself and my children. I wanted a family. I wanted normalcy. But the fact remained that I could never, ever forget what James had done to me. And I felt pretty sure that I would never trust him again.

I pulled out a Preggie Pop as Emerson took her place on set. Mom and I smiled at each other excitedly. The director yelled, "Action!"

Emerson said about two lines to some really cute actor, and then he pulled her in and started making out with her. Not a bad job.

I covered Vivi's eyes with my hand, and she pulled it away, exasperated, saying "Mo-om."

The director called, "Cut! Take five!" He walked over to Mom and me and introduced himself.

Mom cocked her head. "Listen," she said. "You know Emerson's career means everything to her, but is it really necessary for her to be so thin?"

He winced. "That's totally my fault. I suggested she lose a few pounds before filming, but she took things too far. I'll talk to her about it."

"We would really appreciate that," Mom said.

"Yeah," I added. "She keeps making me drink green juice, and it's so gross."

We all laughed.

"I hate to be out of the loop," I said. "What are you filming here?"

He laughed. "Didn't she say? Emerson's playing Edie Fitzgerald, portraying her meteoric rise to stardom after starting out as a poor Georgia girl."

I put my finger in my ear. "I'm sorry," I said, laughing. "It sounded like you said she was playing Edie Fitzgerald."

I looked at Mom. Her hand was over her mouth, so I was pretty sure she was shocked, too.

The director said, "OK. Got to get back to it. Your girl is up."

Mom and I stood there in shocked silence for what seemed like an hour but was probably only five minutes.

"Mom! Mom!" Vivi ran over, shout-whispering. "Did you see me?"

I pinned on my fakest smile. "Darling, you were marvelous. Oscar-worthy. Truly."

I sucked my Preggie Pop furiously, but this time, even that couldn't help. Suddenly, I felt like every person who was supposed to love me most in the world and always have my back had betrayed me in the worst way all at one time. I had done everything for Emerson. James and I had used every contact we could scrounge up to get her auditions, finagle parts for her, arrange publicity when she was going to be in a movie or on TV. How could she humiliate me like this? How could she . . . There weren't any words to describe this feeling. Being betrayed by your husband was one thing. But your sister? Your own sister?

And that voice in my head started all over again. *I'm not in love with you anymore. I'm not in love with you anymore.*

I wanted to run. But it occurred to me that nowhere was safe. I had come to Peachtree Bluff to escape reality, to be somewhere, anywhere I could break free from this humiliation. But now I realized it: There was absolutely nowhere to hide.

SEVENTEEN

moments like these

ansley

After Caroline half ran, half waddled off what had previously been a calming, coastal Georgia set, Emerson kept acting.

I didn't know what to do. Should I defend Emerson? Was this a defensible action? Was it OK because it was her job? A good opportunity? Even if it was, shouldn't Emerson have at least warned Caroline?

I knew that no matter what, Emerson should apologize. And it occurred to me that when I was home by myself, things like this didn't happen. I went to the store, I pulled fabric samples, I went to town meetings, I had heart-to-hearts with Hippie Hal over birds and soil erosion and wild horse preservation. I did not have screaming, hysterical daughters yelling at one another. Caroline had taken the car, which was dicey since she'd had a driver's license for two days. But I hadn't stopped her. She had tried to take Vivi, too, but I told her to let Vivi stay with me. I had the feeling Caroline needed a moment.

I picked up the phone and dialed Sloane. She answered.

"Code Blue," I said.

She laughed. "Mom, I have no idea what Code Blue means."

"It's new. From now on, Code Blue means major situation between your two sisters."

Sloane groaned. "What now?"

"Emerson is playing Edie Fitzgerald in this new movie."

"No!"

"Yes."

"Oh, dear."

"Exactly. So batten down the hatches. What did Caroline say when she got there?"

Sloane paused. "She isn't here."

That feeling in the pit of your stomach never goes away, that dread when you are worried about one of your children. Right now, it was almost consuming. Between Sloane's husband being deployed and Caroline's life erupting and Emerson's all-juice starvation plan, there were a lot of Tums and Tylenol PM consumed.

"Hmmm. I wonder where she is."

"Gransley," Vivi piped up. "You don't know where Mom is?"

I pinned on my biggest, fakest smile. "Oh, sweetie. I'm sure she's just picking up something for dinner."

Realizing that Vivi was beside me calmed me. No matter how she was feeling, Caroline would never leave Vivi.

When Emerson asked where Caroline had gone I told her

Caroline wasn't feeling well, which was the truth, technically. I knew Emerson hadn't handled the situation properly but there was no sense in ruining her shoot. Emerson told me to take her car home, that she would get a ride with the director. I took a moment to silently hope she wasn't sleeping with him.

When we got home, I couldn't help but notice that my car was still conspicuously absent from the driveway. This was not good. A girl who was eight months pregnant didn't need to be driving around this worked up.

"Viv," I said, "could you please get the biscuits we made out of the guesthouse freezer?"

"Sure, Gransley!"

I walked into the kitchen, where Sloane was cooking up a storm, and sighed. This was supposed to be a subtle lesson in entertaining for my daughters. I had set the wide-plank table on the front porch with my hand-painted Anna Weatherley china, my great-grandmother's monogrammed linens, the English sterling silver. We had gotten out the crystal, the intricately carved sterling candlesticks that I saved for special occasions, and Caroline, before she found out what was happening, had created six stunning flower arrangements in silver goblets and lined them down the table. They were a mix of blue hydrangeas, bells of Ireland, sweet peas, and a couple of gardenias she had found blooming in a particularly sunny spot. It was going to be all flowers and candlelight, a perfect table that made me wonder why I didn't entertain more.

"I'm going to bet that Caroline is no longer in a celebrating Emerson kind of mood," Sloane said.

I heard the front door open, and a familiar, deep voice called, "Hell-o-o!"

I looked at Sloane accusingly.

"Oh, right," she said. "I might have forgotten to tell you . . ."

She didn't have to finish the sentence, because Jack appeared in a sport coat with a bouquet of hydrangeas that I assumed were for me.

I looked from Jack to Sloane. "Someone want to get me up to speed?" I took the flowers and said, "Thank you." But the look I gave him was cold. His judgment should have been better. I had let it go that he put the crib together. But I could not have been clearer with Jack about being around my family.

"Your lovely girls invited me to dinner," Jack said. "I hope that's OK. They promised me they would fill you in."

"You would think they would have, wouldn't you?" I paused. "Jack, there is some turmoil around the Murphy home right now." I turned to lead him out the door, trying to keep my composure. "I think we should take a rain check."

I heard the front door open again and braced myself. "I have the best news!"

It was Emerson.

"I am too thin!" she yelled. "Ice cream for everyone!"

She stopped dead in her tracks when she reached the kitchen. "Oh, hi. Sorry, Jack. A little actress life here."

He held his hand up for Emerson to give him five. "I'm always up for ice cream."

My heart raced. I didn't want them high-fiving. I didn't

want my daughters getting attached to him. I didn't want them getting to know one another. I wanted Jack to go.

She ran in place and squealed, "I'm reading too thin on camera. I get to gain three whole pounds!"

I looked at Vivi. "Please don't ever be like this."

She shook her head.

I was so relieved. My child did not have an eating disorder! She was having ice cream!

"First," Sloane said, opening the oven, "let's eat."

"Ohhhh, I smell tipsy cake," Emerson said, inhaling. "Even better." She looked around. "Hey, where's Caroline?"

"Oh," I said. "About that. Someone may or may not have told her that you were playing Edie Fitzgerald."

By the look on Emerson's face, you could tell that she was no longer all that interested in ice cream. "Oh, no," she said. "I wanted the chance to explain."

"With all due respect, sugar," I said, "you should have told her way before now if you wanted the chance to explain." It suddenly made sense why Emerson hadn't wanted us to come to the set. She wasn't being modest; she had something to hide.

"OK," I said again. "Jack, we'll see you later."

"Mom," Sloane said, looking at me incredulously. "It's fine. Quit being so rude."

Dinner was a little strained. Well, actually, very strained. We were all on edge about Caroline's whereabouts but trying to act casual for Vivi's sake. I was caught in a place between mad that Jack had ignored my wishes, irritated that the girls had gone behind my back, and positively over the moon that he was sitting beside me at the table.

The food was so delicious it made up for the weirdness. Sloane had made a beautiful salad with prosciutto, peaches, mozzarella, and thyme from our box garden out back. She had created a lovely cold chicken, perfectly marinated, with thinly sliced avocado and tomato, and paired it with my mother's green bean casserole topped with fresh Georgia peanuts instead of crispy onions because it was Emerson's favorite. And my great-grandmother's tipsy cake, which we got to eat with the stunning mother-of-pearl dessert forks that were a priceless wedding gift from my in-laws, topped it off.

In the midst of our salads, I saw Emerson watching someone. I turned to see a man walking down the street. I realized it was Mark, whom Emerson had started dating her sophomore year of high school, and I had wished she hadn't, simply because you know that something that starts when you're fifteen probably isn't going to last. I had adored him. Mark's great-grandparents had partnered with my grandparents many times in the shipping industry. They had been dear friends. Mark was still in the family business, which, to me, said a lot about him and how much he valued tradition. Plus, he was sweet to her and nice and would make good-looking grandchildren. As he made his way to the front gate, Mark seemed taller than I remembered, but then again, it was possible he had grown in the last ten years. He had a head of sandy-blond hair and blue eyes, not clear like Emerson's but dark navy blue. He was wearing freshly ironed khaki shorts with a Vineyard Vines shirt tucked in and a UGA belt. He was very Southern, not like those men Emerson was always taking up with in LA, with their skinny blue jeans that looked like they belonged on a teenage girl. Mark was darling. But I had a feeling that if he was barking up this tree, he might get his little heart hurt.

Sloane raised her eyebrows at Emerson, who wiped her mouth, stood up, and said, "Come in, come in," motioning toward the still-closed gate. She stood on her toes to give Mark what could only be described as a rather awkward hug. "How are you?" she asked.

"Sorry to interrupt dinner," he said.

"Oh, not at all," I said. I pointed toward Jack. "Jack, Mark. Mark, Jack."

Jack stood to shake Mark's hand.

No one said anything for maybe two seconds, but it felt painfully long. "Mark, please come join us," I said, breaking the silence.

"Oh, that's OK," he said.

"No, really," Emerson added. "I was going to take the kids for ice cream after dinner. Come with me. We can catch up."

He grinned, finally relaxing. "That sounds great."

"Sounds great to me, too!" Vivi chimed in.

I couldn't read Emerson, couldn't tell if she was happy to see Mark or just being polite.

After a few more minutes of eating, Emerson and Mark headed down the street with Vivi and Adam for dessert, since the cake was extra tipsy, while Sloane put Taylor to bed. I frantically dialed Caroline again. And texted her. Twice.

Jack walked into the kitchen.

"What are you doing?" I whispered.

"Why would you be like this?" he asked. His hurt expression really did make me feel bad. "The girls acted like you'd be happy I was here."

"Jack," I said, "you know why I would be like this."

He shook his head. "Ansley, it was fine. Nothing is going to happen. It's all fine."

I didn't know what to say.

"Carter's gone, Ansley. Carter's gone, the girls are grown. We haven't seen each other in decades. It's all fine."

I bit my lip, wanting to believe him, wanting to be able to erase my uneasy feelings as easily as he could. Jack took my hand. "I know. I know that this may never happen. But Ansley, knowing something shouldn't happen is different from knowing it can't. And neither of those things is going to keep me from wanting to be with you."

I smiled sadly, knowing that was true. "I know, Jack. But it doesn't leave us in a different place."

He nodded and glanced down, looking so sad for a moment that I almost wrapped him up and kissed him hard right then and there.

"Ansley, I have let you be for years and years. I've respected you, respected your wishes, played the role that you wanted me to play. But everything is different now. I can't see any logical reason that we have to be apart. I stayed away from you for so many years. Now I'm just done."

I knew what he meant. I knew the feeling. Because I

couldn't count the number of times I had wanted to go to him over the past fifteen years, the number of times I had pictured what it would be like if I showed up on his doorstep, if he pulled me to him, kissed me like no time had passed at all. In my heart of hearts, it was what I wanted. In my head, it was all more complicated than that.

I didn't know how to answer. So I said, "Caroline."

"Want me to help you look for her?" he asked.

I didn't answer. I suppressed this incredible urge to be close to a man, to be held by him, to be safe in his arms. Not just any man. *The* man. Jack. If Carter wasn't ever going to come back, I only wanted Jack.

My phone rang, and a bolt of fear jolted through me. I held up the phone. "James."

"Don't panic," James said when I answered.

Nothing good ever starts with the words "Don't panic."

"What's happening?"

He sighed. "Caroline is in labor."

"Oh, my gosh, but she isn't due for . . ." I did the math in my head. "Nineteen days."

"Yeah," James said. "I know. She isn't happy." He paused. "She's very unhappy that I'm here. She's very unhappy that Hummus isn't here. But on the bright side, she's not freaking out about the hospital germs." He paused. "Obviously, I've already sterilized every surface and put new sheets on her bed. But that's pretty benign, considering."

"Does she want us?" I asked.

"Yeah," he said. "She wants you all."

"Even Emmy?"

"Even Emmy."

My phone beeped, and I looked down at the screen. My brother Scott. Obviously, this was not the time to chat, so I texted him, BABY TIME!!!!

He texted back, Right on! Tell Caroline if it's a boy his name better be Scott.

"Tell our girl we're on our way." I looked up at Jack. "Is this what you imagined? All those times over the years you thought about coming to see me, is this what you envisioned?"

He kissed my hand, which I realized he had been holding all that time. "Ansley, this is what I've dreamed about my entire life. The only thing that could make it better would be to re-wind thirty years and get to start from there." He paused. "Or, well, you know, at least fifteen."

I took a deep breath. I called Emerson. "Hey," I said. "Caroline is in labor, and she wants all of us, even you." I was so ex-cited and distracted I didn't even have time to consider what was happening between Mark and her.

"Oh, my gosh! OK, you guys go ahead, and Vivi and I will meet you."

"OK, then. We'll see you soon."

I grabbed my keys and my purse. "All right, Jack," I said. "I'll let you know if my new grandchild is a boy or a girl."

He looked at me, confused. "Let me know? I'm going with you."

"Jack!" I looked at him in amazement.

He put his hands up. "I'm kidding, Ansley. I get it." He

paused. "In my defense, this dinner wasn't my idea. What was I supposed to say? Those girls are persuasive as hell."

"Just please remember what I said."

He nodded. I grabbed my keys and ran out the back door.

My fourth grandchild was getting ready to come into the world. Three weeks early. But it's at moments like these that you have to trust that the universe knows what it's doing. Any fool could see that our family wasn't at its best. But I couldn't help feeling that all was right with the world.

pipe dream

caroline

Emerson had taken a long time to grow hair when she was a baby. I mean, she had some, but it was really short. By the time she turned three, I was sick and tired of people saying, "What a beautiful little boy."

Mom and Dad did not seem terribly concerned about this state of affairs, which annoyed me to no end. I considered getting her a wig, but she wouldn't even keep a hat on, so I knew that wouldn't work.

One afternoon, when Mom had a dentist appointment and we had a sitter, I formulated a plan. Sloane would distract the sitter, saying that she needed a lot of help with her homework. I would kidnap Emerson.

It worked like a charm. I had Emerson in the stroller and out the door before anyone was the wiser. I was ten, so no, I wasn't allowed to babysit or go out by myself. But, well, as you might imagine, the rules have not always been my primary concern.

I walked to the jewelry store two blocks away, pulled out the allowance I had stuffed into my pockets, picked out a tiny pair of diamond studs, and said, "I'd like to get my sister's ears pierced, please."

The angst-filled teenager with the earring gun gave me a second look. To my surprise, I didn't even have to launch into the neatly planned diatribe I had practiced to talk her into it.

Emerson screamed, of course. But I gave her the sucker I'd brought, and that calmed her down quickly. On the way back to the apartment, someone stopped me and said, "What a beautiful little girl."

Mission accomplished.

What I hadn't counted on was that my mom would come home early or that she would call the police. I mean, yeah, I knew she was going to be mad. But I didn't know *how* mad.

When I left Emerson's film set that day, I knew exactly how mad I was.

There were so many things fighting for position in the forefront of how illogically, inexplicably pissed off I was. I think that term is really vulgar, so when I say it, I'm serious. My sister. My own sister. My flesh and blood. Was playing, on TV, for the world to see, the woman my husband had left me for. It was vile. Despicable. And the media was going to have a heyday with it.

If I could have put myself in Emerson's shoes, I couldn't blame her, really. It was a good opportunity for her. It was a starring role in a film with an A-list director. Just because my dream had crapped out, that didn't mean hers should, too. But I couldn't put myself in her shoes.

She hadn't even had the decency to talk to me about it. Emerson would have accepted this role long before she knew that James was cheating with Edie. But if she had sat me down and explained, I would have . . . Well, I would have been livid.

But she was my little sister. I usually cut her more slack than most people. Eventually.

I couldn't wait to get home and give her a big, fat piece of my mind.

But before I could, I felt this sharp pain in my stomach, one that I recognized all too well. But I was thirty-seven weeks. I was sure it was Braxton-Hicks, my body preparing itself for the real thing.

The pain was getting sharper. And fast. I was going to call my mom, but I wasn't sure I wanted to worry her yet—and I especially didn't want to worry Vivi. So I did something I couldn't have imagined: I called James. I wanted *him* to worry.

"Hello," he answered breathlessly.

"I am not forgiving you, and I do not want to be with you, but I'm pretty sure I'm in labor." I groaned. "And it feels really strange. Not like last time at all."

We've established how I feel about hospitals, but like I said, once the grand event was actually taking place, I ran right in, because, you know, I didn't want the baby to fall out on the floor. I was less acutely aware of the germs but more aware of the horrid fluorescent lights.

Before James even arrived, the doctor confirmed that the baby was breech and he was performing a C-section stat. This baby was coming, ready or not.

I was kind of whimpery, because my midwife, Hummus, who would be flying in next week to wait until the baby arrived, wasn't there, and I wanted a normal birth, and it was three weeks early, and all of that. So I give James a tiny amount of credit for taking care of everything, for scrubbing in and wearing that ridiculous hat and mask.

He held my hand and looked down and brushed my hair off my sweaty forehead and said, "Car, I know you don't want to hear it, but I love you so much. I'm so proud of you. I'm so grateful for all of this."

He was right. I didn't want to hear it. What I did want to hear was how my baby was. "Everything OK down there, Doc?" I asked.

Right about that time, I heard this unfathomably beautiful cry, and he didn't even have to announce what the baby was, because before I saw baby, I saw some sort of yellowish liquid flying through the air. Yeah. So that pipe dream that maybe my kid wouldn't pee on me like Sloane's was not going to come true after all. One minute in the world, and he'd already started.

"Oh, my gosh! It's a boy!" James said. "I was sure it was another girl."

I tried not to feel resentful that James got to hold my son first. He didn't deserve it. But I was tired and happy and relieved, so I let it go. James held the baby up to my face, and I kissed him. "Hi, Preston. Welcome to the world."

"Is he OK?" I asked the doctor.

"He's absolutely perfect," the nurse said. "He's all yours, Mom."

By the time the nurses were wheeling the bed holding Preston and me—he was now cuddled up to my chest where he belonged—my very surprised family was in the waiting room. When they saw me coming down the hall, I heard Vivi first. "The baby is already born?" she asked.

"Sure is, kiddo," James said. "You have a baby brother!"

"Can I hold him, Mom?" Vivi asked.

My mom walked over and took Vivi's arm. "Sweets, let's let Mom get settled in her room, OK?" Then I heard her say, "James, you make sure that vile curtain is gone. Sprint!"

I couldn't help but remember when Vivi was born, what a perfect day that had been. James and I had been so happy, so in love, and I had been certain that we were going to have the best life together. Nothing could come between us, nothing could hurt us. But something had. Irreparably, I was afraid. And so, while I was ecstatically in love with my new son, I was also worried about what his life was going to look like. I could already say that no matter what some judge said, James was not getting my baby every other weekend. That was not happening. Not a chance.

I didn't know that tears were running down my cheeks.

"Are you in pain?" James asked.

"I most certainly am," I said. "I want you out."

"But Caroline—"

"Out, James. I mean it."

"He's my baby, too."

"You should have thought about that," I said coldly.

He made a face like *I* had crushed *his* hopes and dreams. Please. Shoulders slumped, James left, and I smelled the sweet top of my son's head. I knew my whole family was going to come into the room in a minute. But for now, he was all mine. No one else's. And no matter what happened with James and me, no matter what sacrifice I'd had to make to get Preston here, it had all been worth it for this one, perfect moment.

NINETEEN

plain and simple

ansley

Carter and I found out he couldn't have children during a visit to Peachtree. I remember standing in my grandmother's kitchen, dialing the doctor's office on her rotary phone—it was 1982, after all—my heart beating louder with every *click-click-click* the dial made as it returned to zero. Devastated doesn't begin to describe how we felt, but we held it together pretty well. I gained so much respect for Carter, because he didn't let it wound his pride. He didn't act diffident or moody or let it make him feel like less of a man. He simply suggested that we go back to the drawing board. We agreed pretty much immediately that we'd use a sperm donor.

I expected to have a hospital stay after my IUI—a term I much preferred to "artificial insemination." But I expected it to come about nine months later, not in two days. When I started feeling pain in my uterus, I was thrilled. I knew something was happening. I thought that something was a baby, not a massive infection that would soon cause my low-grade fever to spike to almost 104 and make me spend more than a week in the hospital, much of which I don't remember.

Carter never left my side. And he never said anything about the baby.

I remember crying the night we got home, sitting with Carter on the couch in our living room, feeling as low as I had ever felt. But Carter held me and stroked my hair.

"We just have to try it again," I finally said. "It will work the next time."

It was a minor miracle that the infection hadn't ravaged my insides, hadn't destroyed my ability to carry a child at all. As stubborn as I was being, you couldn't help but wonder if a husband who was shooting blanks and a wife who nearly died from an extremely rare complication while trying to conceive weren't signs to hang up the baby thing.

I'll never forget the way Carter looked at me, the shock in his face. "Ansley, no," he said. "We will never, ever do this again."

And then he began to cry, too, something I'd seen only when his father died. I thought it was because of the frustration, the anger, the lack of control.

But he said, "You have no idea how sick you were. What if I had lost you? No matter what else happens, I can't lose you."

That was the moment I realized that what you see in movies, what you read about in books, that isn't the good part. Not at all. The butterflies make you feel giddy and alive, and that's sweet. But it's what happens after that really matters. It's the time you realize that your love has grown exponentially since that first day, when you discover that being someone's wife, being in it for the long haul, having someone there beside you day in and day out, is so much better than any roses on Valentine's Day or any first-date jitters you could ever have.

That was when I was strong again. Because that's what marriage is. When your partner is falling apart, you have to buck up. Plain and simple.

I wiped my eyes and sat up straight. "These are our options, then, love." I took his hand in mine. "One, we adopt. Two, we don't have children."

Carter shook his head. "This is so unfair," he said. "We work hard, we pay our taxes, we rescued those kittens from the subway. Why would this happen to us?" He paused. "Option two is not an option, as far as I'm concerned. We are parents. We are supposed to be parents."

Then he got quiet and looked at his hands.

I didn't say anything else for a minute. Then I said, "So we adopt. That's fine. We'll get on lists, we'll start looking. Hell, we can probably call some of our doctor friends and skip that altogether."

"You and I both know that could take forever," he said. "And then you don't get to be pregnant. We don't get to feel kicks and go to doctor appointments. You don't give birth. We don't stand together in the hospital room ecstatic and overwhelmed."

This was one of those times when our age difference really

showed. We were practically from different generations. Although private adoption was fairly common then, Carter was definitely still leery of it.

"I am aware of that, Carter, but these are our choices. I've already said I'll try IUI again, but you seem to be against that."

Carter was always a determined man. He was steadfast and reasonable, but he got what he wanted. And something in his face told me that this was what he had always imagined, and this was what he was going to get, one way or another.

I watched him closely as he ran his thumb over his forefinger. He bit the inside of his cheek and said, "You could get pregnant."

I wanted to throw something at him. No, in fact, I could not get pregnant, which was why we were in this mess to begin with. I put my arms up in frustration. "Carter, for God's sake." I threw my arms down and started to get up, but he grabbed my hand. "We can talk about this later," I said. "We can think about it some more. I'm just finished with the conversation for right now."

"Sit down," he said gently. "I can't stomach the idea of this, so I will only say it once. I can't ever know about it. I can't ever hear about it. You have to make certain that I never do."

I truly thought the man had lost his mind. One bump in the road, and he had become a raving lunatic. "What are you talking about?"

"You should get pregnant." He motioned toward the door. "We will continue to try. I will have every reason to believe that it is my baby. We will be the only two people in the world who know this. And even we won't be sure."

Now I really looked at him like he had lost his mind. "Carter, you can't be saying what I think you're saying. This is insanity. We will adopt, and that's that. I won't hear of it again."

He took my hands in his and said, "Ansley, this is up to you. What I am saying is that I will never know one way or another, and I will choose to believe this baby is mine, no matter what the doctors say." Then he whispered, "This baby will be mine, no matter what."

He got up, and I said, "Carter, you can't know that. You can't be sure that's how you'll feel. What if you don't feel that way at all?"

He turned back to me and said, "Have you ever known me not to keep my word?"

He walked off toward our bedroom, leaving me feeling cold. He couldn't believe that I would actually do this. Go sleep with some stranger on the street? Of course not. What about diseases, what if someone found out, and so many things that I couldn't even process. Carter was the only man I could imagine who would love me enough to actually go along with this scheme. Wasn't he? I couldn't fathom getting pregnant with another man's baby and keeping it a secret.

I couldn't do that. Could I?

I tossed and turned over that conversation for weeks and actually rethought a lot of things about my relationship in the wake of my husband even mentioning something as crass and vile as my getting pregnant by a stranger.

One night a couple of months later, I was walking home and passed a happy family with one child in a stroller and the other on his father's shoulders. It made me feel so irreparably empty. It steeled something inside me against Carter's idea, too, though. Because that was the way it was supposed to be, I thought. Children were supposed to be created out of love.

As if from outside me, as if from another world and another life, another option came to me. And just like that, I knew exactly what I would do.

TWENTY

right as rain

caroline

Sloane and I have always known that our dad wasn't our biological father. Maybe it should have bothered us more. Maybe we should have spent more time wondering about our sperm donor. But we didn't. Dad raised us. He loved us. We loved him. He was our father. Mom used to tell us this cute story, when we were small, about how mommies were princesses and daddies had special prince dust they sprinkled on mommies to put babies in their tummies. Mommy and Daddy loved each other so much and wanted babies, but Daddy was all out of his special prince dust. So another prince let us borrow some of his so that Mommy and Daddy could be parents.

This was a perfect story, because it was the right amount of information for our little toddler minds to process, and when we went to school and told the other kids that another prince spread prince dust on our mommy, the teacher didn't send notes home.

So prince dust it was.

I was realizing now how very unimportant the prince dust was in comparison with the work of actually being a father. I needed a husband and a partner and a supporter right now, not a sperm donor. I had forgotten what a mess new motherhood can make you. How vulnerable you suddenly are. How exhausted. How utterly alone. And the last time, I hadn't been cut from stem to stern. Were you honestly expected to breastfeed when you had a giant (well, I mean, you know, like a two-inch) incision across where the baby was supposed to lie?

Aside from the pain and the feeling that I was going to lose my mind, life was perfect. I had a brand-new little boy with ten fingers and ten toes and chubby pink cheeks and that intoxicating baby smell. Even three weeks early, the kiddo had been nearly eight pounds, which was still bigger than Vivi had been at full term. It might have been because I was much bigger this time, but it's not polite to discuss such things.

Mom had been utterly amazing, despite the fact that although she was trying to hide it from me, I knew something was going on with Grammy. I had caught her in a few hushed conversations with Uncle Scott.

Every time the baby woke up, she would get him from his crib, bring him to me so I could feed him lying down in the bed, sit with me the whole time so I didn't accidentally fall asleep, change his diaper, and then do the whole thing over again in another ridiculously short amount of time. I was thankful that Hummus was to arrive this afternoon. She might have missed the birth, but we begged her to come help with the baby. I couldn't stand the idea of a baby nurse I had never even met coming to live with us.

I couldn't believe that Preston was already one week old. Even though his father was a schmuck, I still named my beautiful boy James Preston Beaumont IV, as planned. In reality, we were city folk, and James Preston Beaumont was a name you could really use if you lived in Manhattan. In addition to its New York cachet, it also rang of old Southern money, where it had originated, which thrilled my mother.

Mom and I were putting clothes away in Preston's drawers and making up the twin bed in his room for Hummus when she said, "I know you're kind of delicate right now, but have you given any consideration to what you're going to do about James?"

The baby was napping, so I kept my voice low, but I looked at her like she had suggested I take up vampire hunting as a new career. "What I'm going to do about him?" I whispered. "I'm going to divorce his sorry ass and take him for everything he has is what I'm going to do about him."

She nodded, but I knew there was more.

"What, Mom? Just say it."

She shrugged. "I don't know. I told him I would tell you not to take him back under any circumstances." She paused. "But Caroline, being a single mother is a hard life. You girls weren't even that small, and it took all I had."

I looked around. I needed a Preggie Pop. I didn't see one, so I rubbed a tiny Kissy Kissy convertible day gown on my cheek to calm me. It was so soft. "You know what else is hard, Mom? Wondering if your husband is cheating on you all the time. Walking around New York with everyone talking about how you're the idiot who took back the guy who paraded all over national television with someone else while he was married. I don't think I can be that girl."

She shut the drawer quietly and said, "OK. I get it." We stepped out of the room, and she crossed her arms and looked at me squarely. "I know you know everything," she said, "but I am your mother, and I am allowed to have an opinion, and I will continue to do so until I die. So we're clear."

I raised my eyebrows. What was clear was that she was really tired. I could scarcely remember the woman ever standing up to me. I smiled at her. "Go, Mom. Way to assert yourself. Is it the new man?"

She sighed, exasperated. "There's no new man. Only an ambush from my daughters."

Emerson appeared at the top of the stairs, and I could tell she had been crying. In retrospect, she had been kind of weird the past few days, but I was so overwhelmed I hadn't had much time to worry about it.

"Caroline," she said, her chin quivering. Sometimes I wondered if she really got this upset about things or if she was that good an actress.

I didn't know what this was about, but I was sure I wasn't up for it.

"I am soooo sorry," Emerson said, one fat tear falling down her cheek.

My heart started to pound. I sighed. "What else could possibly have happened to be sorry about?"

She hugged me and said, "I feel so guilty." Now the sobbing began in earnest.

And she should feel guilty. I was too busy to be paying attention, but it was definitely out in the media that my semifamous sister was playing my husband's überfamous lover in a new movie. You couldn't blame the people. It made for a fabulous story.

And I was still mad, for sure. But having Preston put everything into perspective. I was a mother. I had a brand-new life to attend to. The miracle baby I had prayed for and wished for and tried to have for years and years and years until I had finally given up had arrived. So I was still angry with Emerson. But having Preston reminded me what really mattered.

"It's my fault that Preston was born early!" Em sobbed.

She was still hugging me, and I rolled my eyes at Mom over her shoulder. I actually hadn't considered that it was Emerson's fault that Preston came early.

"Emerson, I really can't right now, OK? Preston is healthy and fine, and it doesn't matter."

She pulled away from me, those big blue eyes full of water. "I know, but I feel awful. Car, I just need you to understand. It has been so hard for me to get ahead in this business. It's like, all of a sudden, everyone is talented and beautiful and special." She looked me straight in the eye with a steeliness that told me, no matter how down she might be feeling, she wasn't going to give this up. Not yet. Not without a fight. "You can't imagine how terrible it feels to be average." She shuddered as she said the word and I smiled in spite of myself.

I nodded and winked at her. "I'm the one who just gave birth. I'm supposed to be emotional. Not you."

She sniffed, wiped her nose on her shirtsleeve, and hugged me again. "Can you ever forgive me?"

"Em, I have been your biggest fan since the day you were born. No one wants you to succeed more than I do. If playing my nemesis gets you closer to your dream, I'm in."

Her face was so expressive, it was as if the relief was drawn on by a talented makeup artist as she said, "Really? Because I never, ever meant to hurt you. It was just like I was in it and I was so deep I couldn't tell you."

I nodded. "I get it. I forgive you. All is forgotten."

She hugged me again. "You're the best sister in the world."

"I know," I called breezily as I walked down the hall toward Vivi's room to see if she was ready for lunch. This had become my life. One big feeding schedule. I peeked in, but she wasn't there.

Mom followed me down the hall. "Anyway," she said, "back to what *I* wanted to talk about."

"Mom, can't we be done with this?" I sighed. "You don't understand. You and Dad were the perfect couple. You never dealt with anything like this. It's nearly impossible to recover from."

A strange look came across her face. She opened her mouth as if to say something, but she shut it again. Then she said, "Fine. I won't say another word. But you chose him. You knew what he was like. I'm just saying that he's here in Peachtree, it doesn't look like he's going anyplace, and while you're still in anonymous territory, away from those vultures you call friends, maybe you should listen to what he has to say."

I rolled my eyes. "Doubtful, but I hear you."

We made our way downstairs to the kitchen—me gingerly, very slowly, but with much more ease than even two days before. Vivi wasn't there, either. I figured she was in the main house. "Sit down," Mom said. "I'll make you lunch. What are you in the mood for?"

"Tequila."

She laughed. "Grilled cheese and tomato soup it is."

That sounded delicious. "Gluten-free," I said.

I sank down in one of the comfortable dining chairs that was mere feet from the stove. And I figured that now was as good a time as any.

"Mom," I said. "I need to ask you something. And it's kind of uncomfortable."

Oh, yes! I saw it. A Preggie Pop, right there on the counter. I grabbed it and ripped the paper off.

"Ooo-K," she said, drawing out the one word as if it were two.

"When the divorce goes through, I think I'll be fine. I'll probably have to get a job, but I'm sure I'll have enough money that I can wait until Preston is in kindergarten."

"Well, that's good."

"But you know how Dad always talked about the money he was leaving for us? Was there some sort of date attached to our receiving that? Because I think if I knew what was coming down the pike, I could prepare better."

Mom stopped stirring the soup for a long moment. Then she turned to me. "You know, Caroline, I am going to have to look into that. I'll call the financial adviser right away."

She looked kind of weird and pale when she said it. I had this horrifying thought, momentarily, that she had spent it. But there was no way. The house was paid for, and yeah, there were expenses, but she surely made enough to cover those. While I wanted Mom to be taken care of, she had always had this simple life and seemed fine with it.

"I'm sure Sloane could really use it, too," I said.

"Sloane could use what?" Sloane asked.

Oops. "Oh, a break from the kiddos every now and then," I said breezily. I didn't want to put Mom on the spot.

But Sloane needed money worse than I did. She was always cutting coupons, and her kids dressed in hand-me-downs from God only knew who. They were lucky they were cute. I had learned long ago that not everyone needed to be exactly like me to be happy. But I was sure that her life would be better if she could buy those Dove chocolates she liked, even when they weren't on sale. Although Lord knows, she didn't need to be eating them.

Sloane sat down beside me. "Oh," she said. "Hummus is here."

I tried to move, and she said, "Don't get up. She's with Vivi and the boys in the main house. She said she would come back here before Preston woke up from his nap."

I instantly relaxed. "How do you do this, Sloane?"

"Do what?" She took a sip from the bottle of water in her hand. I knew she didn't drink those at home, only at Mom's. She wouldn't have spent the money.

"Take care of your kids alone all the time."

She smiled. "I love it. It's what I'm here for. My job is to take care of them and take care of our house and keep things together when Adam is gone. So that's what I do."

Adam had been deployed the first time when little Adam was only four months old and hadn't seen him again until he was nearly one year. I couldn't imagine that, not seeing your child for that long. It was certainly one of the biggest sacrifices a person could make. Seeing the life my sister lived made me more appreciative not only of everyone in our armed forces but also of the spouses they left behind. Because it didn't matter if your wife was nine months pregnant. When it was time to go, you went.

Mom set a plate with one of those good, smashed grilled cheeses in front of me and a bowl of soup beside it. "Sloane?" she asked. "Can I get one for you while the pan's still hot?"

She smiled like Mom had offered to pay her kids' college tuitions. "That would be amazing, Mom." Then she said, "The only hard part is the worrying." She paused and laughed. "And not seeing Adam. That is torturous. But at least we have Skype. I don't know what people did before Skype."

"They talked to each other!" a booming voice said from around the corner.

I was so happy I could cry. "Hummus!" I said.

I struggled to move, but she, with one hand, told me to keep my seat. She was wearing brightly printed scrubs and those terrible clogs that were supposed to be comfortable. She was a large, sturdy, fleshy woman with a thick blondish-gray ponytail that looked like it could use a flat iron. She wore no makeup and no jewelry except for a plain gold band on her right hand. She was a sensible woman, unlike basically all of her clients.

"Don't get up. I am going to change into fresh scrubs so that Ms. Caroline here doesn't have a fit about airplane germs, and then I am going to go take care of my baby. I will bring him to you when it's time to eat."

"I'm so happy I could cry."

Mom dropped the spatula into the sink. "Me, too!"

Vivi walked in with James, and I mouthed to Sloane, "Oh, yay."

He kissed me on the cheek. Gross. I wanted to wipe it off, but that seemed immature. Today he was wearing jeans and a blue-and-white-striped Johnnie-O shirt that he called his "surfer look." There were no two ways about it. I might hate him, but the man was a hot surfer.

"You look great this morning, Caroline."

Liar.

"Are you feeling any better today?"

I pinned on my fakest smile. "Oh, right as rain, sugar."

"I have soup and grilled cheese for you, Viv," Mom said. "I am going to go find my other grandchildren, and then I believe I'll take a nap."

"Solid plan, Mom," I said. "I think I will, too."

James took my hand and helped me out of the chair. Then he put my arm around his waist and half carried me up the stairs, which was quite nice, actually.

"Thank you for letting me see him today," he said.

I nodded. "He's so perfect. He really is."

James helped me into bed. As I closed my eyes, I heard Preston crying.

"It's OK," James whispered. "I'll get him."

He hurried back, handing me the baby, and lay down on the other side of the bed to watch me feed him. I couldn't help but think that what he had done in bed with Edie Fitzgerald was quite different from this. Oh, that hurt.

I wanted to protest his being there, but I was too tired. So I said, "If I fall asleep, please take him back to Hummus. I don't want him to get used to sleeping in bed with me."

"Oh, yeah." James laughed. "That's a slippery slope."

Vivi had slept between us for years.

My eyelids got heavy, and between the exhaustion and the sweet smell of baby, it was impossible not to drift off. I couldn't move on from the past, and I wasn't ready to let go of the pain that James had caused me. But I couldn't help but think, with him on the other side of the bed and Preston between us, that this was the way my life was supposed to turn out.

TWENTY-ONE

nest egg

ansley

New Year's Eve, like every other important or unimportant holiday, is a huge deal in Peachtree. The town hosts an event called Marshmallows and Goals. There are fire pits all over town, actual bonfires on the island, and firefighters absolutely everywhere. I have this notion that there are so many flames you can see Peachtree from space.

Kids and grown-ups alike spend hours roasting marshmallows and talking about what they are going to do differently on their next turn around the sun. Not me, though. I have lots of goals, but I've never said them out loud to anyone. I like to play it closer to the vest than that.

Which is why I always used to tell Carter not to say anything to the girls about the money. Because you never knew what was going to happen. But he was adamant that they know they would always have a fallback plan. He was wonderful and caring and kind. But when he was adamant, there was really no arguing.

The year after Emerson was born, Carter had finally started to get those big breaks he'd always believed in. He had always done well. We were all taken care of, and that was all that mattered to me. But he was suddenly starting to pick stocks with amazing accuracy, something that can be as much about luck as it is about skill. Carter was a realist, though, and decided to diversify instead of keeping all of the money in the market.

He invested in a large whole life insurance policy with a company that was getting incredible returns. It was a huge security for me, no doubt.

Around 2000, I had noticed some strange patterns in Carter's behavior. He was keeping odd hours, which, according to him, was because he was investing in overseas markets. It made sense, but something still felt off to me.

I wouldn't find out until after his death that Carter's job had turned into almost an addiction for him. The stock market is, after all, gambling by any other name. Looking back over our books, I saw that he had won big, then lost big, then won big, then lost big. I had no doubt in my mind that he would have won big again. But he died. So he never had the chance. And he never told me that he had taken out a mortgage on what I believed to be our paid-off apartment.

The one worry I knew I wouldn't face when Carter died was money. The life insurance policy was there. We would be fine, despite the fact that the rest of our assets were minimal at that moment.

Brad, our insurance agent, had been a good friend for a long time. When he rang the doorbell on September 21, I was unfathomably relieved. The insurance companies were having a tricky time, because who knew who was really dead? But they had determined after ten days that Carter was gone. I was living my second-worst nightmare on a scale that was indescribable. Terrorized didn't begin to cover how I felt.

Brad came in and looked around. The girls were at school. I had finally made them go back to take their minds off their father. What I was going to do to take *my* mind off him I wasn't sure. Brad had sat me down and handed me an envelope. I assumed his grave expression was for his friend who had died in such a gruesome way.

"Ansley," he said. "I have some bad news."

I laughed ironically. "Brad," I said, "it can't get any worse."

Only it did. The economy had been wonderful for years, and the policy had accrued a massive amount of cash value— which Carter had been slowly either taking out or "borrowing" from the policy. As he took the cash out, the face value of the policy diminished, and the money he had borrowed from the policy was also subtracted from the total amount I would receive. Long story short, my millions had dwindled to barely enough to pay the three girls' college tuitions.

My first reaction was to panic, obviously. Not only did I have a giant mortgage that I hadn't known existed, but I had no way whatsoever to support our massive living expenses. And I hadn't worked since Caroline was born. I was a nobody interior designer who hadn't so much as picked up a shelter magazine in ten years. Who on earth would hire me over the big names in the city?

"So what now?" I asked Brad.

He looked at me hesitantly. "I don't know, Ansley. I really don't."

I handed Brad the check.

"What are you doing?"

"Invest it," I said. "I have to have that for the girls' college, and if there's a little interest every year, it will help us get by."

"What are you going to do?" he asked.

I shook my head and looked down at my feet. "I'm going to do the only thing I can do." I sighed. "I'm moving to Peachtree Bluff."

Brad was a true Manhattanite, a real New Yorker, one of the ones John Updike wrote about, who believed that people living anywhere else must be kidding. If you were going to go to Brooklyn, you might as well jump off the bridge on your way. "Ansley," he said, "get serious. Your life is here."

In that moment, so full of pain and dread and confusion, I looked him squarely in the face. "Brad," I said, "my life is over."

At that time, I truly believed it was. Yes, of course, I had my girls to carry on for. But Carter was the love of my life. Without him, nothing made sense.

I tossed and turned over the decision. I could sell our brownstone, but with the size of the mortgage and the instability of the Manhattan housing market at that moment, I would end up owing a ton of money even to get out of it. And what bank in their right mind would have given me a loan? I would need a job for that, and all I was qualified to do was pick sofa fabric. Even at a big design firm, it would take years to build up a clientele to support us. I felt pure, hot panic. I was on my own. With nothing. Which was when I called my mother and told her we needed to come live with them in Florida for a little bit.

"Mom," I explained, "Carter left me with nothing." Actually, he had left me with far less than nothing. Not only would I owe the bank substantially on the brownstone when we sold it, but the debts that Carter owed kept rolling in. And I had no idea how I would pay them.

"Darling," she said, "you don't have nothing. You're beautiful and talented, and you have three amazing girls. In some ways, you are very rich indeed."

I remember the way my breath caught in my throat, the way I nearly choked when I realized that she wasn't going to let me come home. "None of those things is going to feed my children right now, Mom. I am seriously panicking here. If we can come to Florida with you and Dad, just for a couple of months, I can figure out how to get our life set up at Grandmother's house in Peachtree Bluff."

I was lucky. Even then, I knew that. How many people would have had a house that their dead grandmother had left them just sitting there waiting for them to move right into? Not many. But I was mourning, exhausted, overwhelmed, and terrified. I had never, ever felt so alone.

Fortunately, what felt like a lifetime but was probably more like a couple of days later, help arrived in the form of the Victim Compensation Fund. It wasn't as much as I would have thought, because Carter hadn't made as much as I thought over the last few years. I had to pay back what my husband owed to creditors all over the place, which took a huge chunk, but the money gave me hope. We could afford to stay in our house, while it was on the market, until Christmas, when I would move with the girls to Peachtree Bluff. I would sell the house and pay back the bank what we still owed on the brownstone. We would probably even have a tiny bit left to live on while I got back on my feet. We would make it. We would survive.

No thanks to my mother.

Now, needless to say, when Caroline asked me for her money, I felt a little trapped. It was like when Carter and I were trying to have her: there were no great options. I could tell her the money was gone, which would imply that I had either spent it or lost it, neither of which bathed me in a particularly favorable light.

Or I could tell her that her father, whom she loved dearly and thought was completely without reproach, had essentially legally gambled away everything we had spent twenty-one years together building. I couldn't bear to ruin that image of her father for her. My girls had been through enough. They deserved to have their memories.

On the bright side, I had been, slowly but surely, putting whatever I could away every month for the girls for emergencies. I never wanted them to be in the position that I was in, all alone with no one to help them. But I had hoped that it would be something for them after I was gone. It wouldn't be quite as much as their father was going to leave for them but when you combined what I had saved with my life insurance, it would be enough to give them a safety net. They were bright, talented, hardworking girls. All they really needed was enough to see them through a rough patch.

"Earth to Ansley," Jack said.

We were sitting on the floor in my store, each on a colorful striped cotton Dash & Albert rug that would later go in a cabin on Jack's boat, surrounded by pictures of nautical-looking light fixtures. For a home, I would have immediately declared any of these choices entirely too kitschy. For a boat, they were exactly right. These were the moments I liked. I wished we could have a life like this. I could have my girls and their families in one sphere of my life and Jack in another, and the two would never have to overlap. That would be better. That I could handle. If only it were reality.

I held up a photo of a sconce that looked like it belonged in a submarine. "I like this for the head," I said.

He fixed his gaze on my face. "Do you want to talk about it?"

I looked at the photo. "Sure, yeah. We can talk about it. What do you think?"

He laughed. "I meant do you want to talk about what's on your mind? I don't care about the sconce. Like I said, pick whatever you want. The only reason I'm here at all is to spend time with you."

I smiled, feeling that warmth wash over me. "For one, my mother broke her ankle last week."

"Oh, no!" Jack said, looking concerned. "Why didn't you tell me?"

I shrugged. "I think I'm blocking it out. She got into a wreck—her fault." I sighed. "Scott thinks there's something off with her, so I'll be glad to get her here for a little bit." This was the tricky part about being a child. Scott and I thought Mom needed to be somewhere that she had a little bit of care—or at least with one of us. I knew my mother wasn't going to want to leave Florida. I knew she wasn't going to want to live in a nursing home or move out of her house or lose her independence. But she is the mother and we are the children. Our lives had been about her telling us what to do. When was the right time for those roles to reverse?

"Is your brother John involved?" Jack asked.

I laughed so hard I nearly fell over. "Oh, yeah, right. I don't think he and Mom have even talked in like five years." Come to think of it, I didn't know when I had last talked to John. Sometime last year, I decided to see what would happen if I never called him, if he would ever attempt to contact me if I didn't initiate it. I got my answer. I felt a sadness creeping in. The three of us had been best friends when we were growing up. And, yes, I wished Scott and I had more time for each other. But, whenever we were back together, it was like nothing had changed. With John, things were so damaged that I felt like they'd never be right again.

"Oh," Jack said. "That's not good." He paused. "Anything else weighing on that pretty mind?"

I shrugged. "I don't want to stick you with a big secret."

He laughed heartily. "My darling," he said, "a good bit of my life has been centered around keeping your secrets."

I smiled. There was no argument about that. The man hadn't let me down yet. I sighed and told him about Caroline and the money and what had happened to it. "I just don't want her image of her father to be ruined," I said. "That's all."

"You have to tell her the truth," he said. "Maybe not the whole truth. Maybe a watered-down version, like the market took a downturn after nine-eleven, which is true, and it affected all the values, and you didn't get what you thought you would."

I nodded. "So you don't think I should take the blame? I mean, I'm still here to defend myself."

He shook his head. "No, of course not. With all due respect, he's gone, and you're still here. It's not your fault."

"Yeah, that's true technically. But I should have been more involved. I always let him handle everything, and I shouldn't have."

"Well, marriage is complicated."

"It is, isn't it?"

"I wasn't very good at it." Jack smiled. He looked into my eyes. "My heart wasn't in it."

I could feel those nervous butterflies building. "Jack, I—"

"No." He cut me off. "I understand your reservations. Truly, I do. But I don't see how my being in your life changes anything. I'm still the same guy I always was. It's not like if this whole thing doesn't work out, I'm going to do anything to hurt you. I would never."

I knew that was true.

"We aren't getting younger, Ans. Let's give this thing a shot."

I nodded.

"Wait. Is that a yes?" He looked genuinely stunned.

I grinned at him. "I don't really have anything to say yes to, now, do I?"

"Will you please have dinner with me?"

"How about next week when I've recovered from the complete and total lack of sleep that comes along with grandmotherhood?"

He squeezed my hand. "Next week can't come soon enough."

I hated to ruin the happy moment, but I held my hand out to stop his joy all the same. "This is not a green light for you to be a part of my family. This is maybe we'll have dinner and take things really slowly and see how they go. OK?"

He rolled his eyes. "Read you loud and clear."

I held up two photos. "Plain or fancy?"

Jack, completely ignoring me, stood up and wiped his hands on his khaki shorts. "You decide," he said. "I have a dinner to plan."

I clasped my hands together in front of my chest, closed my eyes, took a deep breath, rocked from side to side a little, and raised myself to standing from crossed legs—no hands. I smiled triumphantly.

"What in God's holy name are you doing?" he asked.

"Oh," I said, suddenly realizing that was, perhaps, a little odd. "It's very important to be able to stand from a cross-legged seated position with no hands. It says a lot about your long-term strength." At least, that was what the article Caroline had sent me said.

He squinted at me. "You're serious?"

I crossed my arms. "You try it, smarty pants. It's not as easy as it looks."

Jack laughed. "Next time."

It wasn't until the door had fully closed that I realized I was a little nervous. I hadn't been on a date in more than thirty-seven years.

TWENTY-TWO

the suit

caroline

"Do you remember the day we lost our fairy stones?" I asked Sloane, as she was lying beside me in my disheveled bed in the guesthouse. She was sipping coffee, I was sipping tea, and for the moment, the world was still. And mercifully quiet.

She just nodded. "Of course I do. It was like losing a part of who we were."

It really had been, though I couldn't explain why. It made me feel better to know that even after all these years, Sloane still felt that way, too. Of course, things gain their meaning when we ascribe meaning to them. But I swear it was more than that. Even now, twenty-five years after I had weighed one of those dense, heavy stones in my palm, its mineral flecks sparkling in the daylight, I could still feel the magic coming from it, the power it had. Grandpop told us those stones would keep us safe. And losing them had meant losing a part of our childish invincibility.

"Do you remember the little bag I made to carry them in?" Sloane asked, looking over at me.

"Of course."

Grammy had taught us to sew that summer—or at least attempted to. Sloane had made a little bag, misshapen and uneven, with a pink satin ribbon threaded through the top. Grammy had embroidered all three of our initials onto that bag in a matching pink, and inside we had placed our fairy stones for safekeeping.

"I was never meant to be a seamstress," Sloane said seriously. We both laughed.

We had been playing at Starlite Island one day, Mom and the three of us girls. Emerson was two, Sloane was eight, and I was ten. We had built a tall sand castle and placed our bag of fairy stones on the very top.

"The fairy stones reign over the kingdom of Starlite," I remember Sloane saying.

We all laughed, even Emerson, who repeated, "Fairy stones, Sissy."

She had run back and forth with her pink bucket that day from the sea to the castle to the sea to the castle, filling it up and dripping the water over her sand kingdom just so. Even then, she had such a determined little spirit.

I had realized that Mom wasn't playing with us, and when I looked over, brushing the hair out of my face, I saw her, maybe twenty yards away, talking to a man. I remember that she wasn't smiling, that she didn't seem happy. And neither did he. The look on her face unnerved me.

"Who was that man on the beach that day?" I asked Sloane, lying beside her in bed.

She shrugged. "I have no idea. But I remember who you're talking about. And I remember Mom coming over and making us leave when she was finished talking to him."

Mom had seemed almost scared that day, something we hadn't seen much. I remember wanting my dad to be there, feeling like something wasn't right, as she scooted us all into the skiff we had used to putter over to the island. Emerson was screaming as we got into the boat, because of course, you can't just grab a two-year-old off the beach and take her home with no warning without a tantrum. It's Parenting 101, and the mother of three daughters would have well known that.

"She seemed kind of frantic, didn't she?"

Sloane nodded, taking a slow sip of coffee. "I hadn't really thought about it, but yeah. So much so that we left the fairy stones."

Grandpop had taken us back to the island that evening, and we had searched high and low for our little bag with the stones. Maybe the tide had washed them away, or maybe a bird had snatched our bag. But I remember how devastated I felt, how empty. It was different from the feeling of losing a toy or misplacing a piece of clothing. It was a sadness I felt in the core of my being.

"Remember how we cried over losing those stones?" Sloane asked.

"Of course. And Grandpop said—"

Sloane interrupted. "All that meant was that the fairies sent those stones to someone who needed them more than we did."

I laughed. "I found that strangely comforting."

"Me, too." She smiled at me. "I still do, kind of."

"Wonder who found our stones?" I looked down into my tea as if it held the answer.

"I wonder who found my one sewing masterpiece."

That cracked us both up. A masterpiece that bag was not.

Sloane slapped my leg and said, "Well, my dear, all I can figure is that Hummus found those stones, and they made her a magical baby whisperer."

"I know. What two-week-old baby sleeps for six straight hours?"

Sloane rolled her eyes. "None that I know, you lucky duck."

Six hours! I could survive on six hours. I could *thrive* on six hours and a thirty-minute nap.

"All right," Sloane said. "I'm heading off to rally my troops for breakfast."

I smiled at her, but I had to admit that even remembering that day made me feel a little bit off. And I hoped that whoever had found our stones cherished them as much as we had.

I could hear Hummus's footsteps in the kitchen. James had decided that Hummus needed to stay at least another month. He had no idea what we were having to pay her, but I didn't argue. I had inadvertently let him spend the night two times the week before when Preston was still waking up every two hours. But that didn't mean that I was speaking to him. I wasn't. Only tersely and when absolutely necessary.

We had had a massive fight about Vivi going to school in Peachtree. In the end, Vivi had sweet-talked her daddy. I remembered those days when I could sweet-talk my own dad. Just seeing her with him made me miss my dad so much that I persuaded Vivi to let her father back into her life. Yes, he had hurt her. But he hadn't meant to. He had only thought he was hurting me—which was totally asinine, by the way. Even still, nothing was more important than family. Luckily, she is less stubborn than her mother. So she conceded.

James arrived at the guesthouse on Preston's two-and-a-half-week birthday wearing *the suit*. That was my first clue that something was up. He looked very, very nervous. That was my second clue.

He dove right in. No small talk. "I want to take you out," he said, rubbing his hands together.

I looked down at myself. Every square inch was covered with either breast milk or spit-up. But that wasn't the half of it. Mostly, I couldn't imagine having to sit across the table and look at that jackass for an entire dinner.

"James, have you lost your mind? I'm not going to go to dinner with you like nothing happened."

He leaned on the kitchen counter. "We don't have to pretend nothing happened. I just want a chance to explain and to apologize properly."

"Apologize?" I was skeptical.

"Yes. You deserve an apology. A real, true, long one. And then, if you still want to divorce me, I'll file the papers."

I laughed. "There is nothing you can say that will make me not want to divorce you. You will probably make me hate you more, if that's possible."

"Caroline, I'm trying to show you that I'm sorry. I love you, but I don't know how else to prove it."

I put my finger to my mouth. "Hmmmm. Maybe rewind and don't sleep with Edie Fitzgerald, and definitely don't let anyone find out about it if you do, and even more, don't appear on national television for millions of people to see and judge."

"If I could, I would," he said.

"Remember that for your next wife."

"Caroline . . ."

He didn't say anything else. And I wondered why Edie Fitzgerald wasn't going to be his next wife. Maybe she had dumped him. It would serve him right. All I knew was that as of now, I had only one James Preston Beaumont in my life to worry about. And he weighed eight pounds.

TWENTY-THREE

an old sweet song

ansley

To keep expenses down and make things more reasonable for the community, Peachtree Bluff used inmates to do everything from collecting garbage to cutting grass. This used to unnerve me to no end. I had these three girls, by myself, and what if said inmates escaped and tried to get one of them? I used to scold myself for being so unfeeling. They were serving their time, doing their duty, and paying their debt to society. But when the inmate program had to be canceled because townspeople (Hippie Hal) were giving the inmates contraband, I wasn't sad. No matter how many talks I gave myself, I was still nervous.

I kept chiding myself that night, too, for being so nervous. *Get it together, Ansley*. It was just Jack. Jack, who had been my first date, my first kiss, my first love. That he would be my first date again forty-something years later seemed fitting. And my girls were loving this. Every second.

Caroline had unearthed the Barney's bags stashed in the back of my closet, scolding me. "Mom! What is wrong with you? Have you seen these sandals?"

I winced. "Caroline." I looked around and whispered, "They lace up my *leg*."

Taylor and Adam were on the floor in the corner, gleefully tossing tissue paper out of the shoeboxes.

"But it's a good leg," Sloane said. "You should work it, Mom."

I felt a twinge of guilt, because I was sure these shoes had cost more than Sloane's monthly grocery budget. I constantly asked Caroline not to buy me these ridiculous gifts. To her, they were normal things. Reasonable, really.

Caroline looked at Sloane. "If those kids get drool on those shoes, I am not going to be happy."

Emerson piped up. "I thought the point of wearing those shoes was to make men drool."

We all laughed.

Emerson joined Caroline in the closet, while Sloane moved off the bed and onto the floor, pulling Taylor into her lap and snuggling him close.

"I got to talk to Adam this morning," she said.

Relief rushed through me. "Oh, good! How's he doing?"

She shrugged. "He's OK. He's really homesick."

"How long do you think he'll keep doing this?" Caroline asked.

Sloane looked shocked. "Well, forever, I would imagine. Serving his country is what he has always wanted to do. It comes first."

"Over his family?" Emerson asked.

I gave her a look, but in all honesty, these were questions I had, too. It was hard for me to imagine how someone could sign up for something that caused him to have to spend so much time away from his family. I loved Adam, and I knew how devoted he was to Sloane and his kids. So it was a hard thing for me to wrap my mind around.

Sloane shook her head. "But don't you see? He serves because that's how much he loves us. He serves to keep us safe, to protect us and other families, too. It's what he was born to do. He's very clear on his priorities." She paused and tickled little Adam. "It's what I love the most about him."

We all looked at her for a second, and I wondered if she always felt like that or if sometimes, inside, she longed to beg him to come home.

"That's great," Caroline said. "I know I couldn't do it, so thank goodness someone is tough enough."

She held out a simple black knit dress with scallops around the neck and hem. It had short sleeves and a bit of flare at the waist, which most women in middle age seem to need, myself included.

"That's perfect with the shoes," Emerson said.

She had done my makeup already. Dolled me up with eyeliner and the whole lot. I couldn't remember ever wearing eyeliner.

"Well, go try it on," Sloane said. "He's going to be here in like twenty minutes."

There it was again. The racing heart. The pounding pulse.

But then there was the smile, too. I could feel the smile. I hadn't gotten to wear that smile since 9/11. Maybe it was time.

"Can we have a glass of wine with Jack before you leave?" Emerson asked.

"Oh, yes!" Caroline chimed in. "I have three hours before I have to feed Preston."

I gave her a look. I didn't like her drinking at all when she was breastfeeding, although Hummus had assured me that the alcohol cleared before feeding time and was actually good for Caroline's milk production.

I was so glad no one breastfed when I was having babies. It seemed awful. No one could argue with the benefits, though. I wasn't sure about it making the baby healthy and all that. But Caroline was almost back to her prebaby weight, and it had been only a couple of weeks. And she wasn't eighteen anymore. It was impressive.

"Girls," I said, "I know you're excited, but I don't want you getting attached to Jack. That's too much pressure on all of us."

Caroline rolled her eyes. "Mom, we're grown. It's not like you're choosing a stepdad to come live with us."

I raised my eyebrows, looked from one to the other of them, and said, "Well . . ."

They all cracked up. "We're pathetic," Sloane said. "Our mother can't go on a date twenty years after our father died because we are all living at home again."

I smiled and slipped on the dress. The girls deemed it perfect.

That was all I needed to hear. I was ready. Now was my

moment. "Speaking of dates, Em," I said. "What's going on with Mark?"

She waved her hand. "Oh, nothing. We had ice cream with the kids, Caroline went into labor, end of story."

Caroline raised her eyebrows.

"No, for real," Emerson said. "I don't think he's even interested in me like that. Even if he was, you know my career has to be the priority right now."

I wanted to argue with her, but just because we had a difference of opinion on that matter, that didn't mean she was wrong.

The doorbell rang downstairs before I had a chance to continue the conversation, which struck me as funny, because no one ever rang the doorbell, preferring simply to walk right in.

"I'll get it," Vivi called.

I rushed down the stairs, surprising myself at how excited I was to get my date started. When I peeked into the foyer to get a glimpse of Jack, my mood instantly soured.

"I see you up there," Mr. Solomon yelled through the glass storm door. "Four hydrangeas are missing off my bush, and I want to know where they are."

I walked down the stairs and flung the door open. Man, that guy could get my blood boiling. In the bad way. "Do you seriously think that I wouldn't know better than to cut your hydrangeas? Besides, I have three bushes in my own backyard."

Jack appeared at the door and clapped Mr. Solomon on the back. That infernal dog barked.

"Another day, another grievance to address with the neighbor, huh, Mr. Solomon?" Jack said.

I couldn't help but smile.

Frank wagged his finger at me. "I know you took my hydrangeas, and I'm not going to stand for this anymore. I'm having cameras installed."

I crossed my arms. "Fine," I said. "Then I'll have cameras installed, too. I know you let that yippy rat relieve herself on my cucumbers, and I will sue you if I see that again." Poor Biscuit. I felt bad again for calling her a yippy rat. She was sweet.

He glared at me. "Fine," he said. "Maybe I'm ready to order that survey."

"Fine," I replied, hoping like hell that I was right and the fence was on my property. But Hal had built it for me, and if I knew him, I knew that he would have triple-checked that survey line before he installed it.

Mr. Solomon turned. Needless to say, I didn't tell him good night.

"Well," Jack quipped. "Our date is off to a great start."

"Come in and have some wine," Caroline said.

I grabbed Jack's arm. "No, thank you. I have had enough of all of you, and we will be leaving now."

"We're going to be waiting up for you, young lady," Sloane teased.

"Don't do anything I wouldn't do!" I heard Emerson yell, as we headed down the front walk.

"So what exactly does that eliminate?" Caroline asked.

"Precisely what I was thinking," Sloane added.

"Hey," Emerson said. "I am a career woman now."

As Jack slipped his arm around my waist and whispered,

"Let's take a walk on the boardwalk before we go to dinner," I wondered if I could let him in. Just a little.

But that was what I was here to find out, wasn't it? So, sure, we had loved each other all those years ago. And I could pinpoint moments in between. But what about now? Now was the big question.

"Tell me about the girls," Jack said, as we walked down the wooden planks. "I hope I'll be lucky enough to really get to know them myself one day, but in the meantime I'll settle for your expert description."

I smiled. Oh, those little girls. I couldn't believe they were all grown-up. I *really* couldn't believe they were all grown-up and all living under my roof.

"Caroline is a force of nature," I said. "She has the strongest personality. She is stubborn and headstrong and a hair obnoxious." I paused. "But she loves like crazy. Once you're in with her, you have everything. But when you're out, you're out."

"So things aren't looking good for poor James, then, huh?"

I looked out over the dark water, the mast lights of the sailboats shining like stars fallen closer to earth. "For one, James brought this on himself. For two, he knows how unyielding his wife can be. I don't know why he would dare to think that she would have him back after what he did." I paused. "He doesn't deserve her. He never has."

"I think Caroline is the easiest to figure out," Jack said. "She seems very authentic, like you always know where you stand." He squeezed the top of my arm. "Reminds me of someone else I know."

I almost protested. How could he possibly think I was like Caroline? She was so loud and opinionated. But I guessed I was highly opinionated, too. Just more Southern about my delivery of those opinions. There's that old saying that the people you have the most trouble with are the ones who are most like yourself. So maybe it was true. Maybe Caroline and I were alike. I certainly couldn't see Sloane arguing with her elderly neighbor over four hydrangeas.

"And Sloane?"

"Sloane is the sweetest," I said. I thought back to our conversation earlier about Adam. "But I think she might also be the most steadfast, which is surprising. She is persistent, but she's quiet about it. She gets you to do what she wants, but quite often, you don't realize what she has done until later. She's incredibly creative, too, an amazing artist." I looked out at the sunset, the one that always made me think of my late husband, and said, "Just like Carter."

Jack slid his arm down and reached for my hand. "Let's turn here," he said.

We walked down the dock, which is when I realized that we were going to his boat, not a restaurant.

When I saw it, I smiled. He had a table set up on the deck, the new teak stain shiny and beautiful. It had a white tablecloth and two candles, which I knew must be LED, because it was way too breezy for real candles to stay lit. As Jack took my hand and helped me step over the side, I realized soft music was playing in the background. When I recognized what it was, I started laughing. "Is that Ray Charles?"

But he didn't have to answer. Instead, he pulled me close to him, and we started to dance, just as "Georgia on My Mind" began playing. It was a perfect moment, one that I knew had been orchestrated but still felt totally organic and completely right.

"This song has always made me think of you," he said.

"Really?" I asked. But I understood. It was funny how even now, all these years later, simply hearing a song could put me right back in a moment, right back in the emotions I felt.

He pulled me tighter, and I wondered if he could feel my heart racing through his sport coat. "Every time I heard this song on the radio I used to wonder if you were somewhere thinking of me, too. Even when I was married, I think I always knew that this would never end for me. For me, Ansley, the road leads back to you."

I could feel tears in my eyes, and I rested my head on his shoulder.

"Ahem," I heard from across the deck.

I turned and was surprised to see Kimmy, holding two tiny plates.

She set them down and said, "Your appetizer this evening is a goat-cheese-stuffed fig with pancetta."

I raised my eyebrows at Jack and walked toward the table. "So, Kale Yeah Kimmy is also Caterer Kimmy?"

"Ansley," she said, "it's not happening. I'm not getting one of those cheesy nicknames, no matter how much you want me to."

"I don't think it's really your choice," I teased.

I caught a glimmer of a smile from her.

"I can't believe you'd participate in something so sappy. You old softy."

She definitely smiled now. "I can't sell you vegetables for one anymore, Ansley. It's too pathetic."

Jack raised his glass and said, "To Ansley. The stars may be awfully bright tonight, but none shines as brightly as you."

He smiled that winning smile at me, the one that couldn't help but make me feel a little giddy, and that's when I realized it. "You," I said.

"What?"

"Sloane is exactly like you." My palms started to sweat.

Jack smiled. "That's good," he said. "If you think I'm like one of your children, then you'll be predisposed to liking me."

But I hadn't just liked Jack from the first time I laid eyes on him. Something inside me shifted, and I knew that after this moment, Kimmy was right. Vegetables for one weren't going to cut it anymore.

TWENTY-FOUR

mending fences

caroline

Sloane, Emerson, and I couldn't imagine why my mother would have devoted years of her life to hating her next-door neighbor. I mean, sometimes I give my mom a hard time, but at the end of the day, she's one of the most rational people I know. She has a good head on her shoulders and is always talking us down from one ledge or another. Well, Emerson and me. Sloane doesn't have ledges, because Sloane is a reasonable person.

I had fed Preston, Hummus was watching him during his nap, and I recruited Vivi to help me with a project. "We," I said, "are going to end this feud between your grandmother and Mr. Solomon once and for all!"

She put her sassy little hands on her sassy little hips. "Mom," she said, rolling her eyes, "people have to work out their own problems."

In the most ironic of ironies, Vivi's Georgia friends were

possibly even worldlier than her New York friends. Vivi had an answer for everything, and I was quite sure that I seemed even dumber than usual to her. That was really saying something, because she already thought I was the stupidest person on the planet.

I nodded. "They do, Viv. But sometimes they need a nudge in the right direction."

She smiled. There was my little girl.

"We're going to need Hippie Hal," I said.

It was a beautiful day in Peachtree, and I could walk more than three feet again without feeling as though I would imminently die. It was a good thing. "So Viv," I said, walking down the crepe-myrtle-lined sidewalk, "tell me what's going on at school."

"Nothing," she said, predictably. "Everyone is already talking about what they're going to do for spring break, and it's still like six weeks away."

Spring break. I hadn't thought about spring break. In six weeks, I could probably take Preston somewhere. Maybe Mom, too. Get her out of town, give her a break.

"Oh!" I said. "I know! Let's go to the Cloister."

Vivi nodded. She already had my taste for the finer things. "Can we get our toes done?"

"Sure," I said.

"Can Daddy come?"

I paused. *Um, no. Hell, no, Daddy cannot come.* Had she lost her mind? "We'll see," I said. I meant, *Not on your life, kid.*

We reached the home of Hippie Hal, with row after row of bikes lined up in the yard.

"Can I have one?" Vivi asked.

I looked at the rusting refurbished pieces of crap in the yard. Who would want one of them I wasn't sure, but I said OK anyway.

"Can I ride it to Melanie's house?"

Melanie was a sweet girl in Vivi's class who lived a few blocks away. Melanie's mother was one of my favorite moms at school and had brought a casserole when Preston was born. I knew we would be good friends—if I had time for friends, that is.

I shrugged. "Sure. As long as you're home by dinner."

It was so suburban I almost fell off the sidewalk.

"Hey, Viv," I said, "do you miss New York?"

She thought for a second. "I miss our family," she said. "But I love Peachtree."

I missed our family, too. Perhaps her father should have thought about that before he made an ass out of all of us. And I knew I missed New York. As much as Peachtree had grown on me these last few weeks, it was like a nice vacation. I knew it would end. When it did, I'd be ready to go back. The storm would mostly have blown over, and I would be ready to face whatever residual music was there waiting for me.

Alone.

My stomach flipped at the thought. It was very antifeminist, but I'd never been one of those women who wanted something more for herself. I loved being a wife and a mother. I loved making my home beautiful and going to lunch with my friends and raising money for charities that were important to me. I wasn't like Sloane or Emerson or Mom, who all had these fabulous creative abilities and outlets, passions that they didn't feel like themselves if they weren't doing them. Sometimes it made me jealous, especially times like now, when I realized that I would probably have to go back to work, but I had no idea what that work would be. Either way, it was time to stand on my own two feet. I had learned in the worst way that depending on your husband for everything wasn't the best strategy.

"Pick out whichever one you want," I said. "But you can't ride it until you go back to Gransley's and get a helmet out of the garage."

She took off running. "Look both ways!" I called.

Of all the things I wouldn't miss about Peachtree, I would miss that I could let my eleven-year-old tear off down the street by herself and not think even once that she was going to be kidnapped. That was a load off.

I knocked, and Hal opened the door so quickly I thought he must have been standing there waiting for me.

"Hey there, Caroline," he said, lids heavy, eyes red. He was super-duper stoned. No problem. High or not, we had work to do.

"First," I said, "Vivi wants this bike. Can I pay you for it when we get to our house?"

"When we get to your house?" he asked.

Ah, yes. The window had opened. I knew how to play this now. It was so simple.

"Yeah," I said. "Remember? You and I are peacemakers,

trailblazers, Hippie Hal. We're planning to take down that wall today. Or, well, the fence, rather. Remember?"

He rubbed his long beard for a moment. "Take down the fence," he repeated. "All right. Let me get some tools."

He disappeared inside, reappeared with a grocery bag full of clanging metal, and said, "Oh, Vivi can have the bike."

What a good guy he was. I felt sort of bad about tricking him. Sort of. But not bad enough to tell him the truth, especially now that I was getting what I wanted.

He pushed the hot orange bike down the sidewalk.

"So how's it going with old McClasky?" I asked.

"Well," he said, "she's as big a pain in the ass as ever. At this week's town meeting, she was as feisty as I've seen her about the bikes."

You couldn't help but notice the gleam in his eye. They were fighting. All was right with the world.

Vivi met us before we reached the boardwalk, helmet already on. She took the bike from Hal. "Thanks, Mom," she said, out of breath.

"Thank Hal," I said. "He gave it to you."

She hugged him, which you could see thrilled him to no end.

"OK, Hal," I said. "We've got to work quickly. Mom is at the shop, and I saw Mr. Solomon's car leave like ten minutes ago. I have to feed the baby, but then I'll come help you."

"That won't be necessary," Hal said. "I've got this under control. I built the fence in four-foot sections that screw onto a frame, so it's a piece of cake to take down. I can't say I didn't see this coming."

We both laughed.

When I went upstairs, Preston was still sleeping. Hummus didn't approve of swaddling, so he was spread out in his crib, tiny hands open and relaxed with sweet dreaming. It took everything I had not to pick him up and squeeze him to me.

That was the difference in being a second-time mother. When Vivi was born, I almost wished part of it away. I was so tired. I was so overwhelmed and consumed with the care of this person that I didn't savor it like I should have. This time, I knew exactly how quickly he would be riding bikes with his friends. The diaper changes were short. The sleepless nights were short. The breastfeeding was short. And so I was going to savor every day.

Or maybe I was getting some semblance of sleep this time and that was giving me a fresh and rosy perspective on life. Who knew? But I know for sure that I felt more grateful than I had in a long, long time. Even though James had humiliated me and broken my heart, I knew that I would do it all again. Because without all of it, I wouldn't have Preston. The world would be hideously incomplete.

I looked out the window, the very same window where, the night before, I had been up for a four thirty feeding and had seen Mark tiptoeing out the back door—moments after giving Emerson a kiss good-bye that did not look like anything I'd ever seen friends share. But if her party line was that they weren't dating, far be it from me to meddle. I knew Mark was Emerson's first love. She had dumped him mercilessly when she left for LA, but I always thought she had a place for him in her heart. I tried to deny it, of course. Like any good stage mom (I had to take on that role, because clearly, my mother was anything but a stage mom), I didn't want her throwing away her big, beautiful career on some townie. He was nice and all, but frankly, Emerson could do better. Emerson could do A-list. I saw her with a professional athlete, a movie star, Prince Harry . . . not some regular guy. So if she wanted to deny, I was a happy clam.

Currently, outside that same walk-of-shame window, Hal was working. The poor tomatoes. He was doing his best to salvage them, but they were pretty attached to the fence. That would be the only casualty of this adventure. But I knew that Mom and Mr. Solomon were going to be so, so happy.

Being selfless was not necessarily my strong suit. So I was glad I had tried it out. I could see the appeal.

A few hours later, I was snuggling my precious baby, who was fed and happy and so delicious I could eat him up. We were rocking in the rocking chair, which was making me sleepy. I was about to drift off when a man's voice yelling "You murderer!" reverberated from outside.

I looked out the window to see Mr. Solomon standing over the tomatoes, shaking his cane.

No, not exactly the response I had been looking for. I walked gingerly down the steps, Preston snuggled to my chest.

"Mr. Solomon," I said. "Look! I had Hal take the fence down. Aren't you happy?"

"Happy?" He practically spat. "Happy? You killed my prize-winning tomatoes."

They were all sort of lying there in a heap.

"Didn't kill them," I said. "Simply reconfigured." I paused. "And it's OK. Kimmy is coming over later with stakes to tack them up."

He still looked extremely flustered, which was when Mom pulled into the driveway.

She burst out of the car. "Where is my fence? Frank Solomon, what have you done with my fence?"

"It wasn't me! It was her." He pointed his cane at me.

I bounced up and down with Preston. "Could we keep our voices down a touch so as not to traumatize the baby?" I asked.

"Look," he said to Mom. "My babies are ruined!" He pointed his cane at the tomatoes.

"You think you have problems? Now I have a full view of your disastrously unkempt yard."

I looked over. The yard wasn't going to be in *Southern Living* or anything, but it wasn't horrible looking. They were both being pretty unreasonable, if you asked me.

"I want it back up," Mr. Solomon said.

"Are you serious?" Mom asked. "All these years of fighting and hating me over this fence, and you want it back up?"

He sniffed. "I rather like the fence. It's good for growing tomatoes. And I don't like seeing into your yard."

"The feeling is mutual." Mom looked at Mr. Solomon intently. "So if I put the fence back up, you won't terrorize me anymore? You won't say it's four inches on your property or threaten to watch me with security cameras or any of that?"

Mr. Solomon put his hand out for Mom to shake. "I'm too old to fight anymore. I'd rather be friends."

I've never seen my mother so astonished. And honestly, I mean, I had thought this would help, but I had no idea how much. I knew I was good, but I had no idea I was *this* good.

As Mom shook Mr. Solomon's hand, her phone rang. She put her finger up and walked across the yard to talk.

"Mr. Solomon," I said, "do you promise you're invested in this truce?"

He nodded. "I promise. I like getting your mother's goat. But I think I'd rather drink coffee with her on the porch sometimes than have to take an extra blood-pressure pill every time we're in the yard together."

"That's nice," I said. "I know she feels exactly the same way." Mom returned, her face white.

"What's wrong?"

She shook her head, and I could see that there were tears in her eyes. "They've taken away your grandmother's driver's license." She paused, looking totally defeated. "I'm going to bring her here until we can figure out our next steps."

"Oh, Mom," I said, looking back at the main house. "Seriously? We're like *Full House* on steroids over here."

"I know," she said. "But what else are we going to do? John certainly isn't going to take care of her." She rolled her eyes. "Scott can't. I'm not going to just dump her in some home."

Uncle Scott had spent his life traveling the world. He'd never married or had kids, because nothing had ever been tempting enough to slow him down. He was a travel writer, and his life depended on his ability to jump on a plane to Ibiza one day and a boat to Virgin Gorda the next. It was a cool life, but even as a kid, I had known it wasn't something I would ever have been able to do.

I didn't know John well enough to comment, sadly.

Mr. Solomon didn't say anything. He turned to walk back inside his house. But later that night, when I opened the back door, there was a small vase with four blue hydrangeas in it. It was a beautiful peace offering, and you couldn't help but notice how my mom smiled when I handed her the flowers.

Even I couldn't believe how easy it had been, after seven years of feuding, to mend fences. All it had taken, in fact, was tearing one down.

TWENTY-FIVE

the most natural thing

ansley

I am the official town decorator. I know. I'm a big deal. Whenever the library needs new carpet or the museum's reading room needs to be updated, I am the person they call. It was my first paying gig when we moved back to Peachtree. I donate a ton of my time, too, because in the laundry list of positions I fill, this is one of my favorites. It appeared that I would be adding another role to that laundry list: caretaker. It isn't somewhere a mind ever wants to go. But I guess that at fifty-eight, with an eighty-three-year-old mother, I knew this was coming. Maybe not today and maybe not tomorrow, but I had to have known that my mother wasn't going to be able to live on her own forever.

I think that's what hit me the hardest, realizing that her needing me, depending on anyone, was the beginning of the end. There was no question that my brother Scott got his independence from my mother. She was still living alone, cooking alone, driving alone. She still did her own grocery shopping and went to Zumba and walked her dog. Scott had taken the dog, much to my disappointment. But when I told Caroline that my mom was coming to stay, she had printed an article for me about a new study on how, while it was previously thought that dogs and humans couldn't pass viruses and bacteria back and forth, they were now realizing that this wasn't true—and dogs carry hundreds of viruses not usually found in humans.

I tacked one on the fridge, over hers, that said that children who grow up with dogs or cats have stronger immune systems—because they are exposed to hundreds of viruses not normally found in humans.

But honestly, despite how much I wanted a dog running around the house again, between the three daughters and the four grandchildren and now the mother, I had enough to take care of. So I let Caroline think she had won that one.

When I walked into the living room that morning, everything was quiet. Sloane was on the floor with Adam, sorting plastic animals by color.

"Wow!" I said. "Adam, you are so smart!"

He grinned up at me, plunking a green dinosaur beside the other green dinosaurs with enthusiasm.

"So you still think you're going to do this homeschooling thing all the way through?"

Sloane nodded. "Absolutely. Then if Adam is transferred or deployed for a long time, I'm flexible. The kids won't have to switch around to a bunch of different schools."

Emerson walked down the stairs, eyes blurry, hair in a messy bun on top of her head.

Now that my mother was coming, Emerson had to move upstairs with the rest of us to make room.

I patted the couch beside me, and she snuggled up under my arm, head resting on my shoulder. She had always been my most affectionate child.

"That's so good, Adam," she said.

She smelled of perfume and alcohol.

"Aunt Emmy!" he shouted. "Watch this!"

She looked like she was resisting the urge to cover her ears. "How can Adam bear to miss this?" she asked. "How do you do it, Sloane? You are Superwoman."

Sloane smiled. "This is what I chose, so I accept it. Plain and simple." She shook her head. "But his twenty years are up in four more, and I sure do hope he chooses civilian life. This military stuff is a hard business."

"Do you think he will?" I asked.

Sloane laughed. "Realistically? Not a chance. He loves it. It's his passion."

Caroline came in about that time. Except that Caroline doesn't really come in. She makes an entrance; she arrives. She was all dolled up, her hair fixed, her makeup done. It was shocking to see her in wedges and a dress after a few weeks of lounging around.

"You look fantastic, sweets," I said. "Where are you going?"

She looked at me like I was dense. "To pick up Grammy, obviously."

"Yeah, girl. Work that driver's license," Sloane said, laughing.

"I don't know," I said. "Grammy has already been in one accident this month."

Caroline shot me a look. "I'll have you know that I got a perfect score on my driving test. I parallel parked for the first time with an eight-months-pregnant belly. So I don't want any lip from any of you."

I was so proud that my daughter was doing something selfless. I had been dreading having to leave this quiet morning with my grandson and daughters to go to the airport alone. Even though I joke about Caroline being difficult, I would be happy to have my firstborn all to myself for a little while.

And Mom would be thrilled. She and Caroline had always had a special bond, like Vivi and me. I don't know how that happens, except that being a grandparent is like being a parent but with decades more perspective. I had felt guilty about Mom having to fly by herself, but Scott insisted that he couldn't go, and Mom insisted that she didn't need me flying there to come get her only to get right back on a plane to come home. "They have people for that," she said. "They are paid to take care of old people like me."

Mom and I had had our share of disagreements in the past, the largest, of course, that she wouldn't let me come home when I needed her the very most. I never told her how I wished she would have been there more when my girls were young, taken a greater role in their lives. But she had raised her three children. She was finished. I think it was more of an internal struggle I had, a difference in how we parented, in that she continued on with her life and we fit in on the fringes where we could. I knew I would never be that kind of parent. And I wasn't. Not even now that they were all grown up.

I remember thinking when I was young that there was no greater gift than losing yourself to raise your children. People complained and moaned about it, but to me, it was a privilege. I don't regret one single day that I spent with them. I knew that this would be exactly the same thing. I would lose myself again, the self that I had clawed and scraped to recreate after Carter had died, but I would find something else in caring for my mother. Just like when my girls were young, I knew I would never regret one moment I had spent with her, would always cherish that I had been the one to get to be there for her final time on earth, no matter how long that time was. I knew already from being a mother that sometimes the days would be long. Some days would be hard, would wring me out, would lend me that tiredness I felt from the roots of my hair to the soles of my feet. But the years? They would be inexplicably too short. And so, even on the toughest days, I would be grateful. I had the gift of time. I had the privilege of more days to work through our differences, to say the things that so desperately needed to be said.

Emerson, Vivi, and I had done a yoga video that morning whose main theme was surrender. Life, we had been instructed, was as much about surrender as it was about control.

Surrender, I thought. It was a tricky thing. Letting go. Trusting another person more than you trusted yourself. Knowing he would be there for you. Believing that the universe would send you the right thing. When your husband is killed in a way so excruciating that you can't bear to think of it, that you have nightmares of being burned, buried alive, suffocating on smoke for years and years and years, surrender is no longer in your vocabulary.

When you find out that someone you had trusted more than anyone else on the planet hadn't bothered to let you in on the very real financial distress that was facing your family, letting go was a tricky concept.

But when your three daughters and four grandchildren were living under your roof, your eleven-year-old granddaughter mastering Warrior Two right beside you, and contrary to your fears, it was going swimmingly, and your old boyfriend came back and was living on his dump of a boat presumably to be near you, and your mother was coming back home and you didn't know what to expect but you were less nervous than you thought, you start to think that maybe, just maybe, this surrender thing might work for you. Maybe you can learn to live your life in a different way, in a better way.

My phone beeped. Sandra. It was a group text to Emily and me. It was such a shocking change from nothing but my girls over the past few weeks, I almost did a double take. Don't kill me . . . Did you see the *Ladies Who Lunch* previews for tonight?

I rolled my eyes. That was the last thing I would want to know about. That show is off limits in my house. And you know I don't have a TV!

Emily: Even with all the kids??

Sandra: It looks like James dumps Edie . . . For Caroline.

Me: What?!

Emily: She might want to see it. Maybe.

Sandra: We should watch first. Make sure it's all above-board.

Me: James and Caroline are going out. I'm babysitting. Can't come.

Sandra: We'll come to you.

Emily: Gary will set it all up. Livestreaming.

I was going to be in so much trouble. Curiosity killed the cat, and I was only human. Curiosity was going to kill me if I didn't figure out what this was all about. When Caroline burst through the door, I threw my cell phone across the counter.

She gave me a weird look. "Mom? You OK?"

"Oh, yeah." I smiled, trying to look nonchalant. "I'm just nervous about Mom coming."

She raised her eyebrows. "About Grammy coming? Or riding with me?"

I laughed, but really, riding with her was something to be nervous about.

I took a deep breath and followed her out the door. And it occurred to me that being a parent is one giant leap of faith.

eligibles

caroline

I may be thirty-four years old. And I may love my sisters more than life. But I still like having my mom all to myself every now and then. I am the firstborn child, after all. Sometimes I want a few minutes of going back to how it was for those short, fleeting years before Sloane was born, when it was just Mom and me hanging around all day until Dad got home. As I used to call them when I was little, the good old days.

Now, of course, I wouldn't trade my sisters for anything. But it was difficult to transition from being an only child and having all of Mom and Dad's love and attention.

"So," Mom asked, sliding into the passenger seat of her SUV. "How you farin'?"

I smiled. It was one of those habits that even years as a New Yorker hadn't cured her of. I kind of liked it.

"Well, I'll be honest." I turned to back out of the driveway.

"During all those years of fertility treatments and IVF and praying for a baby, this wasn't exactly how I pictured things. But I have a new baby. And he is perfect."

"The universe has a funny sense of timing, that's for sure."

I rolled my eyes. The universe. My mother was in the front pew of the church, pearls on, the three of us in smocked dresses beside her, every Sunday morning for most of our childhood. It wasn't like I had this strong faith or anything, but I liked that she did. It bugged me that she had lost so much of herself when she lost our dad. But I didn't want to get into it today.

"Do you think that's what made James cheat?" It was the first time I had said it out loud. Because it was a reason men cheated, wasn't it? We had spent six years, ever since Vivi was three and it became apparent that I was not getting pregnant on my own, doing every fertility treatment under the sun. From Clomid to Chinese herbs, acupuncture to IVF, the big, the small, the Eastern, the Western, and everything in between. If someone had gotten pregnant doing something, I tried it. And nothing. No baby.

It was the most stressful time in our marriage. No doubt about it. I can't count the number of months I cried over an EPT, the number of months James had tried to persuade me to give myself a break.

I took my eyes off the road long enough to see Mom shake her head. "Caroline, no." She sighed. "I want to think only the worst of him right now because I'm mad at him, but the way he took care of you and supported you through all of that . . . I'm not sure many men could have taken it."

It brought tears to my eyes. "Did you ever think about adopting, Mom?"

She shrugged. "Sure I did. But your father didn't love the idea of that." She paused. "I hope that doesn't color him in a negative light. It was a different time. It wasn't even about the baby, really. It was such an invasive process. He didn't want anyone delving into our histories, all of our financial details . . ."

She trailed off. James had been so good about that, saying that we could adopt. And at first, I thought we should. I don't know if it was the hormones or my basic personality or what, but once I started down the fertility road, I couldn't stop. I became obsessed by being pregnant again, of experiencing giving birth. I almost idolized the idea. When one doctor would sense my desperation, would tell me that he or she wouldn't let this lunacy continue, I would go to the next one and the next.

James tried to talk to me about it, but it was like he knew this had gotten bigger than me. He knew I couldn't hear him, not really. He had to let me do this. He was always good about knowing that.

One night at dinner, the three of us were discussing how we would celebrate Vivi's ninth birthday. And I said, in my usual way, "Wonder how we'll celebrate your tenth birthday when the new baby gets here?"

Vivi was calm but strong. She reminded me a lot of Sloane in that way. She burst into tears at the dinner table and looked at me with the most beautiful yet terrorized face I'd ever seen and said, "Do you even love me anymore? Or only the new baby?"

She ran from the table, and I let her leave. I was stunned, as though she had slapped me across the face. No words could have cut more deeply or hurt me worse. She sliced right through me in the way only a daughter can do to her mother.

I didn't cry or really even react much. I just turned to James and said, "What have I done?"

He squeezed my shoulder and said, "We understand, Caroline. It's a hard time for you."

I shook my head. "I have damaged my relationship with the child I do have in favor of the one I don't."

That was it. It was the last day I went to a doctor except for a regular checkup. The last time I took hormones, injected myself with drugs, anything. That's how I am, though, I think. Sometimes something big has to happen to snap me out of it. But once it does, I'm done. It's over.

"Thanks for everything, Mom," I said now. "You were so great."

She squeezed my arm. "I knew what you were going through. I wanted to protect you from it, but of course, I couldn't."

"It was better my way. At least there was something wrong with me. I could be in control. I can't imagine if I'd had to wait around for James to decide what *he* wanted to do."

Mom laughed. "That is what you would think about. Men can be very sensitive about these things, but your father was really fine. He was totally on board. He wanted our babies to at least be mine, and he was very grown-up and stoical about the whole thing."

"Mom, did you worry that Dad would love Emerson the most?" There. I'd said it. Sort of. We always used to joke that Emerson was Dad's favorite child. But even the joke stung just a little. She was the only one who was biologically his, after all.

She laughed again. Harder. "You need to turn right at the next stoplight." She laughed again. "Honey, no. Of course not. I can promise you, from the bottom of my heart, that he did not love Emerson the most. It's different for men. They don't carry the babies. Either way, they sort of spontaneously come into the world. He was so grateful for you, because we weren't sure we'd have any children. And then Sloane and Emerson were both just beautiful icing on a beautiful cake."

I smiled and turned right into pickup and dropoff, which was a comical name for a section of the tiny airport that could have easily been someone's house. There were no cars anywhere. Just us.

I put the car in park, and Mom said, "Whew! We survived!"

I held up my phone. "I didn't even text and drive. Impressive, right?"

"You'd better not ever," Mom said. She was very serious about three things: we were not allowed to text and drive, take shots, or skydive. Otherwise, she was OK.

So maybe my parents didn't have favorites, or maybe they did. But I was pretty certain, as I walked into the tiny airport a few minutes later, that I was Grammy's favorite grandchild. When I met her at baggage claim, she was on one of those contraptions that you rest your leg on and wheel around. It was shocking how agile she still was, in her blue tracksuit, pearls, and Ferragamo tennis shoes. Her hair was whiter than the last time I had seen her, curled and set like the good Southern woman she was.

"How do you do it?" was the first thing she said to me when I saw her.

"What, Grammy?"

"How do you manage to look like a million bucks right after a C-section? There is no rational explanation for it, yet here you are, stunning as ever."

This was why I loved this woman.

"So," I said, wheeling her two suitcases through the lobby, while she looked like she was having way too much fun on her scooter. "Give it to me straight."

She nodded. We had always had that connection, that mind meld, where we used very few words. "Well, darling. You made your bed. You're going to have to lie in it. For heaven's sake, that son of yours can't grow up without a father."

I turned my head toward her. "But Grammy—"

"But nothing, love. We honor our commitments. We just do."

Very awkwardly, as there was no one else around to help—I didn't know how they kept this airport open—I finagled the two suitcases out the door and held it for my grandmother. "He didn't honor his commitment. Not at all."

She waved her free hand at me. "Well, darling, all men are morons. You know that. For heaven's sake, you just gave birth to one. But you have to be the bigger person. Lord knows he isn't capable." She took a deep breath. "It's going to be harder than hell. But doing the hard thing, even when it hurts, is what makes you strong."

I thought about my sister Sloane, how she sat in her room every night after the kids went to bed and wrote her husband a letter. A real letter, detailing the events of the day. Her life was one huge sacrifice after another, and while, yeah, Adam's calling was a noble one, it was still a choice. It was still choosing to protect your country over being with your wife and kids.

But she loved him. So she stuck by him. Although she was quieter and calmer and more reserved, I had no doubt that she was one of the strongest people I knew.

Mom turned, saw us, and said, "Mom!" running to Grammy.

"Oh, it's my favorite girl," Grammy said.

Mom and Grammy had had their differences in the past. But I felt like they were in a better place. I hoped so, anyway. Otherwise, this was going to be a long recovery.

Mom hugged Grammy and practically carried her into the backseat. It was a good thing the woman barely weighed one hundred pounds. Emerson had always had her string-bean build.

My phone beeped, and since I wasn't yet driving, I checked the text. It was a silly selfie of my husband, daughter, and son. We love you, the text said. The biggest of us can't wait to take you out to dinner tonight. You looked so gorgeous when you left. I've been thinking about you all day.

I didn't need anyone telling me what to do. Not even Grammy. But it occurred to me that it was her voice, telling me it was OK, that crossed my mind when I texted back: What time?

I might not ever be able to forgive James. And that would be OK. But if I didn't give our family another shot, I knew I'd never be able to forgive myself.

I REMEMBER TELLING SLOANE when I was a senior in college that I was sick of boys. She was very supportive. It took me a good fifteen minutes to realize that she thought I was telling her I was a lesbian. What I was really trying to say was that I was sick of kegs and kids who couldn't hold their liquor. I was ready to find someone I could really settle down with, fall in love with.

He couldn't be just anyone, of course. He had to be the kind of man I had always envisioned myself marrying. He had to be the kind of man who would support me, who would want me to stay home with our children like I'd always dreamed. In retrospect, I see how much I was asking for. But at the time, it didn't feel like much. It had worked out for my mom. (Well, until the whole Dad-killed-by-terrorists thing.) Why couldn't it work out for me?

I was way past the time when I thought picking up some random stranger in a bar was going to cut it. And online dating back then was still for people who lived in their parents' basements.

So I did what many more women in my position would do if they were as crafty as I am. I combed every "eligible bachelor" list in the city for the previous few years. I figured out who these men were, where they liked to go, what they liked to do. I wasn't trying to bag one, necessarily. But if I was ever in the position, I'd like to have a fighting chance.

So when I was at an art opening for yet another one of my friends who fancied herself an artist, sipping my chardonnay, standing around on my sample-sale Jimmy Choos in a dress too tight for my own good, it took me a moment to figure out who he was.

I thought I'd noticed him because he was so devastatingly handsome. I was actually intimidated, which is really saying something. He had effortlessly fluffy dark hair and eyes that, although I wasn't close enough to see what color they were yet, I knew already wouldn't let me go. His suit was perfectly tailored.

Jolie, artist du jour, came over and gasped. "Oh, my gosh! That's James Beaumont!"

I replied, "Who?"

But I knew who. Number seven, four, and eleven on three of my latest "eligible bachelor" lists. Lawyer. Son of a lawyer. Grandson of a lawyer. Family was Southern, but great-grandfather had made his way north to find fortune—which he had.

Jolie was all breathless and flighty. "Do you think he'll buy one of my paintings?"

I shrugged nonchalantly. I set my gaze on James, like I always did when I was interested in a man. And like they always did, he turned his gaze to meet mine, at which point I looked away demurely.

"Want me to ask him?" I said.

I looked back up, and he was still staring at me, which was a pretty good sign that he might be interested. I walked over casually, took a sip of chardonnay, and said, "This is my favorite piece in the entire collection."

It spoke to me. The blues and tans and whites, the way they swirled in that perfect combination of water, sea, and sky.

"I think it's mine, too," James said, grinning at me. I could feel my heart pounding, and I felt thankful that I hadn't inherited that awful blushing tendency from my mom.

I examined the painting, and James examined me.

"I grew up spending my summers in Peachtree Bluff, Georgia," I said. "This painting feels like that to me." I turned to meet James's gaze.

"You're a good agent," he said.

I laughed. "Oh, no. I'm not an agent. I'm a senior at NYU. I just love Jolie's art."

He reached out his hand, which Grammy would have pointed out was rude. He should only have reached for my hand if I offered mine first.

"James Beaumont," he said.

"Caroline Murphy," I replied.

"So, Caroline Murphy, would you hold it against me if I bought this painting? I don't want to steal your favorite."

"Oh, not at all," I said. "College living doesn't provide much room for six-foot-tall paintings."

Thirty minutes later, James and I were sharing oysters and champagne. When he asked about my parents, I heard myself say, "My dad was killed in the second tower."

I couldn't believe I had said that. I never said that. Which made me know that I must like this guy, eligible bachelor or not. He stopped mid-sip, mouth agape, and I think he actually dropped his oyster shell.

"You mean like the World Trade Center?"

I nodded and took a sip of champagne to swallow with my tears. It was still so raw and so fresh. I wondered if it would ever go away.

"God, Caroline," he said. "I'm so sorry."

This was when I usually said something like *So many people lost loved ones that day.* But I didn't. Instead, I said, "Me, too. He was one of the good ones."

James didn't ask me back to his place, and I didn't ask him back to mine. He didn't kiss me, either. But he did walk me home, slowly, holding my hand the entire way. We talked for hours that night. We talked about art and politics, religion, love, our favorite episode of *Friends*, the new BlackBerry and how we couldn't live without it. We talked about his brother and my sisters. Man, did we ever talk about my sisters. In fact, we talked so much that I wasn't sure we'd ever have anything to talk about again. And when he didn't try to kiss me, I assumed he considered me a friend.

I thought I would be bummed because I'd let one of my "eligibles" slip away. Instead, I was bummed because for the first time in my life, I really, really liked a guy, and he didn't like me back. So I thought.

The next morning, I awoke to a soft rap on the door. "Hang on," I called quietly, trying not to wake my roommates, swiping a toothbrush through my mouth. Not even the UPS man needed to deal with that. I had no makeup on, my hair was disheveled from sleep, and I was wearing these ratty flannel PJs Mom had gotten me when I first went off to college.

I opened the door expecting to see a brown uniform and hear "Sign here." Instead, I opened the door and could feel myself blushing, Ansley-style.

James, in a pair of blue jeans and a button-down shirt, peeked his head out from behind the massive painting.

"No!" I exclaimed. There was no way I would ever have been able to afford that painting in a million years.

"I saw the way you looked at it," he said. "And I knew it had to be yours."

He was still standing in the hallway. He stepped forward two steps and slid the painting against the wall of the apartment.

My heart was pounding so loudly I forgot to be embarrassed about the dishes in the sink or the months of magazines stacked on the coffee table.

"Do you know what else I knew?"

I shook my head.

James took a step closer, pulled me to him, and said, "That you had to be mine."

Then he planted one on me that I knew I'd never forget. I mean, it was like planets colliding and the world stopping and the earth shaking all at once. Needless to say, I was glad I had brushed my teeth.

I fell for him so hard and so fast, realizing pretty quickly that all of my lists and qualifications never would have mattered. Because when you fall in love, real, consuming love, you're done.

Six months later, I graduated and "rented a room" in the apartment of one of my friends so my mom wouldn't know I had moved in with James. Well, at least she wouldn't have to know for sure. I married him nine months after that. And I can truly say that I never looked back. Not once. From the very first time I laid eyes on that man, he was it for me.

Which is what made it so particularly difficult to swallow that I hadn't been it for him.

gmos and soul mates

ansley

When I was remodeling the house in Peachtree Bluff, you know, getting the general old-lady vibes out of it, one of the first things I wanted to do was replace the windows on the second floor. It had this grand and glorious view—and some of the smallest windows you've ever seen. Three of the windows were across the front. It wasn't that many, but the Peachtree Historical Committee would have to approve the changes.

I knew they wouldn't.

The same crew redid everything else in the entire house for me, and we got to be great friends.

So when Leonard the contractor said, "Ansley, I need you and the girls out of the house tonight," I didn't think much of it. When he added, "You'll probably want to spend the night out, because the guys and I will be here at two a.m.," I started to get suspicious. I looked at him sideways, and he said, "Trust me.

Something has to be done here, and if anyone realizes it, you're going to have to be able to swear you didn't know a thing about it. So I am not telling you."

I laughed. "Say no more, Leonard. Say no more."

I wished I had witnessed Leonard and his crew installing, as silently as possible, three giant windows at two in the morning.

Six months later, when I thought I was in the clear, that damn Carol Glover came to me with a photo. "Ansley," she asked, peering at me suspiciously, "what on earth happened to the windows?"

I looked at the picture and then at the house and then at the picture and then at the house. There was a vast and gaping difference to anyone with a trained eye—or an old photograph. But I squinted and said, "I'm not sure what you mean."

She crossed her arms. "Ansley Murphy, I know you can see the difference."

I put my hands up in confusion. "I don't know about a single thing that has ever been done to those windows, Carol, so you're asking the wrong girl. Too bad Grandmother isn't here to consult."

I looked at her, teary-eyed, and she rolled her eyes, but she relented. I haven't heard about those windows again directly, but the historical committee has made it clear via snide remarks that, no matter the culprit, they are less than thrilled that the windows do not match the originals.

Caroline was less than thrilled about her date with her possibly soon-to-be-ex-husband. She couldn't say that, of course, because Vivi was there. I'd give Caroline credit. She was as feisty as they come, but I hadn't heard her utter one negative word about James in front of her daughter. I had to catch myself every now and then.

"So are you and Dad going on a date?" Vivi asked.

"No, sweets," Caroline lied. "We're going to dinner to discuss some things."

Vivi crossed her arms. "Are you getting back together?"

"All right, love." I stepped in to save Caroline from the line of questioning. "Let's go downstairs and make supper." Then I whispered, loudly enough for Caroline to hear, "And then we'll go get real ice cream with dairy and gluten in the cones and everything."

"Even GMOs?" she asked.

"Probably even a few GMOs," I said.

"I'm not hearing this," Caroline called.

Hummus swept in with Preston. She winked at me. "You get Vivi squared away, and I'm going to get this little guy down, and then . . ."

I winked back. That was code for *and then we would sneak into the guesthouse den while Caroline was out and watch Ladies Who Lunch*. As soon as Caroline stepped into James's car, I texted Gary: The Eagle has landed.

We were all chuckling and thinking we were funny. But if we weren't careful, this could end very, very badly.

Getting Vivi into bed by nine took some finagling, but I persevered. Getting my mother into bed by nine took no effort at all, as she was exhausted from traveling. I vacillated about whether to include her in our scheme. But she was too close with Caroline—and too likely to forget that she wasn't supposed to say anything. I couldn't take the chance.

Hummus held my hand while Sandra poured wine, and Gary and Emily wrangled cables and successfully plugged in the TV, hooked the laptop to it, and streamed the three words we were not allowed to say in our house. Emerson and Sloane silently came and sat on the couch. It was as if we were at a very dark, very macabre wake, fearing every minute that the deceased was going to jump out of the coffin.

It felt like time was standing still. The nausea started about halfway through. On-screen, James was at a party with Edie and the rest of the "ladies." Edie, classy girl that she was, got into a fight with a friend about the person who did their spray tans and threw a glass of wine in her face.

James, evidently, wasn't a big fan of this move. "Have you lost your mind?" he hissed, eerily calm.

"Did you hear what she said to me?" Edie screamed. "Why are you not on my side on this?"

And then the moment happened. "Caroline would never, ever act like this. Ever."

Edie screwed up her face. "Caroline who?"

"My wife!"

Edie put her hands on her hips. "Are you serious with this right now?"

"I'm totally serious. I am going home to beg my wife's forgiveness, and I don't ever want to hear from you again."

"James, wait!"

He put his hand to his forehead. "What is wrong with me? She's the love of my life."

"Me?" Edie asked.

"No!" He practically spit. "Caroline!"

He turned, and she called after him, "But James! We're soul mates!"

The camera pointed toward James as he walked out of the penthouse, down onto the street below, and as his back became very small, it panned to a shot of Edie sobbing on the shoulder of some blond girl with too-long extensions. And then the previews for next week started.

I didn't know what to say. It's highly unnerving to see your son-in-law on television with someone who is not your daughter. And I was more certain than ever that if Caroline ever saw James on that show, she would not consider getting back together with him, despite what he had said. It was so tasteless, so tacky. It was, in short, the opposite of everything Caroline stood for. And I started to wonder if watching it at all was a huge mistake.

Gary was already hauling everything to the car when Emerson finally had the forethought to say, "Quick! To the main house!"

Hummus grabbed the baby monitor off of the end table, and we all made a run for it.

"So what do we think?" I asked the faces sitting around my living room. "Are we Team James or not?"

"Come on, Mom," Sloane said. "You've never been Team James."

Sandra put her fingers to her lips. "You know, as someone who divorced her husband because he cheated, I wonder all the time if my life would have been better if I had stayed. My kids would have been together. There wouldn't have been issues over holidays and baptisms, birthday parties and family dinners. If I could rewind, I think I might have given him another chance."

I looked at Hummus. "What?" she said. "He writes my checks. I'm not allowed to comment." She paused. "But Caroline is better than most anyone I know at living her truth. She won't let public opinion affect her either way."

"No," Emerson said. "She won't. But she will let *our* opinion affect her. It's fine to be Switzerland sometimes, but I think this is when we take a stand."

The back door opened, and everyone panicked. I laughed uncomfortably. "Oh, Emerson. Please tell us that story about the director who wanted you to play a pig in the commercial."

She looked at me like *Really?*

It was the best I could do under intense pressure. We all laughed uncomfortably as Caroline walked through the door.

"Hi," she said, looking around. "Did you have a party without me?"

"Of course not," I said. "Sandra, Emily, and Gary popped by for a glass of wine."

"Actually," Emily said, picking up her purse, "we need to be leaving now."

"That's my cue," Sandra said.

Hummus picked up the monitor. "I'll go peek in on sweet baby."

"So . . ." Sloane ventured.

Caroline sat down and crossed her legs, her beautiful shoes, tied in a bow at the front of her ankle, making them look longer and even more slender. "It was fine," she said. "It made me less nauseated than I thought, and I do believe that he's sorry . . ."

There was a trailing off in her voice and an uptick that made me know she wasn't finished.

"But?" I said.

"But I don't know if I can do it." She sighed. "It's not only that he cheated. He told me he didn't love me anymore. I'm not sure I can get past that." Caroline looked down at those impeccable shoes. "I'd have to live with him. I'd have to look at the man I pledged my heart and my life to and know that he slept with someone else and, far worse, that he believed he was in love with her and not with me. I'd have to know that I am the laughingstock of New York City, that every time I walk down the street, everyone is saying what a loser I am. Do you know how that feels?"

"That's awful," Emerson said. "It's so awful. Maybe you could move somewhere else?"

"No," Caroline said, "New York is my home. It always has been. I belong there."

I heard a now-familiar squeak, and my mother wheeled into the room. "Well," she said, "maybe you should ask all of them if you'll still be the laughingstock of New York City. They watched the show tonight." Then she scooted back to her bedroom.

Emerson, Sloane, and I looked from one to the other, stunned. Talk about throwing the grenade and running.

Caroline closed her eyes and took a deep breath. I braced myself for what would come next, but she simply said, "And?"

"And he announced on TV that Edie Fitzgerald was a total moron and you were the love of his life," Emerson said.

Sloane nodded. "Yeah. So if you're worried about the show, maybe you shouldn't be."

Caroline nodded and stood up. "OK. Good night."

That couldn't be it. Not possible.

She turned and said, "I'll film a YouTube video to let you all know what I decide."

"That would be kind of funny, actually," Emerson said. "She could do her own miniseries on YouTube in response to *Ladies Who Lunch*." She gasped. "I could play her!"

That was the scariest thing about Caroline. She was totally unpredictable. I would have expected her to freak out knowing that we had watched the show. But she didn't. She let it roll right off. But tomorrow someone would use up all of her coffee creamer, and she'd blow a gasket. If I'm honest, I know she's hard to live with. And while she has a lot of good qualities that I'm sure make her a great wife, James had to have had his hands full. No doubt about it.

"Girls," I said, "I think I'll take a quick walk." This was my favorite time of night on the water, when the stars were bright and the air was crisp. Evening walks had been one of my favorite traditions—back when I had an empty house, that is.

I think I denied, even to myself, that I purposely walked

down the boardwalk in the direction of Jack's boat. I could see his legs propped up on the stern, a newspaper in his hands. As my footsteps got closer, he turned and, when he saw me, grinned broadly. But he didn't move for a second. Then, slowly, he folded the newspaper, climbed out of the boat, and walked up to where I was.

"Well, hi," Jack said.

"Hi," I replied. "Just taking a walk. It's such a nice night."

He nodded. "So you weren't hoping to run into me?" He winked.

I blushed. I was terribly transparent.

"Are you OK?" he asked.

I nodded. "Yeah. Just needed a deep breath."

Jack squeezed my shoulder. "Those are good every now and then." He paused. "Do you see how good I'm being? I'm trying to stay away to avoid becoming one of those pathetic TV characters who won't get a clue."

I laughed. "You're doing a good job. I think I'm the pathetic TV character tonight."

He smiled. "In that case, can I walk with you?"

I nodded. "Sure."

We walked in silence into the dark night. The sunset earlier had been hot, fire-orange and brilliant, giving way to an iridescent crescent moon. It looked to me like a perfect half. *A perfect half.* I grinned to myself. Why, oh, why could I not keep myself away from him? I was too old to be acting like this.

The shops were closed, and the restaurants had served their last patrons. The boardwalk was totally deserted. We walked a few yards, and I leaned over the railing and looked into the night sky, feeling infinite, feeling eternal, feeling so very small and unimportant in the scheme of this great, wide universe. It was perhaps my favorite feeling.

"Well, I'd better get back and clean up my mess," I said.

I turned around and bumped right into Jack. Before I could think about what was happening, he kissed me. Not a little kiss but a big, wrapped-in-strong-arms, dipped-toward-the-ground kiss to remember. And I did remember. In some ways, it was like my mouth had never left his, like my body had never forgotten exactly how it felt to be in his arms and was simply acting on muscle memory.

Jack and I had had so many perfect moments together since he came back into my life. Romantic moments. Sunsets and starlit dances, rainy coffee runs and long, lingering stares. But this, when I was distracted by my daughters' worries and he wasn't expecting me at all, was the perfectly imperfect moment. In my life now, perfectly imperfect seemed exactly right. And for the first time in a long time, I could honestly say that it felt wonderful to lose control.

TWENTY-EIGHT

more than words

caroline

Sloane and I were seven and nine, it was snowing, we were bored, and I wanted to go sledding.

I remember how she scrunched up her nose at the idea. She did it so much when she was young that her nose had a little red line across the bridge.

"How will we go sledding?" she asked. "There aren't any hills."

We may have been short on hills, but we had steps. It was basically the same thing, if you asked me. Emerson wasn't quite one yet, and while Mom was putting her down for a nap, the best thing happened: Mom fell asleep.

"Grab that cardboard box out of the closet, Sloane!" I said.

She did, and I wrestled the plastic purple toboggan out of the storage area outside our house. Dad would pull us down the sidewalk in it when there was a lot of snow like there was that day.

My strategy was simple. Lay the cardboard down the steps like a trail, cover the cardboard with snow, slide down. I was very confident in my plan. Well, I mean, kind of confident. I still instructed Sloane to get our bike helmets.

"OK," I told her. "When we get to the bottom of the steps, we have to fall off to the side."

"Fall off to the side?" Another nose scrunch. (I realize now that that little red line was because of me.) You could tell she was becoming less convinced that this was a good idea. "But won't we get hurt on the concrete?"

I poked her down jacket. "Nah. We're padded."

That was the optimistic part of the day. The part before the screaming and the bruising and the "You are so lucky you didn't break any bones."

But it was worth it for that one moment of glory. I was in the front, holding the rope to steer, and Sloane was in the back, holding on to me for dear life. And right before we made our maiden—and final—voyage down the steps, Sloane yelled, "I can't believe I let you talk me into this!"

Now I finally understood how she felt back then. Because I couldn't imagine that I had let James talk me into *this*. I mean, yes, I realize that I was, in some ways, culpable in this situation. I had told Vivi that we could go to the Cloister for spring break. It was really close by, but I didn't feel anywhere near ready to leave Preston. He was only two months old, for heaven's sake. I didn't leave Vivi until she was eighteen months.

But my milk had dried up all of a sudden, so it wasn't like I was an integral part of the whole feeding thing anymore. And James promised that Hummus could stay one more week. We'd only be gone two nights. That was all I would agree to. But even two nights under the same roof with James would be tricky.

"I got us the penthouse at the Beach Club," he said that morning, standing in Mom's kitchen, smiling very proudly. "Vivi can have her own bedroom."

My heart stopped beating. "Excuse me? If you think I'm going to stay in the same room with you, then you really have lost your mind."

"So what will we say?" he asked, sliding a stool out from under the island and sitting down. I pulled a bag of sliced pepperoni out of the fridge and started munching. I had three pounds to go, and I was to that point where the only thing that was going to singe them was no carbs. So, sure, I could have been having a grilled chicken salad. But my thought was why not live a little?

James sighed and shook his head. "Caroline, honey, honestly. You are going to die. You just had a baby. Give yourself a break. You don't need to live on processed meats over three pounds. It will come off."

Under normal circumstances, I wouldn't need to live on processed meats over three pounds two months after I'd had a baby. But for some strange reason, being left for a twenty-year-old model had not made me feel my best.

I sighed. "I don't know what to say, James. She's eleven years old. She knows you left me for another woman. How about Mommy and Daddy are getting divorced, so they don't sleep in the same room?"

He looked down at his feet. "Don't say that. Please don't say that."

To be honest, I hadn't filed the papers yet. There must have been some reason for that.

"Fine," I said.

"Fine what?"

"Fine. I won't say that. I will sleep in the same room with you with a line of pillows separating us."

He grinned. "Well, baby, that's a start."

A few minutes later, in the passenger seat of the highly impractical convertible James had procured for me after I got my license, I could feel tears coming down my cheeks. It was too soon to leave my son, even if it was only for two nights. James squeezed my shoulder, which grossed me out. I had told him not to touch me with those hands. That was not a good sign for our future.

"He's going to be fine, sweetheart. He's too young to realize you're gone. Five months from now, he'll be screaming bloody murder every time we leave. That's when things are going to get tough."

"Yeah, Mom," Vivi said. "You need a little bit of time to yourself."

I wiped my eyes and turned to grin at her. She'd had a hard few months. Vivi deserved some time with both of her parents. She deserved for it to be about her.

"So," I said, "we have Pilates first thing when we get there."

"Look fourteen," James interjected.

"Oh, right," I said. "You have to be fourteen to go into the gym, so we neither confirmed nor denied your age."

Vivi laughed. "Then is it sparkly manicures and pedicures?"

"Yes!" I said. "Do you think I should get sparkles, too?"

"I do," James interjected. "You definitely look young enough to have sparkles."

You couldn't blame the man for trying. It was a pretty obvious ploy, but I didn't hate it.

"Then horseback riding on the beach," James said. "And then your mom and I are going out while you do dinner and a movie with the other kids."

"Yay!" Vivi said.

"Wait," I said, trying to keep my voice even so she wouldn't catch on. "I thought this was supposed to be family time."

"But Mom," Vivi said, "I want to do the kid stuff at least part of the time. It's so fun. And you and Dad can have a boring grown-up dinner and talk."

She caught her dad's eye in the rearview mirror. They planned this, the little sneaks.

Three fights over the Pandora station and two bouts of James thinking he knew better than Waze later, we had arrived. You would think that after living on the sound for months, the water wouldn't affect you so much. But looking out the window onto the beach was still incredible. At Mom's, we had sand, of course, and sea grass, and the water quietly lapped the sandy shore. But the majesty and power of the ocean, roaring to the beach and then retreating, was a surprise every time. It never got old. And it never ceased to remind me that the world was large and, in the scheme of things, my problems were nothing.

We were all sitting on couches in our penthouse living room. I loved the Cloister. My aesthetic was much lighter and brighter, but I still appreciated the heavy Oriental rugs, the dark stained beams on the ceiling, the deep reds and blues of the décor. They felt very Old World, very Sea Island, very much the Cloister.

"Caroline?"

"Yes?"

"Are you up for tennis yet?"

"Tomorrow?" I asked.

Usually when we played, it was Vivi and James against me. In New York, I did cardio tennis three mornings a week at our tennis club and then had a match every Friday afternoon. I don't like to brag about my skill level, so let's just say that if I'd indulged my fantasy about taking a racket to Edie Fitzgerald's head, I'm pretty sure her modeling days would have been over.

"How about you and me versus Dad?" Vivi asked.

Yes, I thought. *What happened to you and me versus Dad?*

I remembered giving her the talk about having her father in her life, about how I would give anything to have my father back, just for one day. For the second time, I realized that while I hated this situation, I was largely responsible for it.

"Pilates time!" I called, retreating toward the bedroom.

Vivi jumped up. "Yes! Getting my clothes on."

James followed me.

When I turned, I said, "What do you think you're doing?"

"Just wanted to talk to you."

"No," I said. "I am changing. You may wait outside."

"Caroline, come on. I've seen you naked for like the last fifteen years."

"Yes," I said icily. "That was before you were seeing other people naked."

I was proud of how I looked in my leggings and top. The shirt was tight at the bottom and blousy throughout, which was perfect since I hadn't totally gotten my abs back yet. But the Pilates would help. Tennis, too. It was always fun to quit doing something for a while and then see how sore you were when you got back to it.

Vivi looked so cute. Her outfit was exactly like mine, only neon green, not black.

"All right, girls," James said. "I'm going to the driving range and will meet you back here after the spa."

As much as I missed Preston, I had a great afternoon with Vivi. We needed this time to relax and really talk about friends and school and everything in between. Over sparkly pedicures, we agreed that while we loved Peachtree, we were both on board with moving back to New York.

"I understand that Daddy might not be living with us," Vivi said. She was so grown-up. "A lot of my friends' parents are divorced." She paused. "But Mom, it sure would be cool if he were living with us."

Talk about feeling like the worst person in the world. That was the moment I decided that I was really going to give it a shot. I was not going to make snide comments. I was going to attempt not to hate him so much—although, God, I sure did hate him—and I was going to give this thing a fair shake. I didn't want Vivi to be one of those kids with divorced parents. If she was, it would be because I could not move on. And we would all have to be OK with that.

So we added blowouts onto our spa day, and I wore James's favorite dress and slid on those strappy shoes he liked so much. And when he came in, handed me a glass of wine, put his arm around my waist, kissed my cheek, and said, "You look so unbelievably beautiful," I didn't slap his hand away or say something nasty.

I smiled and said thank you.

James took my arm, and we walked the short distance to the Georgian Room. A bottle of my favorite champagne was already chilled and waiting at the table when we sat in the floral upholstered chairs and slid under the white tablecloths. Everything about dining at the Georgian Room was impeccable.

I eyed the bottle of champagne and said, "So, James, trying to get me drunk?"

He shrugged. "It's a gamble, because you'll either get drunk and be nice to me or get drunk and hate me more."

He was right. It was a gamble. But champagne was a good choice. It usually made me bubbly, too. Usually. Now, not that time at the fund-raiser for 57th Street Primary when that damn Jenna outbid me at the last minute on those estate sapphire earrings she knew I wanted. That night, being a little champagne-drunk made me feisty.

"I wasn't going to give you this yet," James said, "because I don't want you to think it's a bribe."

He pulled a tiny box out of his pocket. My heart raced. I loved a good tiny box. Which is why I got so mad about the earrings.

"But then I decided that giving you this will prove to you how serious I am about working things out. Because I know right now there's like a ninety percent chance you are leaving me, and I want you to have it anyway."

He slid the box across the table. I opened it, and I think I went blind. Seriously. It was a single emerald-cut diamond with two teeny baguettes flanking it. It was huge but not so huge that it looked too clunky like some sort of ungroomed ice rink.

"Whoa."

I slid off the emerald I always wore on my right hand, put the diamond on, and lifted my hand to show him across the table.

"Wow," he said.

"This is seriously amazing, James. Thank you." I paused. "Now there's only an eighty-five percent chance I'm going to divorce you."

He laughed cautiously, and I laughed wholeheartedly. He was treading lightly, as he should have been, because I was incredibly leery of the man. There was no doubt in my mind that if we got back together, I would spend the rest of my life looking over my shoulder. I mean, my shoulder would be more toned from wearing this massive diamond, but still, I'd be looking over it.

I took a sip of my champagne and admired my new jewel. "It really is quite spectacular," I said.

Then I stopped cold, my champagne in midair. I set the glass down too forcefully and glared at James.

"Oh, my God. This was an engagement ring. You bought this for Edie Fitzgerald because you were going to ask her to marry you. I can't believe you!"

"Hold up," James said. "I had Craig make the ring for you. If you'll look inside the box, it says, 'Designed especially for Caroline Murphy Beaumont.'"

Ah, yes. So it did. My longtime jeweler, Craig, was always on point.

James reached for my hand across the table. "I don't get how you can be so sweet one minute and so cruel the next."

And that's when I realized that I might have run from Peachtree Bluff like my hair was on fire, but somewhere in there, a little Southern must have gotten in.

With his hand on mine, I felt that spark that I used to feel, that jolt of electricity that made me know that our being together was so right. And it made me realize how long it had been since I had kissed him, made love to him. It was another gamble. Because I might think of Edie Fitzgerald and how my life was shattered, how I had to leave town and come to my mother's house so as not to be the laughingstock of Manhattan.

As I cut my very rare, very perfect steak, James said, "So where do we go from here, Caroline? What can I do to prove how much I love you and how very sorry I am?"

I didn't say that the ring was a good start.

"I'm trying, James," I said. "I swear I am. But this nearly killed me. You can't imagine how vulnerable you feel when you're six months pregnant and all alone. It is terrifying. I'm not going to forget that soon. You're going to have to be patient."

He nodded. "I've cleared my schedule through July." He grinned.

I smirked, then looked up and said, "I don't want to know details. I don't want some bullshit explanation of why you did what you did or some self-reflective crap. The more I know, the more I'll have to dwell on." I paused. "But James, you didn't tell me that you were having an affair and you were sorry. You told me you didn't love me anymore and you were leaving me. How am I supposed to move on from that? How do I know you aren't going to quit loving me again next week?"

I hated to cry. Couldn't stand it. But I could feel tears in my eyes as I said it. I had spent so much time, understandably, I think, worrying about the outside world, thinking about what people were saying about me and how I looked, that my primary emotion these past few weeks had been humiliation. I hadn't spent all that much time fully feeling how devastating it was for the person who was supposed to be your everything to cast you off like you were nothing.

He looked up at the ceiling for a moment as though I might forget my question if he didn't make eye contact.

"What are you doing?"

"I am trying to answer you in a way that doesn't sound like a bullshit explanation." He put down his knife and fork and took my hand. "It wasn't about you. It was about me. I felt like I'd made a mess of my life and I hadn't amounted to anything or lived up to my expectations. It was like I was breaking out of my rut or something. I made things about us that were really about me." He took a sip of wine. "This sounds insane, I know, but it was like I was living two separate lives, and I couldn't process how this would affect you. It was like the whole thing was a delusion, and I was going to get to keep the life I had while still doing this horrible thing." He shook his head. "You're right. Whatever I try to say sounds idiotic. But I realized that feeling your heart race because someone famous was giving you all her attention is not love. Someone who has your back, who gets you through the hard times . . . that's love."

I could see his eyes welling up, and I knew that this hurt so badly because I loved him so much. It felt impossible. I was pretty sure I could never trust him again. But I also knew that I wanted to be with him—although being with him would be forever, unalterably changed. There was no good answer here. It made me feel sick.

"When I figured out what I had really done," James said, "when I realized that the entire world was going to know that I had destroyed my family, it was like I was running headfirst into a moving train and I couldn't jump off the tracks to get away. I had to convince myself that I was in love with her, that love had made me do this horrible thing." He sighed. "Otherwise I had thrown my whole life away for absolutely nothing."

It was something. But I wasn't sure it was enough. I knew

I could find someone else, probably pretty quickly. On paper, he would probably be as good as James. But in my heart, I knew that no one else would ever measure up. I would spend my life comparing every man with the one I had fallen so hard for. Young love is only for the young. Nothing else compares.

James took my hand across the table and said, "I know you have no reason to trust me, Caroline. But if this horrible couple of months has done anything, it has reaffirmed that you are the one and only love of my life. We were made for each other, and I've known since the day I met you that I don't deserve you. But I promise you that I will never hurt you again."

I closed my eyes, took a sip of champagne, and tried to let his words sink in, tried to let them fill up some of the emptiness that I felt. But I knew already that it would take more than words to fill up the holes.

We skipped dessert after a peerless meal, and James said, "So we have an hour and a half until we pick up Vivi from the movie."

He looked at me questioningly.

I took my last sip of champagne, and I knew it was probably too soon. I knew it was something I might regret. But it might be exactly what I needed.

Because as much as I loved James for his heart and his head, the physical had always been a big part of our relationship.

"You are," he said, kissing my neck as my dress fell to the floor, "even more beautiful today than you were when I met you. Even more than before the babies, even more than the night I first laid eyes on you."

I finally kissed him. It felt like something opened up inside me, something that had been closed for a long time. As he whispered "I love you," I felt like one day, someday, I might be able to say it back.

TWENTY-NINE

the zookeeper

ansley

The St. Timothy's youth group has for the last twenty-six years earned all of the money it needed to take its annual ski trip by "flocking." Flocking is a tradition that makes the decorator in me cringe and makes the rest of me laugh. The youth group puts dozens of plastic pink flamingos in someone's yard. In order to get the flamingos out, said person has to make a donation and then has the option of paying an additional amount to have the flamingos put in someone else's yard.

My house has been flocked every year that I've lived in Peachtree. And for good reason. I don't pay to have one person's yard flocked. I pay to have ten. I have to. Because if my yard was flocked and then the flamingos showed up in Mr. Solomon's yard immediately afterward, he would know I did it to him. Our deal is that the youth group randomly flocks Mr. Solomon's somewhere in there. Sometimes it's the tenth yard, sometimes the seventh, sometimes the fourth. It irks him to no end, which brings me an endless amount of joy. I get to be a fly on the wall when he is out there shaking his cane at those kids and his little dog is barking at the plastic pink birds.

Now I wished I could be a fly on the wall at the Beaumont family vacation to the Cloister. Caroline had just called for the nine-hundredth time to check on Preston, and she sounded happy. But that could have been because she was going to go play tennis for the first time since the baby. Or it could have been because, although Emerson is the professional, Caroline is a fabulous actress. Sometimes, in fact, I thought she pushed Emerson so hard because, deep down, she wanted to be a star— she just didn't want to work for it. Some people would have seen that as a flaw, but I never did. She never wanted to work, and she found a way not to do so. It was perfect, if you asked me.

Well, you know, perfect until the man left her.

I had Mom propped up on the couch in the living room, a pillow under her leg, and was carrying a glass of water for her, a sippy cup for Adam, and a bottle for Taylor. Taylor was too old for a bottle, but Sloane couldn't quite gear herself up to wean him, and I thought it was probably OK for her to take a break on this one thing. I could see the weariness of being away from her husband starting to take its toll on her. And she had a long, long way to go.

I was thrilled that one of her summer friends, Natalie, had called to say she was in town. Sloane didn't want to go out to dinner, but if I had to see her in those sweatpants and that T-shirt one more time, I was going to scream. Caroline had said not to worry. She would schedule an intervention. I had held her off for a couple of weeks, but this was Caroline. She would intervene on the sweats situation sooner rather than later.

I had followed Sloane up to her room and said, "Please go to dinner with Natalie, sweetie. You need to get out of the house and have some fun."

"But the boys . . ."

I gave her an offended look. "The boys are with their grandmother—and their great-grandmother."

Sloane laughed. "Yeah. That's great. So you can take care of Grammy and the kids. Sounds like a blast." She paused. "OK. I guess I could go. I'll call her back."

I was a hypocrite. I knew that feeling of not wanting to go out and make the effort. I knew firsthand that it was easier to sit at home and eat Lean Cuisines. But I also knew that when you did go, you almost always felt better when you got back.

I had thought in the back of my mind that Emerson might help me. But she'd said, "Please, Mom. I'm going out."

Oh, that helpful, helpful girl. I was fairly certain that I would never get a grandchild out of that one; however, I was pleased to say that although she was still on the concerning side of thin, Emerson had gained some weight. I bet she could actually conceive a child if she wanted to—maybe.

So here I was. Friday night. Mom. Adam. Taylor. This wasn't necessarily difficult, except for the fact that Taylor was absolutely everywhere. The boy was in constant motion, as they always are at that age. There was no way to contain him, so I had to chase him around the house while also attempting to entertain Adam.

I had made Adam these colored tongue depressors with magnetic strips on them and given him a big bowl of paper clips. "You put the paper clips with the same color as the tongue depressor on the magnetic strip. See?" I placed a blue on the blue, a red on the red, and so on.

There was no end to what you could do with a glue gun.

"Okay, Gransley!" he said excitedly.

I turned to run after Taylor and said, "Mom, call me if he needs me."

Thirty seconds later, she called, "Ansley!"

I grabbed Taylor, who wiggled and squirmed the entire time, and ran back into the living room. "Everything OK?"

"I sure would love a spot of ice cream with a bit of chocolate syrup."

Wow. Really? I glared at her as Adam said, "I want ice cream! I want ice cream!"

"Oh, no!" I said. "The ice cream has gone night-night already. And we are getting ready to go night-night, too!"

Mom said, "What do you mean it has gone night-night? I just saw it in the freezer. Are you feeling all right?"

This was the thing about my mother. One moment she seemed sharp as a tack, and the next she wasn't sure of her own name. I didn't know what was going on with her, but I was quite certain that the doctor Scott took her to had missed something. She fought me on it every day, but I would wear her down eventually. She was going to that neurologist.

I shook my head. "Later, Mom."

Adam let out a low scream. "I want ice cream!" he said, banging his fists on the floor. "I want ice cream right now!"

Great.

"Adam," I soothed. "How about we go get into the bath, and Gransley will let you eat one of your special Popsicles in the tub? Wouldn't that be funny to eat it in the tub?"

I laughed delightedly, holding my breath. The Popsicles were really some concoction that Caroline had made since she was on this disgusting diet. They were made of spinach and berries and green powder mixed in the blender and frozen. I think they were supposed to be dessert. She was probably going to kill me for giving them to the kids, but I was dealing with one tantrum at a time right now.

Taylor squirmed out of my arms and promptly ran over to the bowl of paper clips, dumped them onto the floor, and started kicking them all over the living room with his feet. It was actually shocking how far they were spreading. What was not shocking was that Adam started wailing again and pushed his brother onto the floor, and then they were both wailing.

"Ansley!" Mom shouted. "Could you please get them out of here? This noise is giving me a horrible headache."

I don't know what happens to people when they get old, but I hope it never happens to me. It's like you lose all sense of respect and decorum. You no longer care about anyone else's feelings or what they're going through. It's all about you. At least, it was with my mom.

"I'm going to get Popsicles," I called. "Who wants to come with me?"

I had to get them to stop crying, because there was no way I could carry two screaming children upstairs and get them into the bath. So I thought I would melt into a puddle of relief when I heard "I do!"

It wasn't the children, though. Nope. They were still wailing. It was Jack.

"I thought you might be able to use some babysitting help!" he hollered over the din. "But I see you have it all under control, so I'll be going now."

We both laughed, me kind of pitifully. I was so relieved.

Jack reached into a paper bag he was carrying and pulled out a yellow case with a clear top. He opened it to reveal a bunch of pieces of thick rope, all cut short. "So he can't strangle himself or the other kid," Jack half joked.

Adam quit crying. "Wow! Ropes!" he said.

"What do you say?" I asked.

"Thank you," he sang.

Taylor had paused his crying for long enough to figure out what was going on, but he resumed. Until Jack handed him a level, that is. "Look," Jack said, moving the level back and forth. Taylor was mesmerized by the green bubble.

"The best part is," he said, "these can both go in the bathtub! So let's go on up."

I slid the Popsicles back into the freezer, figuring that a double crisis had now been averted. I watched in amazement as Taylor let Jack pick him up and Adam followed the two of them up the stairs.

I made Mom a bowl of ice cream and drizzled chocolate

syrup on top. I walked into the living room, where she appeared to be dozing, and said, "Here, Mom."

She looked at me like I had three heads. "What is this?"

"The ice cream you asked me for."

"I would never ask you for ice cream. I don't care for ice cream, and especially not that sorry excuse for chocolate fudge."

I felt like the last couple of weeks had been categorized into good days and bad days. Today was a bad day. The worst part about the bad days was that I missed my mom. I wanted her back. I wanted her to laugh with me and give me guidance about Jack. Maybe tomorrow. But definitely not today.

I wondered, briefly, what it would be like if Carter were still here. Would we be in Peachtree Bluff? Would we still be in New York?

I'll admit, I took my time going up the stairs. I was wiped out. I didn't know how Sloane did this. Youth helped, I supposed, but Adam was gone so much that she didn't have help a lot of the time. I was thankful, not for the first time, that the girls were older when Carter died. That hadn't made it perfect, but it had definitely helped.

I could hear the bath running, and I could only assume that Jack had drugged the children, because they were sitting cross-legged on their towels by the tub. I walked in, leaned against the wall, and smiled as he said, "Where should we go on our magic carpets next?"

I was glad Sloane wasn't there to hear Adam say, "Iraq to see our daddy!"

I couldn't imagine how difficult that must be for these children. But they likely wouldn't remember this particular deployment. Sloane would, though. It was hard for me to imagine that every other year of her life would be spent without her husband. But this was the life she had chosen, she was always reminding me. She knew what she was getting into when she married Adam. But I wasn't sure that made it any easier for him to be away.

Taylor tried to get up, and Jack said, "Taylor! You're going to fall off your magic carpet!"

And he was suddenly still again.

"Let's take a bath in the river," I said enthusiastically.

"Do you think there are snakes in the river?" Jack asked.

We had managed to get them both into the tub with no tears before I relaxed back, sitting on my heels, and said, "Jack, you were a godsend tonight. I don't know how you knew to come over here, but I am so glad you did."

I realized that having him here, with my family, was nice. It wasn't scary and it didn't feel strange.

He squeezed my hand. "Truth be told, I wanted to see you." He paused. "Getting to play with my grandkids was a happy coincidence."

I could feel the blood draining from my face.

"I'm sorry," he said, squeezing my hand again. "I didn't mean *my* . . ."

He trailed off, and I heard a door slam followed by "Mooooommmmm!"

I had really had enough wailing for one night. The kids were plenty. I wasn't sure I could deal with Emerson, too.

"We're up here, honey," I said.

She appeared at the bathroom doorway so quickly she must have sprinted up. "Mom!" It was then I realized this was an excited wail, not a devastated one. Whew!

I patted the floor beside me. "What's the good news?"

This daughter of mine was so emotional. I wondered if I had babied her too much after Carter died, if I had overcompensated for his death by spoiling her, trying to make up for her lack of a father with too much of my own time and attention.

"Em!" I heard Sloane call.

"Up here!" She was still grinning.

"Have you told her yet?" Sloane asked, slightly out of breath.

I looked at my watch. "You're back already?"

Sloane shrugged. "I said I'd go out for a drink. I had a drink. I got dressed, I wore shoes, I even wore lipstick. It was a big deal."

I smiled and shook my head, secretly thankful that she was home. "So what is this news?"

"Mom, I'm up for a role. A big, huge, giant role. Biggest of my career in a real, big-screen movie."

I gasped. "No!"

"It's such a good opportunity for her, Mom," Sloane chimed in.

"Well, great! Take it." I was so excited. Emerson deserved this.

"I'm glad to hear you say that," she said. "Because there's a catch. I have to do *Playboy*."

I could tell that Jack was trying not to laugh, while my mouth was hanging completely open. You're supposed to try not to run your children's lives, but sometimes you must intervene. "Emerson Murphy, under no circumstances are you going to be in *Playboy*."

She put her hands on her hips and said, "Oh, no, Mom. It's not what you think. It's a promotion for the movie."

I could feel the utter shock on my face. "I don't care if it's to end world hunger, you're not posing for *Playboy*, and that's final."

I looked at Jack, who was now having trouble controlling his laughter.

"But Mom," Emerson said. "It will be a wonderful bonding opportunity for us."

I cut my eyes at her. "What do you mean, 'for us'?"

"The movie comes out next Mother's Day, so they thought it would be cool to do a mother-daughter spread. We'll be partially clothed, and you look so great, I figured it would be fun."

I could feel now that my face was completely on fire, and I was having trouble taking breaths. Jack was laughing in earnest now.

No words. There were truly no words.

"Look," Emerson said softly. "I know it's kind of out of the box for you, but this is major for me. I mean, it's a real, big-screen movie, for heaven's sake. They are going to run layout ideas by us, and it will be totally tasteful."

"Ansley!" Mom called from downstairs. "I'm ready to go to bed now. Can you come get my pajamas on and move me in there?"

I felt like I might faint. I don't know how the words came out, but I heard myself call, "Just a minute, Mom!" Then I said, "You can't be serious, Emerson. This is . . ." I didn't fin-

ish, because I didn't know what it was besides totally prepos-
terous.

Jack helped Adam out of the bath as Sloane said, "Looks
like this is all settled. I can't wait to see the spread. I'll go help
Grammy."

"This is going to be so good for my career," Emerson was
saying, following me as I followed Sloane.

I made my way to the landing, towel still in my hand, still
too stunned to speak.

"I really appreciate your being so on board with this," Emerson said, as she walked down the steps behind her sister.

My mouth hung open, "Emerson, I did not say—"

"I was totally wrong," Sloane was saying. "I thought she'd
have a fit."

"But I . . ." I started, but I was having trouble finding the
words. I couldn't tell if all the blood was in my head or if all the
blood had left it, but I couldn't formulate thoughts. I was trying
to say, *But I am having a fit. Can't you all hear me?* It was like
the bad dream where you're opening your mouth to scream for
help, but nothing comes out.

"I'm going to help Sloane get Grammy to bed," Emerson
called cheerily. "You're the best mom in the world!"

I felt Jack's hand on my shoulder as I, with a very weak
voice, called, "Emerson!"

Sloane and Emerson were both at the bottom of the stairs.
They turned simultaneously and yelled, "April Fools!"

I balled up the towel in my hand and threw it at Emerson.
To my surprise, it hit her squarely. She and Sloane were laugh-

ing so hard they had disintegrated into a pile on the floor at the bottom of the steps.

"Your face!" Emerson gasped between her hysteria.

"Oh, my gosh!" Sloane practically cackled. "That was even better than I thought it would be."

I sat down on the top step and put my head in my hands. "I am truly traumatized."

Jack squeezed my shoulder.

I turned to him. "Did you know about this?"

He laughed. "No! I had no idea. But to say it was the best five minutes of my life is not an understatement."

"I am not speaking to any of you. Not a single one. You are all on my bad list." I put my head back in my hands.

"Why don't you let me get the boys to bed?" Jack asked. "You've had a big night."

I noticed with relief that he didn't call them his grandkids again. Thank goodness. What was I supposed to say to that? We were barely dating. We had kissed one time. He had given one bath. This did not a grandparent make.

Even still, I couldn't have done it without him. "Thank you," I said. "I don't know why you keep coming back here to this madhouse."

Emerson and Sloane were still bursting with laughter like a couple of howler monkeys.

It made me think of the Simon and Garfunkel lyrics, *Something tells me it's all happening at the zoo.*

I understood now why the zookeeper was very fond of rum.

EVERYONE IN TOWN PLAYS bingo in Peachtree on Tuesday nights. Everyone. It starts at six so the kids can participate and goes on long into the evening. Mr. Jones is the best in the business at calling out letters, there's a full bar and a fun band, and like I said before, everyone in town plays. Everyone, that is, except for Caroline when we first moved back to Peachtree. Sloane and Emerson would beg her, tell her how much fun it was, come home with funny stories of what happened. But she wouldn't budge. She'd look up from her *Vogue* magazine like they'd asked her to help clean fish guts off the boardwalk and say, "These people's IQs must be even lower than I thought."

She wouldn't go, that is, until she met Peter Hoffman. Peter was Alma Jeffries's grandson, and he was a god among mere mortal teenaged boys. He would have to have been to catch Caroline's attention. He came to town that Christmas, and let me tell you, she had one look at him, and he was going to be all hers.

Caroline was an attractive girl, but she has gotten prettier as she has aged. Even back then, she had something, this power over people. That first time he laid eyes on her, Peter Hoffman asked Caroline to play bingo. She said yes, much to the delight of her sisters.

Much to the horror of her mother, everyone in town was talking about how Caroline and Peter were making out behind the Shriners building downtown while the final card was being played. But I decided that I would trade the humiliation for the happiness it brought my sullen daughter.

Peter was from Connecticut, and they kept in touch for a

few months, but once the whirlwind of college began in earnest, Caroline had enough attention from enough boys to keep her occupied for quite some time.

The briefness of their encounter might have explained why I didn't recognize Peter right off when I passed him on my way to the store.

"Ansley!" he called, jogging back to meet me at the door.

I turned and looked, and right about the time he said "Peter Hoffman," I realized who he was. And then I felt silly, of course, because it was clear I hadn't recognized him.

"Peter," I said, hugging him. "Come on in! I've got to get the store opened up."

"How are the girls?" Peter asked.

Was it remotely possible that he hadn't heard, that he hadn't passed a tabloid and seen my daughter's name in it? When he winced, I knew that was not, in fact, possible at all.

"Sorry about Caroline's husband," he said. "That's really shitty." He put his hand to his mouth. "I'm so sorry. That was inappropriate. It just flew out."

I laughed. "It's OK," I said. "It's extremely shitty."

"So where is Caroline?" he asked.

"Oh, she's here. At the house. They're all here, in fact."

"For a visit?"

"Something like that."

Peter picked up a gold tray shaped like a leaf and ran his finger across it. "I like this," he said. "I think I'll get it for my mom."

He picked up three of my Turkish towels. "And these for me. I love these things. They dry so quickly."

I smiled, wondering if this was a ploy to get more information out of me. "So . . ." he started. "What's the deal with Caroline? Is she in mourning? Do you think she'd like to, I don't know, grab a drink for old times' sake?"

I scanned his towels and smiled. "I don't know," I said. "But you know she has a nine-week-old baby."

He nodded. "Sure. But I love kids."

I thought about the bath fiasco the night before and wondered if he would have loved kids then.

"Well," I said, knowing that I was meddling, "we always have a glass of wine on the porch at nine. Why don't you swing by and ask her yourself?" I paused. "That's pretty risky, you know. With a nine-week-old baby, how do you know she isn't still huge?"

"Because I know Caroline."

We both laughed. He left, the bell tinkling as he did. There was so much to do. Unbox inventory, pay bills, dust the knickknacks, call Barbara Cosgrove and see when that shipment of gorgeous lamps would be in. But I didn't do any of that.

Instead, I walked to the front of the store. I sat down in a beautiful, custom-made Society Social chair covered in a vibrant blue patterned fabric. Then I watched the water roll by. It was impossible not to think of Carter in these moments, not to wonder what would have been if he hadn't died. If I'd insisted that he come to Emerson's dress rehearsal that morning, if he hadn't been able to catch a cab, if security had been a little tighter at the airport, if he had sprinted as fast as he could to evacuate the minute the first plane hit. There were so many if onlys. I could go on forever, imagining scenarios as numerous as the ripples in the sound.

I thought of Jack, and I realized that there were so many if onlys that sometimes it left out any space for the what could bes.

I ran my hand up the chair and realized that I would order four of them for Emily and Gary's family room in this exact fabric but in pink, not blue. It was such a strange room configuration that any way you put a couch, it looked terrible. Four chairs would be perfect.

The night before, Jack had said "my grandchildren." Those two words were enough, in my mind, anyway, to put a stop to anything that was starting to brew between us. This was the reason I hadn't wanted to be with him in the first place. I didn't want him so involved in my children's lives.

Sandra was walking down the street to the bank next door. She poked her head in. "Hi, love."

"Hi," I said.

"You OK?"

I nodded. "Taking a moment away from the madhouse."

"I'm heading to work," she said. "Want to do lunch?"

Did I ever. I nodded. "Yes."

I loved being a mother and a grandmother. I even loved caring for my mom, mostly. But just like when I'd had three babies, sometimes you needed a moment to be you.

When Leah walked through the door and saw me sitting in the chair, she said, "You stay. I've got this under control." Then she walked back over with a swatch book and whispered, "Could you pick a fabric for Hal's new drapes?"

I laughed. Who would've thought that after all these years, Hippie Hal would be my interior design client? His home was incredible, this masculine mix of bamboo and worn Persian rugs, thin and threadbare like I liked them. It had a very British Colonial feel to it, almost like being right inside *The Most Dangerous Game*. He needed to do some sprucing up, and I was more than flattered that he came to me.

I got up, stretching my legs, and said, "I've got to run this bedding down to Jack's boat. If Hal comes in, give him these three options. He has a terrific eye."

I loaded a dock cart with two sets of twin sheets, one set of queen, three white cotton blankets, and three plain white bamboo coverlets. The Euro shams were freshly steamed so I gingerly placed them on top, with the neck rolls holding everything down. I was a fan of big, fluffy comforters, but on a boat, simplicity is best. Anything that can hold moisture is a liability.

I lifted the handles of the cart, trying to ignore the pain in my lower back. There was no doubt that carrying my grandchildren and helping my mother had taken a toll on me. It reminded me that, no matter what else was going on, I had to exercise and take care of myself. I didn't want to be one of these old crippled grandmothers by the time Emerson had babies.

As I walked down the dock, my heart felt heavy. Jack and I were firmly in a gray area, and I had this feeling that he and I had differing opinions about which way we needed to go. Between my mom and the kids, it was too much. Of course, there was that ever-present fear of letting him get too close to my family. The damage could be irreparable; it could ruin my relationships with my daughters forever if things went south.

But then there was my heart. My heart told me he was the one—or, well, the other one. My heart told me he would never hurt me. As I pushed the cart, I realized that it is so often this way. The head wants one thing, the heart wants the other. How I wished I could get them to do the same thing at the same time.

I barely recognized Jack's boat. It was sparkling, clean, seaworthy even, a murky oyster scrubbed and steamed to reveal the pearl inside. I had replaced the old overstuffed fabric couches with sleek, stylish, low-profile leather furniture that still looked manly and boatlike and would stand up to the water. The disgusting carpet had been replaced by shimmering teak floors. The quartz in the kitchen, appliances, and granite in the bath were all new and brought the boat up to date while still maintaining its integrity. The gorgeous wood inside had all been shined and polished and looked fresh and fabulous.

Jack emerged from the cabin looking as though he should be on a yacht advertisement. He had on navy Top-Siders and a navy-and-white-check button-down with the sleeves rolled up hanging out over his shorts.

"There's my girl," he said.

My insides went soft. "Am I?" I said.

"Are you not?"

There it was. That amused look that made my heart race. He stepped off the boat and onto the dock. "Let me help you with this stuff. You're going to be excited," he said, as we carried the bedding into the master bedroom. "Look." He pointed proudly. "New mattress."

I smiled. "That is so wonderful. Now you aren't sleeping in mildew and bed bugs."

"It wasn't that bad." He took the pillows and set them on the bed. Then he swooped me up in his arms and kissed me. And just like that, all of my worries from a few minutes earlier floated away like fresh dew in the early-morning sun.

"I missed you," he whispered, kissing the tip of my nose.

"I missed you, too."

And I knew I had. There was simply no reason to keep fighting it.

We made the bed and tucked in the coverlet, tight and smooth.

"It's beautiful," I said. "A beautiful room on a beautiful boat. Who the hell would've thought?"

Jack pulled me to him, and we admired my handiwork.

"You know," he said, "I've been thinking now that she's seaworthy, I might take her out on the open water."

I gasped. "Is she ready for that?"

I was actually wondering if *I* was ready for that. I liked having Jack right here, where I could find him.

He nodded and held up his fingers. "Scout's honor."

We both laughed.

"And so," he continued, taking my hand in his, "I was wondering if you would consider joining me on the maiden voyage of the *Miss Ansley*."

I gasped and hit his arm. "You did not name your boat after me."

He grinned. "Oh, I assure you, I did. The guys will be here to change the name this afternoon."

I laughed. When a man named his boat after you, he was in. "I don't know," I said. "It sounds fun, but isn't that kind of a lot of . . . pressure?"

He looked at me, puzzled, his eyebrows meeting in the center of his forehead. Then he laughed, catching on, and said, "Oh, Ans, we never had any trouble with that." He shrugged. "And there's no pressure. If you don't want to, we'll wait."

Oh, but I wanted to.

He smiled and pulled me in close to him, kissing me with all the fervor he had when he was a teenager. In so many ways, he was that same kid. "I'd hate to make it awkward," he said, unbuttoning my blouse, his mouth still on mine.

My hands found the button of his shorts, and I wondered, briefly, if I could still do this. It had been sixteen years, after all. But I was sure it would come right back to me. Like riding a bike . . .

As he lowered me onto the bed, I said, "Jack, no!"

He looked at me, alarmed.

I laughed. "Oh, no. Not that. I just had all these shams and coverlets pressed."

He rolled his eyes and kissed me. And I can truly say that I didn't give that bedding another thought.

defying physics

caroline

After that semester I spent in Peachtree Bluff after Dad died, I was at NYU summer school so fast it would have made your head spin. Back to my friends. Back to the not-so-fresh air, the crowds, the noise, the excitement, the center of the universe, basically. I didn't even glance in the rearview mirror. (Well, I mean, the theoretical rearview mirror. As we've established, I didn't drive.) I was so ready to get out of there. Ready for freedom. And my sisters would tell you that they were quite ready to get rid of me, too.

That first weekend back in New York, I realized that against all odds, I was starting to feel a little bit, well, family-sick. I wasn't *home*sick. I mean, I was home. But I missed my sisters. So I picked up the phone, called my mom, and asked if they could come stay. She, of course, said yes, but she couldn't talk Sloane into returning to New York. She wasn't ready. Instead, Mom bought me a ticket back to Peachtree Bluff.

I didn't and couldn't, obviously, but it still made me happy at the end of the long weekend when Sloane and Emerson begged me to stay. I knew Mom wanted to beg me to stay, too, despite what a pill I had been, but that would have been bad parenting.

When I got home from our family weekend at the Cloister, I could tell that James wanted me to ask him to stay. But I didn't. Because, yeah, we'd had a decent vacation, but that was a long, far cry from moving back in together. Surely he knew that.

When I walked into the main house, Vivi ran upstairs to see the boys. And it was like the jig was up. Mom, Grammy, Sandra, Emily, Emerson, Sloane, and Hummus were all sitting in the living room.

"We're sorry," Emily said, pointing at Sandra. "We know we aren't family, but we're dying over here."

I laughed.

"Holy hell," Sandra said, before anyone could say anything. She motioned for my hand. "That is the biggest rock I've ever seen. It's gorgeous."

Grammy shook her head. "Don't let him buy you."

"I'm not letting him buy me," I said. "For him, it was a show of good faith that he's in this even though he knows I may not be."

Emerson motioned, her mouth open. "That is seriously insane. Like you shouldn't wear it in public."

"OK," Mom said. "How did it go? Did you decide anything?"

I told them about the weekend, the dinner and the horse-back riding, the fun family activities. I omitted the sex, although my sisters would weigh in on that later.

"I think," I said, "that I'm going to give it another shot. Vivi, Preston, and I have a few more months in Peachtree, and I'll try to make a decision one way or another before we go back to New York." I sighed. "But I do believe he's sorry, and I do believe he wants me back. So that's good."

"That's big of you," Sloane said.

"Yeah," Emerson chimed in. "I'm shocked."

"The long and short of it is that I don't know what's going to happen. So stay tuned . . ."

Mom shifted nervously on the couch.

"What?"

"You might be mad."

I sat on the arm of Emerson's chair. She handed me her wineglass, and I took a sip. I felt like I might need it.

"I ran into someone today," Mom said. "And he's coming to say hi to you at nine."

I could feel the confusion on my face. "Who?"

"Peter," she whispered.

My heart raced. "Peter Hoffman?"

She nodded. I laughed. Oh, my gosh. I'd had the hots for Peter Hoffman big-time. We'd had a fun Christmas break in Peachtree and one awkward hookup once I was at NYU. But I wouldn't hold his nineteen-year-old hookup skills against him.

"Oh, I couldn't possibly go out with him," I said.

But two hours and two glasses of wine later, I was singing a different tune. When Peter Hoffman walked up onto the porch, as handsome and tall as I remembered him, and wrapped me in that big hug of his, I wondered why I had ever let him get away. *Oh, that's right*, I thought, *James*.

"You look great," he said.

"Likewise."

I took in his perfectly fitted straight-legged pants—which I knew my mom would hate but I loved—and custom-made shirt and flashed him my most generous and beguiling smile. *What am I doing? I told James we would try to work it out.*

"Do you want to grab a drink and catch up?" he asked.

"It has been ages."

I turned to Sloane and Emerson. Why not? I mean, we were only catching up. It wasn't like we were procreating.

Plus, I should get to have a last hurrah before I made my final decision. On the walk to Full Moon, one of the nicest bars in town, I discovered that Peter was a literary agent in Greenwich, who commuted to the city. "Greenwich" to me equaled "married with kids." So I could only assume that he was divorced.

But over drinks, I discovered that he had never married. He had dated two different women for three years each, the second of whom had been the reason for his move to Greenwich.

"But I could be persuaded to move back to Manhattan." He winked at me.

Suddenly, I was on guard. Did that mean he wanted to move back to the city with me? This was moving a bit fast. My mind was racing, trying to change the subject. But I was suddenly completely blank.

"You ruined me for anyone else," Peter said lightly, before I could start talking about the only topic I could think of: cheese.

I laughed. "Oh, Peter. That's not true."

He stopped and looked me dead in the face and said, "Yes, it is, Caroline. That night we had together was so magical, I couldn't ever forget you. I still can't, which is why I'm here. I'm hoping you'll give me another shot."

I looked down into my wine, my happy, fun buzz suddenly gone. "Oh, Peter," I said. "That is incredibly nice of you to say."

I had to think. And quickly. Peter was a nice guy. A cute guy. A fun guy. But that night was not magical, and he was certainly not worth ruining my kids' lives over. But what do you say?

I put my hand over his gently. "Peter," I said, "I really like you. But my life is complicated right now. I have a lot of decisions to make. But I promise you, if I decide against James, you will be the first person I call."

That was probably true-ish. No, it wasn't. I would not call him if James and I got a divorce. But that was a nice thing to say. Actually, a nice thing to say, the thing the old Caroline would say, was that I was not interested in dating him ever and that if James and I broke up, he had freaked me out so thoroughly that I would never go out with him, because I would be afraid he was trying to trap me into marriage.

But, see, the South had gotten the best of me. And now I was a nice girl who tried not to hurt people's feelings. Well, mostly. I was getting ready to hurt Sloane's. I'd held my tongue, because I knew she was having a hard time, but this sweat-pants-and-beer-gut look was over. Tomorrow.

I thanked Peter and said I needed to get home to the baby, even though I had put him to bed and, because of Hummus's magic, was assured he would sleep until seven a.m. I ran into Emerson and Sloane on the walk home.

How lucky. I'd been wanting some time with these girls all to myself. Sloane needed a boost. I could tell. Besides getting her into shape, I was going to get her out of the house more. Before I went back to New York, that is.

"So," Sloane said, "how was the sex?"

I looked at her like she was nuts. "We just had a drink!"

"Noooo." She laughed. "With James."

"Oh," I said. "The sex with James was great. The sex with James was never really the problem."

Emerson winced. "Well, actually . . ."

I laughed. "OK. Yeah. The sex *was* the problem. Just not the sex with me."

"I miss it so much," Sloane said.

"I can't imagine," Emerson said. "I would die. Seriously."

"You can't even have phone sex," I realized out loud, suddenly aware of how very grim my sister's life was every other year. "That is horrible."

"Yeah. But we have sex letters."

Emerson and I both burst out laughing. "Excuse me? Sex letters?" I said.

"Oh, my God," Emerson said. "You mean to tell me that

when you're up there every night demurely writing, those are *sex* letters?"

She nodded and giggled. That was the thing about Sloane. She always surprised you.

"What do you say in a sex letter?" I asked.

"Well, I'm not going to tell you," she said. "But after a while, they can get stale, so I've serialized them."

Emerson stopped in her tracks. "Serialized them? Like a novel? Like a slutty little novel?"

"Little Sloaney is a slut," I said. Then I got serious. "Speaking of," I said. "First thing in the morning, we are starting boot camp."

Sloane groaned.

"I'm serious," I said. "I love you, and I'm not going to watch you walk around here in sweatpants anymore."

"I'll be in charge of postworkout smoothies!" Emerson said gleefully.

"You should see these new Pilates moves I learned at the Cloister."

"From the instructor or James?" Emerson asked.

We all laughed.

I knew already that we'd stay up too late, that we'd all hate ourselves when our alarms went off at six so we could work out before the babies got up. But this was the thing about sisters. No matter how much you laughed, no matter how many hours you talked, no matter how many months you got to spend together, it never seemed like quite enough.

AS PREDICTED, THE HANGOVER sisters—as an LA waiter had nicknamed us at a brunch nearly five years ago—did not exactly perform at their peak the next morning. We had barely made it over to Starlite Island on our paddleboards, but when we got there, it was so beautiful it was worth the effort.

We had decided to forgo towels or mats. There was nothing like being on the sand, feeling your hands and feet in it, getting it in your hair. We were beach girls. We had been raised like this. We waded through the chilly water and onto the island, sliding our paddleboards far enough up on the shore that they wouldn't be carried out to sea.

"Oh, hey!" I said brightly. "We could do paddleboard yoga!"

Emerson looked like she was going to kill me.

"Or not," I said.

We sat on the beach for a few minutes, the water lapping around our feet. I hugged my knees to my chest, looking back at the house, the one we'd been looking back at our whole lives. It was amazing how even though it was so close, when you got over here to Starlite, you felt so very far away.

Sloane leaned her head on my shoulder. "It hasn't changed at all, has it?"

I shook my head.

"Exactly like when we were kids," Emerson said.

It soothed me, that thought, that while the world seemed to be spinning too fast around me and I had lost my grip in so many ways, some things, the best things, stayed the same. Sloane took my hand, and I took Emerson's. "It's nice to know that all these years later, we're still the Starlite Sisters."

And it was.

"The skinny Starlite Sisters," Emerson said, groaning. "So get your tails up before I wimp out."

We sort of half-assed our ab work and sipped sparkling water to settle our stomachs and hydrate us during the leg work.

I didn't even yell. There was no energy for that. But the few people walking down the beach all had plenty of energy to stare at us as if we had grown extra limbs. It was exercise, people. Get a grip. If you did it, you would recognize the action.

"Ohhh," I groaned, rolling over onto my back, the cool sand feeling soothing and refreshing.

Emerson sat up and leaned her head almost to the ground to sip her water through a blue-and-white-striped paper straw. My paddleboard had a cooler on it that I, very smartly, had stocked with hangover essentials to get us through. "I'm too weak to lift my can," Emerson said.

"Why did we do this?" Sloane asked, groaning. "Why would I let you people talk me into this?"

I rolled onto my side and looked at her. "Because a few months from now, you need to be doing a little better than sex letters. Got it?"

Paddleboarding back home felt less taxing, since the breeze was so nice. So, no, we weren't really paddling fast enough to get our heart rates up and call it cardio. But it was so peaceful early in the morning. It was like the whole world belonged to us.

As we pulled our paddleboards back up onto the dock,

Sloane said, "Since we worked out this morning, can we drive out and get McDonald's?"

Peachtree didn't allow chains of any kind in its downtown, so you had to drive a few miles for fast food. I mean, other people did. I hadn't had fast food since 1998.

Emerson looked at me warily. "Can we?"

I scoffed. "Emerson, I expect this from her. She's one of them now." By "one of them," I meant a Southerner, of course. "But I expect more from you."

Emerson flopped dramatically onto her mat. "Do you know how long it has been since I have had a cheeseburger? I mean, a real one with a bun, not a lettuce wrap? And cheese, and ketchup with sugar, and all that stuff?"

"You weaklings!" I chided. "When you all have mad cow disease from cows fed their friends as a snack, I will not take care of you."

"But think about the fries," Sloane said. "Do you remember them, Caroline? Thin and the right amount of crispy, with plenty of extra salt?"

I didn't want to. But I remembered anyway. They were oh so delicious. And hot. My head was pounding, and my stomach rolled.

"And a Coke?" I whispered. "A real, sugary, delicious Coke?"

Sloane nodded. Emerson sighed with happiness.

"If either of you tells Vivi, I will deny this until the day I die. She has never had fast food, and if I have anything to say about it, she never will."

Emerson laughed, and Sloane actually clapped. "Well, Caroline Beaumont," Sloane said, "I never thought I'd see the day."

"I'll drive," I said, suddenly able to taste the flavors combining. The cheese and mustard, the ketchup, pickles and onions, all on that fluffy bun. With gluten! And that skinny patty that wasn't too overpowering. I couldn't believe I was doing this. But, you know, when in Rome.

Before I could get into the car, I saw James walking up the driveway. Shit. How was I going to get out of this? He couldn't very well know that I was getting fast food.

Before I could even say "Hi," he said, "So I heard you were on a date last night?"

That he was asking it like a question boded well for me.

"Who told you that?"

"I'm sorry. You were out on a date, and the biggest issue to you is who told me?"

Sloane took a step toward James and said, "Excuse me. Did you forget the hell you've put my sister through the past few months? Were you around while *Ladies Who Lunch* was airing, while every idiot with a Twitter account was talking about her? And it sure as hell wasn't her fault. Did that occur to you?"

The Pilates and hangover combination must have made Sloane strong.

"Well, I—I . . ." James stuttered. "I just heard at coffee that you were out with Peter Hoffman, and it made me jealous."

I rolled my eyes. Those old men at the Palm House made the beauty-parlor women in *Steel Magnolias* look tight-lipped.

"Who cares, anyway?" Emerson said. "It's just Peter the Panter. It was a drink. She doesn't even like him."

"Wait," James said, laughing. "Peter Hoffman is Peter the Panter?"

Sloane burst out laughing. "Oh, my gosh. I had totally forgotten about that!"

We all cracked up, and I guessed our laughter must have driven Hummus downstairs.

"You are going to wake the children with all this noise," she said.

I burst into tears. It was absurd. Very Emerson-like. But this was Hummus's last day. She had been a savior. And now she was going to be gone. I hugged her, and she squeezed me to her ample chest.

"You are going to be fine, my sweet being. This isn't goodbye. This is simply the beginning of a new chapter."

I felt another sob in my throat. It was a new chapter where I was going to go back to being a real, full-time, on-my-own mother.

"I need to leave for the airport in twenty minutes," she said, turning to walk back upstairs.

As if on cue, Preston started crying. "I'll get him," I said.

"Does this mean the adventure is off?" Emerson whined.

"No," I said. "This means get Taylor and Adam and move Preston's car seat into the minivan."

"Where are you going?" James asked, following me up the steps.

"It's sister stuff," I said. "You wouldn't understand."

"Oh." He looked dejected. But really, it wasn't my job to protect his feelings. That ship had kind of sailed.

I picked Preston up out of the crib, and James said, "I'll get his bottle ready."

I smiled. "Thanks."

Vivi, bleary-eyed, walked into the room. "What is all the noise downstairs?"

"Say good-bye to Hummus," I said, my voice catching in my throat again.

Vivi walked into the hall, where Hummus was rolling out her suitcase, and said, "'Bye, Hummus." She squeezed her around her thick middle. I loved that woman. How could she leave me like this?

"'Bye, sweet being," Hummus said to Vivi. Then she turned, blew me a kiss, and said, "Live your truth, Caroline."

I was getting choked up again, and James looked like he might gag. "I guess I'll take Hummus to the airport," he said, handing me the bottle.

"That would be great."

James put a manila envelope on the counter. "I didn't want to," he said. "But I drew up the papers. The ball is in your court now, Caroline. I'm not signing until you're sure."

It was like being punched in the gut. For a moment, I couldn't breathe. So I nodded.

Preston cooed, and I rubbed my finger across his forehead, my new diamond sparkling in the morning light. I sat down on the couch and said, "Good morning, baby boy." As soon as he spotted the bottle, Preston started to cry. It was uncanny.

"I know," I said, lowering the nipple to his mouth. "I feel the exact same way."

"I'm hungry, too," Vivi said.

The morning had started so well except for the whole hangover thing. And now this was always going to be the morning James gave me the divorce papers. Unless . . .

I had an idea. "Don't worry about changing out of your pajamas," I said. "Brush your teeth, and then go down to the van." I grinned at her. "We're going on a field trip."

So yes, it wasn't even eight in the morning. But I ordered six cheeseburger Happy Meals with Cokes all the same.

Then I turned back to Sloane. "Can Taylor eat a cheeseburger?"

"Yeah, he's almost two," she said. "Might as well indoctrinate him now." We all laughed.

"Mom," Vivi said. "Have you flipped your lid? You don't let me eat this stuff."

"I know," I said. "That's what makes it a fun field trip." I winked at her.

"When God smiles, don't ask questions," Emerson said.

We all ate in silence, sitting in the parking lot.

"Mommy," Adam said. "We're having cheeseburgers for breakfast?"

"We sure are."

After we finished our burgers, I drove through Krispy Kreme, and we each had a hot glazed doughnut for dessert. I hadn't had fast food in nineteen years, gluten in six, or refined sugar in at least five.

I kind of hated myself when I was done, but, well, this was a day I knew my kid would never forget. She would always remember eating doughnuts and cheeseburgers in the back of a minivan with all the people she loved most in the world singing Meghan Trainor and Taylor Swift. So would I. And I had a feeling that ten years from now, this would stay with me, but those divorce papers wouldn't.

It sort of made up for the fact that I'd had only one pound left to lose and now I was sure I had gained five in this one meal. I wanted to hate myself for it, but, you know, sometimes even uptight, regimented bitches like me deserve a break.

I did not want to weigh myself the next morning. There was no point in seeing the damage I had done. But because I am obsessive and like to punish myself, I did it anyway. I stepped on the scale, one eye closed, and held my breath for the bad news.

I had lost two pounds.

I had eaten doughnuts and McDonald's, and I weighed one pound less than before I got pregnant with Preston. It was a moment that defied physics. It made me feel like anything was possible. If I could eat like crap and still lose weight, then maybe I could forgive James, too. Maybe we could move on and clean up the mess we had made out of our life together.

It wasn't like me to be forgiving and pliable and sweet. It wasn't like me at all. But it wasn't like me to eat fast food, either, and that had turned out OK. I was thirty-four years old. And I decided that maybe it was time for me to start making some different decisions. Maybe it was time for me to try something new.

the good old-fashioned way

ansley

Peachtree's motto is "A Place to Call Home."

I'd never thought about it that much, but my subconscious must have. Because when I contemplated what Carter had said to me that night when I got home from the hospital after my IUI, this mandate about the creative ways in which we could get this baby, home was what I thought of first. I wanted to go home. I couldn't get pregnant by a stranger. I needed to go home.

So that's what I did. It was fitting that when I arrived in Peachtree that night in 1982, without a word to my grandmother, it was pouring rain. Because that was how I felt, like everything in me was streaming down and together, a waterfall too powerful and scary to be beautiful. I had talked myself out of it on the plane more than a few times. But now I was resolved. I was strong. Nervous. But resolved.

I hadn't called him before I came. I knew that if I called, he would know something was up. So I held my breath when I rang the doorbell, hoping the warm light streaming from the windows meant that he was home.

I'm sure the sight of me on the front stoop, rain pouring off the light jacket I had packed for emergencies, wasn't something he expected. But he didn't seem terribly ruffled.

"Ansley," he said, pulling me in through the door. "Come in out of that rain."

He unzipped my jacket and helped me out of it, and for a moment, I thought I wasn't going to have to say a word. Something sparked between us like the electric start on a gas stove, just like it had all those years ago. You could almost hear it pop. If I had leaned in, I know I wouldn't have had to say a single word.

He pushed my hair, wet around my face from the space the hood couldn't cover, behind my ears as I studied him. That same strong jawbone, those deep brown eyes, so soulful and warm and wise. And I knew it wasn't only Peachtree that was like coming home.

It was Jack.

He had moved into his grandmother's house after she died, couldn't let go of his connection to this place. I couldn't help but think that in some small way, it was because Peachtree was his remaining connection to me. Or maybe I flattered myself.

I didn't know where to start, but he didn't say a word. He walked to the fridge and handed me a beer. "Long flight?"

I shrugged. "Not too bad."

"How's New York?"

"It's fine," I said. "I've come to like it more, but I miss the South."

He nodded. "You'll always be a Southern girl."

"How's Peachtree?"

"Same old. I'm moving to Atlanta next month. I got a job offer there that I can't refuse. Life by the sea is magic, but it's time to move on."

I felt a knot growing in my stomach. I liked him here, in Peachtree, where I knew where he was, what he was doing, where to find him if I needed him. Part of me wanted to beg him to stay. Part of me wanted to stay, too.

We made small talk for another few minutes until I thought I would burst. Then the enormity of it hit me, the enormity of what I was going to do. I hadn't truly decided if I would tell Jack what I was up to. Maybe I would feign an affair, fly in to see him once a month until I got what I wanted, never let him know that he had a child. But now that I was here, staring at that face I had said "I love you" to so many times, that face I had promised to always be there for, I knew I couldn't do it.

"I don't know why I've come here," I said.

I turned to walk away, but Jack grabbed my arm. "You've always been a bad liar."

My eyes filled with tears. "It seemed like something I could do. In New York, in my living room, with my husband, it seemed like something I could ask of you. But now, back home, standing here, I know it's absurd. And it certainly isn't fair."

Jack looked at me with those dark, piercing eyes of his, those eyes that held both the weight of adulthood and the light of a child. And, more than knowing that what I was here to ask him was insane, I knew that if he agreed to what I was going to ask, I was in serious jeopardy of falling back in love with him. Standing here now, inches from him, so close that I could feel his breath on my skin, I knew that in a lot of ways, I'd been in love with him the whole time, never really fallen out of love with him. And that's what makes love such a complicated emotion. Because I knew Carter was the man I was supposed to be with. I knew he was the man I was supposed to grow old with. But that didn't keep me from still having those same first-love feelings for Jack.

"It doesn't matter what it is, Ansley. You know already that I'd never tell you no. I can't. I've tried, but I don't have it in me."

I bit my lip and shook my head. "Then I won't make you tell me no. I need to go now."

He smiled sadly, then turned, walked to the refrigerator, pulled out two more beer bottles, popped both tops, and handed me one, even though I'd had only a couple of sips of the first. He smiled at me, that amused look on his face, and I found myself wondering how I'd ever let him out of my sight, how, even though I was so young, I had been stupid enough to throw it all away, to throw him away.

Jack took a swig of beer and said, "We both know you aren't going to go. What do you want from me? You know I'll give it to you."

I took a sip of my beer, noticing how cold and bitter it was, how it burned as it went down my throat. Standing in Jack's kitchen was so intense that all my senses seemed heightened. I know I will remember it on my deathbed as a defining moment, the best and the worst of my life. I took another swig of beer for courage and sighed. I shrugged, and I could feel the apology in my shoulders.

"Children," I said. "I want children."

He studied me for a long moment, puzzled. "But why would you come to me . . ." He trailed off, and it was as if you could see him putting the pieces together in his mind. "You can have them. *He* can't have them."

I nodded.

His eyes were glued to my face, searching. "You want my sperm or something? Is that why you're here?"

I couldn't form sentences to explain what I wanted. So I simply said, "I am a delusional woman. I don't know why I would have come here."

He wrinkled his forehead, still studying me. "Wait a second. You're here because you want to have children with me." He grinned. "The good old-fashioned way?"

You would think that a man in this position, in Jack's position, would look baffled and bewildered. But he didn't. In fact, I couldn't really describe how he looked. Contemplative, maybe. Pleased, perhaps. But not bewildered. Not at all. It was as if he knew that this very thing was going to happen, only he didn't know when. And now here we were.

"I'm going to guess he doesn't know you're here," Jack said.

Carter knew I was here, of course, if here meant Peachtree.

But he thought I was visiting my grandmother. That was the deal, after all. He wouldn't ever know for sure. Only I would know.

I bit my lip, remembering too late how sexy Jack thought that was. This couldn't be an arrangement of attraction. He couldn't say yes because he wanted to sleep with me. I took a step back, trying to seem professional. "Well, no, not exactly."

I paused, and as I felt his eyes on my face, it was like my veneer cracked. Everything inside me that had been so oozing and raw for all this time came out and spilled all over him, because, whether I said it or not, he knew it. He knew it all. He always had. And that was the problem.

He laughed that laugh. My very favorite one. The one where his eyebrows rose a little, the one where he was both annoyed and astounded by me. God, I loved that laugh. And I found myself realizing what a mistake all of this was. I didn't need to carry a child. Carter and I could adopt, and he would have to change his vision of what the day we became parents would look like. It would take a few years, but that would be fine. That would be better. It would be cleaner. No emotions involved.

Jack rubbed his hand down my bare arm, and I could feel a shudder run through me. A cold one, one that said I needed to go, because this was way more than a deal. This was way more than a business transaction. This was a man I had loved, a man I had trusted, maybe more than anyone. There was no way I could do this.

"So what's my part in all of this?" he asked.

"Nothing," I said, a shake in my voice. "And that's the hard part. I will have the baby and raise it with Carter, and you have to keep this giant secret for the rest of your life." I laughed now, too, realizing the layers upon layers of absurdity as I said it. "It's very fair," I said, laughing again, feeling myself backing away toward the door, hoping it was the stress that had made me this much of a raving lunatic. "You get nothing. I get everything."

He nodded and took a sip of his beer, not moving, not reaching out to me, but still, somehow, rendering me motionless with the intensity of his stare. "All I've ever wanted," he said, setting the bottle on the counter, "is to give you everything."

He pulled me close to him and whispered, the moment before my lips met his, "If this is how I can do that, sign me up."

As I wrapped my arms around him, his lips feeling so familiar and so very, very right, lightning flashed and thunder boomed across the earth. Panic ran through me like a shot of whiskey as I realized that this was far from a business transaction and far from making a baby. It scared me to think what it meant for my marriage as Jack slid my dress to the floor like he had done all those years ago. It scared me more to realize that I hoped I wouldn't get pregnant right away.

THE DAY I MOVED with the girls to Peachtree, a crew of twelve men I didn't know was waiting on the lawn to help us unpack. Their wives had made banana bread, chicken potpie, squash casserole, pans of brownies, five-star pie, and award-winning jam to stock our freezer. We were mystified, devastated, and, most of all, exhausted after the drive from New York to Georgia—in a U-Haul van, no less.

I was used to the girls bickering in the backseat for hours on end. It drove me out of my mind, but what drove me more out of my mind was when they didn't bicker at all. They didn't say one single thing. Because they were too sad. We all were. And I knew that moving them away, taking them out of their environment, was going to be incredibly difficult for all of us. But I didn't have a choice. I couldn't afford to stay in Manhattan, but they could never know. And so, as is so often the plight of a mother, I would take the blame for something that wasn't my fault.

When I saw all of those people waiting for us, ready to help, it made me feel like I was going to live; it made me feel like it was all going to be OK. And it made me unendingly, eternally grateful for my wonderful neighbor, Mr. Solomon, who had organized this grand welcome for us.

Now I was telling this story through tears and my handkerchief at his funeral. Only weeks after we had made up, only weeks after we had mended fences, literally and metaphorically, he was gone.

To lighten the mood, I told the fence story, too. And when I said, "Mr. Solomon, instead of calling the surveyor, grew tomatoes up that fence. Big, ripe, juicy tomatoes—and didn't share a damn one with me," everyone in the church laughed. I wasn't sure it was appropriate to make people laugh at a funeral, but I was glad I did.

Jack was waiting for me in the pew. He squeezed my hand. "You did great," he whispered. It felt so normal, so right.

I choked back my sob. The irony of how incredibly much I missed a man who had made my life a living hell for years on end was not lost on me. But this is how it is, I guess. Even the people who drive us up the wall earn a spot in our hearts. And most of all, I was glad we had made up before he passed away. I would always remember those four blue hydrangeas by my back door. I would always be grateful that I took the time to leave my own five-star pie in return.

Sometimes in the ebb and flow of life, the tide rolling in and out, as Hal would say, we forget to take the time to think about the people who really make us who we are. We forget to say thank you, to tell the people we love that we love them. I couldn't help but think of my own mother, propped up on my couch, her great-grandchildren, I was sure, doing a fabulous job of entertaining her. At eighty-three, no matter how you sliced it, no matter what happened, I wasn't going to have her much longer. I wasn't going to have her around forever to ask her advice and laugh with her and love her. Same with my brothers.

Having her come live with me wasn't terribly convenient. I was overwhelmed, to say the least. But now, when I realized again that life was short and time was fleeting, I was grateful that I had her here, that I would get to be the one to spend this time with her. Even on her bad days, I knew it was precious. For the girls, their kids and, most of all, me.

I knew already because of Carter that there was never

enough time. And as I looked at Jack, who, as he reminded me often, had always been there for me, I wondered what I was waiting for, what was holding me back.

The choir sang, and all of a sudden, I felt very blessed. I knew already from having children and grandchildren that time moved quickly; the days were long, but the years were short. And I knew for certain that no matter how many fights they had or how many times I had to change sheets or clean up dirty dishes or babysit all day for one grandchild after I'd been up all night with another, I would look back on these months of having my children home with me, back where they belonged, with incredible joy and wistfulness. These were the good times, even when they were hard.

I silently thanked God for bringing them to me again, that all was well, that they all were well, that despite some bumps my girls and their families were healthy, strong, and no worse for the wear. It was my first prayer in many years, as after Carter died, I had felt certain that God had forgotten about me.

I had no idea yet how ironic that prayer would seem. I had no idea how all of our lives were about to change.

THIRTY-TWO

the end of the world

caroline

After my dad died, Sloane and I used to talk, in hushed tones, between ourselves, about how the day he was killed had felt strange, like nothing was off and yet everything was. I always wondered if it was retrospect that gave us that insight, if it was only in hindsight that we realized that something about the day felt a little bit eerie from the beginning.

Ever since then, I've been leery of perfect days. And this morning in Peachtree was perfect. On the walk from the guesthouse to the main house, I smelled that smell, the one that always reminded me of summer, one of the many things I really couldn't duplicate in New York. The fresh scent of gardenias. I stopped to smell one, Preston strapped to my chest. I pulled a few off the bush and put them to Preston's nose.

"Smell that?" I said. "That's gardenia." I kissed the top of his head, which smelled even sweeter. "If you're like your mommy, you will always remember the smell of gardenia, no matter where you go. Although there's no telling. I guess it's possible that you could end up living in the South one day."

I laughed at the thought.

As I made my way to the back door, I spotted the tanned legs and dark hair that could only belong to one man in town: Kyle. He was laden with this really cool coffee carrier he had made out of an old Coke crate.

"Hi, Kyle!" I said.

"Caroline," he said. "Coffee for all!"

I motioned for him to follow me into the house. He did and started unloading.

"The usual for your mom, the rooibos decaf latte for you, caramel macchiato for Sloane—"

I stopped him there, putting my hand on his. "No more," I whispered. "She needs something low-sugar and low-calorie. Work your magic."

He smiled and saluted. "Will do. And a half-caf coffee with skim milk and two sugars for Grammy."

I silently counted the coffees. "Where's Emerson's?"

"I passed her on the sidewalk and gave her hers."

I cocked my head to the side, studying his face. Something in it changed when he talked about Emerson. Interesting. I could feel my mouth and eyes getting wide. "Oh, Kyle. Do you like her?"

He put his arm around me. "Well, sure, I like her. But not like *that*."

"Mm-hm," I hummed skeptically. I'd seen that look before.

"Well, she's all about that career right now, but hey, looks like I'll be single soon. I mean, I'm ten years too old for you, but if you need a Murphy fix, I'll be available." I decided to see how it sounded, try it on for size. Not terrible. But certainly not great.

He squeezed me to him. "Thanks, Caroline. I really appreciate that."

We both laughed, and I patted him on the back.

He said, "All right, Car. I'll see you tomorrow. Let me know when you're single." He winked, and we both laughed again, much harder this time.

It wasn't funny, but somehow it kind of was.

Preston still strapped to my chest, I got out a pan and started making eggs. Vivi walked in behind me, saying nothing. She sat down at the island and opened a textbook.

Grammy was laid up on the couch, waiting semipatiently for her orange juice. Adam was in the den with Grammy watching *Mickey Mouse Clubhouse*—Mom had finally broken down and bought a TV—and Taylor was upstairs with Sloane folding towels. I could hear his sweet giggles drifting down the stairs, a sound much like music, a sound that I knew I would remember well after I was Grammy's age.

Emerson, the overachiever in the family, was out for a jog, and we had all made a pact that after she returned, we would let the kids run around in the front yard while we attempted to do our Pilates. It would be touch and go, but it would be better than nothing.

We were perhaps more exhausted than even on our hangover morning, because the night before, I had done the unthinkable. With my sisters, I had watched every one of Edie and James's episodes of *Ladies Who Lunch*. I didn't want to, but I knew I had to. I had to have all of the information before I made my decision. I had to know what I was up against. Seeing them together on TV destroyed me. The way they looked at each other, the way they laughed. It was so much worse than I had imagined, and the fact that he had declared his love for me at the end didn't make up for it.

Vivi disappeared out the back door, and I watched her go into the guesthouse.

I hadn't seen James yet, and when Sloane walked into the kitchen, she said, "What have you decided about those papers?"

I shrugged. "Is it even a decision? Is there any way we can possibly come back from that? The image of the two of them together will be forever burned in my brain." I turned to the side and scraped the eggs off the pan with a spatula, keeping the heat as far away as possible from Preston. "I can't stand the idea of going back to New York, of my friends asking me about it and my fake friends having fake sympathy, people whispering when I walk past about how my husband had the affair with Edie Fitzgerald and I was the idiot who took him back . . ." I trailed off and looked out the window. "I'm hurt, and I'm humiliated. I'm not sure if that will ever heal."

Vivi walked in through the back door as Emerson jogged in through the front, sweat around her ponytail, the back of her shirt wet.

"Are we ready?" she asked.

I pointed to the stove. "Eggs first."

Emerson sat down at the island, and I pulled out a big stack of paper plates and started doling out eggs and strawberries.

"Viv," I said, "could you please take this to Grammy?"

She jumped off the stool.

"What about the papers?" Emerson asked.

"We were just talking about that," I said. "I don't think there's any way I can move on. I think we should make a clean break. It will be easier on everyone that way."

"You should go to therapy," Emerson said. "Oh! Oh! You can consciously uncouple like Gwyneth."

I rolled my eyes. "I'm not sure I'm the conscious-uncoupling type. I'm more the give-me-half-your-money-you-loser type."

Vivi came back in, and we buttoned it back up.

"How come Gwammy gets to eat in the wiving woom?" Adam asked.

"Because she has a broken ankle, my love," Sloane said. "It's very, very hard for her to walk into the kitchen."

"And she's old," Vivi whispered. We all smiled.

It was a perfect morning, by all accounts. Everything seemed right, despite my bad news. Any decision at all felt like a relief. But we would say later that something was in the air. We were all on edge, for no reason we could discern.

I chalked it up to Mr. Solomon's death in the house right next door, to the idea and remembrance that our time here wasn't guaranteed. But in hindsight, I know that it was something more.

I retrieved a Dollar Tree bag from the pantry and doled

out the obscene amount of bubbles and sidewalk chalk I'd picked up the day before. It would buy us at least twenty minutes.

I laid out an extra mat for Preston, who cooed and kicked at the air. Mom would be home any minute. We thought about waiting for her, but we decided against it.

If we had waited, we would have had a few more seconds of normal, a few more seconds of that happy, easy morning, with no makeup and plenty of free time, when life felt like those summers when we were children. The worries were few, the cares far between.

My back was turned to the fence, and I was getting everyone stretched out before we started. Which was why I didn't see what was behind me. But I saw Sloane's face go white. And I saw Emerson grab her hand.

I turned, and my first instinct was to get Adam, which I did. I scooped him up and ran into the house, putting him on the couch with Grammy. She was snoozing, and his TV channel was still on.

When I saw those uniforms, I knew I didn't want it to be his first memory. I didn't want him to look back on his life and know that the very first thing he remembered was those two men telling him what I could only assume would be the worst news of his life, news that would steal his childhood and haunt him forever.

I knew what that was like. We all did.

And I knew this drill. I knew that one of those uniformed men was a soldier, and one was a chaplain. We had been told about this, debriefed. I knew what that meant. Or, at least, I thought I did.

I ran back outside, into that peaceful, sunny day, where Vivi was blowing bubbles and Taylor was giggling, where Preston was lying calmly on his back, discovering his hands. Where my sister was quiet but sitting on the ground, her head in her hands, my other sister wrapped around her.

"We have to pray for the best," the chaplain said. "We have to know that, either way, this isn't the end."

It might not have been the end of the world, but it was the end of Sloane's world. It was the end of our family's world. Life was too short, I remembered yet again. Life was too short not to live by your own terms, not to make up your own rules. As the sob came up in my throat so violently it nearly choked me, as I wrapped up my sister on her other side, all at once I knew exactly what to do about those papers.

THIRTY-THREE

tatters

ansley

Peachtree has a group of "funeral fairies." When someone dies, they are the women who swoop in, hold hands, wipe noses, make casseroles, organize visitations and postfuneral food. They are the ones who slip the spouses a Valium, tip the priest to forget that old Harry was a drunk who hadn't set foot in a church in decades, and organize a crowd for the graveside if it was someone who was less than well liked around town.

When I saw my three girls sitting on the front lawn, those men in uniform standing in front of them, I turned for a moment to look out over the water. It was as though I was outside myself, watching what was happening. We knew that this was a possibility. When you are in a military family, you were trained to dread this day. But why Sloane? After all the nightmares, the terror, the trauma that she experienced when her father died, why would those funeral fairies have to visit her?

We all went through it when Carter died. But Sloane's experience had been the worst of all. So bad, in fact, that it was one of the greatest shocks of my life that she decided to date someone in the military. Knowing how scared she was and how much unknown was involved in that life, I was surprised that she would take the risk.

But, as I well knew, we don't get to choose whom we love.

Caroline finally saw me, and she ran out through the gate to the sidewalk, where I was standing. I was frozen there, as if what was happening on my front lawn was a picture. I was seeing it, but none of it was happening to me. It was outside of me, like a dream I couldn't imagine was true but I also couldn't wake up from.

I thought I was crying, so I was surprised at how strong my voice was when I said, "How did it happen?"

Caroline shook her head. "He's MIA. It might be OK. He might still be alive."

I felt a sense of dread in the pit of my stomach, knowing that this could potentially be worse for Sloane than if he were dead. The uncertainty, the fear that he was being tortured, that instead of going out with one, clean, painless shot, he was being killed slowly. It was more than I could bear. I remembered that feeling all too well.

I hadn't known if Carter was dead. I wanted to believe that he had been killed instantly, but what if he hadn't? What if he was buried under the rubble, still gasping for air, still holding on to hope that someone would find him? That, for me, was the very worst part.

I should have asked more, heard more, known more. I should have been begging for information and wanting to know every detail, but it didn't really matter. There was nothing that any of us could do. I should have been feeling this unimaginable aching pain for Adam. But instead, as so often happens when you're a mother, I was thinking about my child, about her hurt, about how her life had changed. Adam was in God's hands. But Sloane was still in mine.

Emerson helped me scoop her up off the lawn and take her upstairs. She wasn't sobbing anymore. She was eerily quiet. I wanted to take that quiet for calm, but I knew better. I remembered that quiet. It was a panic that defied anything your body was capable of doing, any sound it was capable of making. It was an otherworldly quiet, one that I had hoped none of my daughters would ever experience.

I tucked Sloane into bed, although I'm not sure why. She wasn't sick. But it felt like the right thing to do. Your mother tucking you into bed is taking care of you. I sat beside Sloane and said, "Emmy, please make Sloane some tea."

"I don't want tea," she whispered. "I just want Adam." And that was when the sobbing began again.

I knew what I was up against now. I knew about the sleepless nights, the crying anywhere, anytime, the inability to eat or drink or even think. This was going to be a living nightmare. Again.

Mothers are supposed to know what to do, but there's no handbook for this. There's no appropriate response for something this horrible. So I sat and held Sloane's hand. I sat there until the sun set and the moon rose across the water. I sat there, looking out the window, praying for good news but that even if it wasn't good news, it would be news that arrived quickly. It was more out of habit than anything. Anyone could see that God had betrayed my family yet again. We were on our own.

Somewhere in there, Sloane fell asleep, though she wouldn't be asleep for long, I knew. I got up, and Emerson met me in the hall. "I'll sleep with her tonight," she said, "in case she wakes up and is scared."

I hugged her. "That would be so sweet."

I wasn't sure who had taken care of Grammy, Taylor, and Adam today, but there was no doubt that Emerson and Caroline had had their hands full. I tiptoed down the stairs to check on my mother, but before I got to the hallway to her bedroom, I noticed a man sitting on the front porch.

"Hi," I whispered as I opened the door.

Jack stood up to hug me, and for the first time, I broke down and started to cry.

"How could this happen?"

He shook his head. "It's so awful. Can I do anything?"

I shrugged. "I don't think there's anything anyone can do. I think this is going to be months on end of my taking care of Sloane and the children." I sighed and felt the tears in my eyes when I said, "I'm not sure this is the right time for us."

Jack pulled away from me, a genuinely shocked expression on his face. "What does any of this have to do with us?"

"Jack," I said softly, "don't you understand? My life has to be about them right now."

He sat down on the porch couch and rubbed his face with his hands. "Ansley," he said. "Don't you know that I understand that? It's not like I'm going to be suggesting we run off for a weekend in Paris or anything. Would I like to date? Sure. And we'll have time for that someday. But right now, we'll have this instead. I'm fine with this. I want this." He paused. "I want this more than anything."

Tears streamed down my face again. I thought of how good he had been with Adam and Taylor, how sweet he was with my mom, how patient he had been with this circus of a life I was leading. But my throat constricted with the fear that Jack was getting too close. I thought back to Jack calling Adam and Taylor his grandchildren, which, technically, they were. And my conviction returned.

I shook my head. "I can't handle it right now, Jack. I just can't."

"Why would you do this, Ansley? This isn't a good reason. It isn't an excuse. You need me now more than ever. Let me be here for you and the kids. Why are you so damn intent on pushing me away?"

"Because I've done it alone for sixteen years!" I shouted. Then I lowered my voice to a whisper. "Because every time I'm with you, I remember that I cheated on my husband, that you are the father of my two eldest daughters, that my entire life is a lie!"

He looked as though I had stabbed him in the heart. "A lie that you created, Ansley. You. Not me." I could see that he was biting the insides of his cheeks. "They're mine too, Ansley." He looked around before he added, "They are my children. And my grandchildren. I want you, Ansley. More than anything. But I want them, too."

I shook my head almost violently. "Can't you see, Jack? That's what I'm afraid of. What they know and when they know it has to be on my terms. Your being here puts my entire life at risk."

The hurt in his face was so pronounced I had to look away. He shocked me by saying, "You're right."

"What?"

"You're right. It does. It puts your whole life at risk." He took my hand. "But it puts my whole life at risk, too. If I told them, if they found out and it wasn't the right time in the right way, I'm out. It's over. If it doesn't go well then I never even have the chance to get to know them. No matter what, I would never ever risk that."

"How can I really know that?"

"You can't. You just have to trust me. I would think that now, forty-three years in, you'd be able to do that." He looked down and licked his lips. "I couldn't stand it," he said. "After I knew that Caroline was born, I couldn't stand it, knowing that out there somewhere, I had a child. And that the woman I loved and this child of mine were with this other man."

I could feel the tears running down my cheeks, but by this point, I wasn't sure what they were for. This was an awful story, sure. But it paled in comparison with what my daughter was going through right upstairs. "I'm sorry," was all I could squeak out. It was woefully inadequate but yet, at the same time, all I could truly offer him.

He crossed his arms and leaned back on the couch cushions, pushing his hair back with both hands in a way that, to anyone else, might have seemed like nothing but to me seemed like utter agony. "I came to New York," he said.

My heart was beating in time to his words, a metronome keeping rhythm to a song I wished I didn't have to hear. Simply knowing where this story could go, what a nightmarish disaster could have transpired, put the fear of God in me for what could happen in the future. And I understood what he was saying about it being a risk for him, too. But it wasn't the same thing. Not even close.

"I don't know what I thought I was going to do. Talk to you, work things out in private, lay eyes on Caroline." He looked so pitiful that I could feel my heart breaking for maybe the hundredth time that day. "I was going to come to your apartment, assuming that Carter would be at work. But while I was thinking about what I would say to you, I took a walk through Central Park. It was cold that day, and I remember stuffing my hands into my pockets, blowing out my breath, wondering if you were really happy, allowing myself to envision the possibility that maybe you would choose me, that you would take me over him."

"Jack, I—"

He cut me off, but I could barely hear him, my heart was banging so loudly in my ears, the tears choking me.

"As luck, or what I believed at the moment to be fate, would have it, I saw you. In this city of millions of people, I saw you and Caroline and Carter. You were pushing the stroller, and he was holding her, and you were all laughing. He had his arm around you, and you looked like a postcard or a movie or something. It was all so perfect. And I knew you were happy. I knew you had what you wanted. And so I walked away, not for the first time and certainly not for the last. But once Carter died, and certainly by now, I can't see why you keep pushing me away. So I have to assume that you don't love me. Plain and simple."

I could tell that in the midst of this monologue, Jack's sadness had switched to something more akin to rage. So I softened my tone and said, "Can't you understand—"

But he cut me off again. "What I understand," he said, "is that I've been waiting for you for a lifetime, Ansley. I've been there for you at every turn. I have pined and prayed and hoped." He was so worked up he had to catch his breath. "I only assumed that our being thrown back together like this was the sign I had wished for. I want to be here for you, but you won't let me. You're always going to see me in the same way."

I could feel tears in my eyes. But really, this was so far from the most important thing going on in my life. My daughter was in tatters. That was all that truly mattered.

But it didn't keep it from feeling like I was in tatters, too, when he said, "I'm done, Ansley. I'm gone. I won't be here waiting anymore. I have nothing more to give you. You have taken it all."

He stood up to walk away, and everything in me wanted to follow him, call him back, something.

I understood how horrible this moment with Jack was; it

registered with me that my life had just crumbled around me again. But when your children are in pain, that's all you can think about. And the difference between Jack and me was that this was a sensation he'd never know. And I realized that it might be too steep a barrier to cross.

———

SAVING SEA TURTLES MIGHT be all the rage in coastal towns now, but in Peachtree Bluff, we've been doing that for well more than a century. My grandmother still had dusty photos of men and women, dressed in full wool outfits that looked anything but beachlike, building barriers around turtle nests as early as 1905. The Turtle Brigade, as they called themselves, would walk right over the bridge to where the landscape changed from sound to beach and go to work.

Back then, I didn't realize the value of what they were doing or the sanctity of these little lives. I used to wonder if all of that was necessary. Did the sea turtles need barriers around their nests? Was this something that we should even be doing? Or were the turtles perfectly capable of taking care of themselves?

I remember asking my brother why people were interrupting the circle of life, why they were changing biology. He explained to me how people help the turtles. And then Scott said, "But Ansley, you'll learn that humans don't think they are a part of biology. They think they are above it."

I never forgot that night, sitting beside him on the beach, watching the Turtle Brigade go to work. I never forgot what he said. And I realized when Caroline was born that I thought I was above biology.

The day Caroline was born, everything changed. Everything always changes, of course, when a new life comes into the world. But for me, it was more than that. Because I knew the moment I held her in my arms that it wasn't only my life that was changing. It was my marriage, too.

We never talked about it. That was the deal. But I could see the way Carter studied her, the way he examined her features, looking for something, anything, that would prove that maybe it had been a miracle, maybe Caroline was his after all. Those first few months, when she had those big blue eyes, people would say, "She looks exactly like her daddy."

And she did look like her daddy. Her real daddy. She looked exactly like Jack. It was somewhat eerie, actually, how little she resembled me, how little it mattered that I had made the egg, that I had been the one who had done the work of growing her for nine months and would continue to put every ounce of who I was and what I had into raising her, long after she was the age where she actually needed to be raised.

At times, I almost felt like Jack should have warned me that he possessed the world's strongest genes. Then again, I had to consider that it was only in my mind, that her clear resemblance to a man few people I knew had ever met was nothing more than a figment of my imagination.

For the rest of our lives together, it would be the thing that sat, heavy and unspoken, between Carter and me; it would be the thought I could hear him thinking. Which is why nothing could have prepared me for the night, when Caroline was nine months old, when he came to me and said, "Do you think we should start trying again?"

It had caught me so off guard I said, "Trying what?"

He laughed. "For another baby, of course."

I know I looked at him like he was delusional. He rubbed his big, rough thumb over Caroline's dainty cheek and said, "She's so perfect, Ansley." He stared at me, that deep, penetrating stare that disarmed me so fully. "You did such a good job with her. Why wouldn't you do it again?"

Fear coursed through me that he was challenging me, that he could see inside me, hear my thoughts, know that while I was in love with him, in love with my life and my family and fully committed to all of the above, ever since that rainy night in Georgia, Jack had been the tune that I could not get out of my head, the hum that constantly ran in the background.

But he couldn't know. I'd never told him, never talked to Jack, never visited him, never done a single thing to betray my thoughts. And so, in some ways, I realized that refusing to do what I had done before would be an admission of my feelings, a confession that no, Caroline's father was more than a hazy memory from my past, and yes, we were dancing on some dangerously thin ice.

I looked up at him and said, "Carter, are you sure about this? Are you certain you can go through this again?"

He smiled at me encouragingly and leaned down to kiss me. "As long as I have you," he said, "I can do anything."

As I stared down into Caroline's sleeping face, I knew that I had already begun to feel that pull on my body, that maternal feeling that nudged me, that whispered in my ear that one would never be enough. I already knew that I would want another baby to love. But I had never imagined that Carter would go through all of this again. I had never considered what, in the end, this complicated decision might cost me.

only one

caroline

Once Dad was gone, my sisters and I always used to wonder when Mom would start dating. We had seen friends' parents do it. We knew what that looked like. While the idea of my mom moving on with someone else made Sloane's stomach turn, it was something I was endlessly fascinated by. I think I always knew the chances were good that she would find someone else. And I, for one, felt almost strangely comfortable and happy that it seemed Jack might be the guy she finally chose after all these years.

I watched Jack walk off the porch that night. I ran out the back door and got to him before he could get too far down the sidewalk. I was, sadly, out of breath. But for the first time in a long time, I didn't care about what I looked like or what I felt like or what my situation was. I cared about my sister, my mom, my nephews, my children. My family. In this new phase of my life, I couldn't see my family without Jack. I knew that if my mom was honest with herself, she couldn't see a family without Jack, either.

Before he said anything, Jack wrapped me in a hug. "I'm so sorry," he said. "I can't imagine."

I shook my head. "I can't imagine, either. This shouldn't happen to Sloane. She's too good a person. I want things to go back to the way they were before."

He nodded. "Yeah. Me, too."

I pushed the hair out of my face. It was a windy night, the sunny, clear morning giving way to a blustery evening. "She loves you, you know," I said.

He shook his head. "I thought she did. I always thought she would, anyway." Jack sighed, tears coming to his eyes, too. "But I think she's right. I think our time has passed. I need to move on."

I nodded firmly. "You do."

He looked puzzled.

"You know . . ." I started. Even heartbroken and exhausted, I was crafty, after all. "Georgia has strict rules against living on boats."

His eyes widened. "What? Why has no one told me this?"

"They usually give you a bit of a grace period in Peachtree, mostly because Dockmaster Dan wants the cash, but it is against the law, and eventually you'll have to move."

"So you want me to move?"

Jack took his jacket off and wrapped it around my bare shoulders. I hadn't realized I was cold until I was warm again.

I laughed. "Yes." I paused. "I don't know about your financial situation or anything, but I know of a great house on the market." I raised my eyebrows and pointed behind me.

It was Jack's turn to laugh. "Caroline, I can't buy the house next to your mother's."

"No. I get that. It's super expensive."

He smiled. "Let me rephrase. I *can* buy the house next to your mother's. But I probably shouldn't."

"Why not? No one else is living there. Seems like a shame to let that prime waterfront Peachtree real estate fall into the hands of someone else." I gasped. "What if it's some man who sweeps Mom off her feet?"

I could tell by the conspiratorial gleam in his eye that that did it. "What if it is?" he asked. And his tone was all I needed to tell me that the man would be him.

"She has always, always wanted to decorate that house," I said.

I pulled a scrap of paper out of the pocket of my dress. "This is the number of Mr. Solomon's son. I suggest you call him before it hits the market. This thing will go in a skinny minute."

"So you were just carrying this around with you?"

I shrugged. "Truth be told, I was going to ask James to buy it for me as a summer house. He could suck up a little bit. But if you buy it, we'll come stay with you."

He laughed. "Caroline, there is only one of you."

"So I've heard." I turned to walk back toward the house, realizing that I had Jack's jacket. I chased him back down the street and handed it to him.

"Thanks," I said. "She's a tough one, but once you wear her down, once you get inside, no one will ever love you more." Then I whispered, "If you can bear it, give her one more chance."

My eyes welled as I said it, realizing what my poor mother had gone through these past few months, what she had sacrificed. She was barely working, every time she went to the grocery store she had to buy four different kinds of string cheese and eleven brands of fruit snacks, we were constantly drinking all of her favorite coffee without replacing it, and quite often she was the one who ended up doing all six loads of laundry per day that this family produced. And she never complained. At least, not to us. I'm sure Sandra and Emily got an earful. But she never let us know if she was unhappy. Which made me think that maybe she wasn't.

As I walked up the front path, I turned to look back over the water. The beauty of it was a surprise every time. The marsh grass growing on the islands, the ancient cedar trees that formed paths and trails that we spent hours traveling on when we were young. I couldn't explain why, but somehow, in that perfect evening moment, I knew that Adam was going to be OK. They were going to find him. They were going to bring him home. I had no basis for this thought at all. It was just that when you were in Peachtree, it simply felt like everything would be all right.

THIRTY-FIVE

serenade of summer

ansley

Carter, Caroline, Sloane, and I had gone to visit my grand-mother in Peachtree Bluff when I was six months pregnant with Emerson. Grandmother's health had been slowly fading for years. Like an oil painting left too close to a window, you weren't sure it was less vibrant. It was only in looking back that you realized how vivid it had once been.

Carter and I were in a wonderful place in our marriage, which was a good thing, since the realization that I was preg-nant had not gone like I had imagined. When I told him, ec-static tears streaming down my face, the first thing he said, as icily as I've ever heard him, was, "How could you?"

I remember how alone I felt then, how the breath caught in my throat. But I went to him, sat on his lap, and said, "Car-ter, it's your baby. It's our baby. After all these years, it's our miracle."

I remember wrapping my arms around him and how he didn't wrap his back. And I realized in that moment, with horror, that he didn't believe me. The pain of that pierced through me, and my first reaction, as it often is in these situations, was anger.

I jumped up off his lap, crossed my arms, and said, "Are you serious right now? You think I went out and got pregnant by someone else without telling you? Do you know how this has weighed on me, how the life we have lived has nearly torn me apart? Do you honestly know me so little that you believe that about me?"

I turned to walk out the door. I had no plan, really. Sloane and Caroline were both spending the night at friends' houses, and I knew that I could leave tonight, check into a hotel, and worry about tomorrow tomorrow.

But mercifully, Carter grabbed my hand. He looked at me warily. "Ansley . . ."

"Carter . . ."

He took a deep breath. "Is this even possible? Are you sure?"

I grinned. He was getting it now. "Carter, I swear to you on our children's lives."

It was the fourth time I had seen him cry in all our years together. I wanted to wait to tell people, but Carter just couldn't. I didn't stop him from calling friends and family. I knew this pregnancy was different for him. Of course, it meant more. I knew instinctively that Carter would be more attached to this third baby than our first two. I prayed that it was a boy, so that if the girls noticed a difference, they would always believe it was because of the baby's sex, not because it was the only one that was biologically their father's.

We had celebrated straight on through, and by this sixth month of pregnancy, it felt like we had been on some sort of extended honeymoon. Carter couldn't stay away from me, couldn't get enough of me. He worked less, stayed home later in the mornings, took the girls to school, made sure my every craving, need, and want were met. I was the queen. It was magic.

Being pregnant with Emerson had restored something in our marriage, something that, like a perfect accessory that completes a room, I hadn't even known was missing until I got it back.

Caroline and Sloane had gone over to Starlite Island with their grandparents, who were also visiting for the long weekend. I remember the sky that morning when I woke, how it was a baby blue, the way it mingled with the rising sun, tinting the clouds perfectly pink, swirled together like cotton candy on a stick. It had made me smile, that baby pink and blue, like God had colored the sky for me that morning, for this baby I was growing inside me. Carter and I had laughed about it. It would be, unbeknownst to me, the last time we laughed on that trip.

An hour later, we were walking down the boardwalk, toward our favorite breakfast spot on the water. I was already tasting pancakes. Carter was pointing out boats that belonged to friends or famous people he knew, marveling that this little map dot had become such a yachting destination.

I saw him from the other end of the boardwalk, like a blurry apparition, but I knew Jack was in Atlanta, had moved there. I hadn't seen him since after the night I told him I was pregnant with Sloane, told him that I couldn't talk to him or see him anymore. It was too hard. There were too many feelings, too much at stake, so very much for me to lose. And I could feel him wanting more. Jack had tasted what it was to have me, had decided that the life he never wanted, the life that he and I would never have, was maybe what he wanted after all.

It was the last time I had seen him. Of course, I couldn't come to Peachtree Bluff without thinking of the man I first fell in love with all those years ago on that sandbar a couple of miles across the horizon. But as we got closer, I knew it was him. I could feel my heart pounding, and everything in me wished that I had broken my vow and called him just once. I should have told him that I was pregnant.

He smiled and waved. I was still fairly small, and if you saw me straight on or from behind, you might not even notice. Carter reached his hand out to Jack.

"Good to see you," Jack said.

I felt his eyes travel to my stomach, and that sick feeling set in. He was studying it like a hidden picture, searching for the clue that would complete the puzzle.

And then he said, "Oh, my God. You're pregnant."

Our eyes met, and in that moment, I knew he knew he had done the wrong thing. I laughed lightly and said, "Well, geez, Jack. I'm not that old!"

He laughed, too. "Of course not. Congratulations. I know you two are absolutely thrilled."

I could feel Carter's eyes on me and then on Jack. When he dropped my hand, I felt my heart race again. When Carter started walking toward the other end of the boardwalk, I knew he knew. I wasn't sure what to do. Run after him? Give him time?

It was the one thing that Carter made me promise, that he would never know who Sloane and Caroline's fathers were. I couldn't imagine it, couldn't wrap my mind around the idea that he could live his life never knowing. As I suspected, it began to weigh on him. Yet he didn't want to know who the man was. Even before we married, we never talked about past relationships, where we'd come from, who had shaped that path. It didn't matter. What mattered was that we had found each other, that our future was the two of us.

And so we compromised. I told Carter that the father was someone from my past, someone I had once loved, someone who never wanted children of his own but had agreed to give me, give us, the one thing that we wanted so badly. Carter was angry at first, said that I had been irresponsible, that I had risked our family by letting the other man know he had children. I didn't argue. He could never understand.

But now he understood. In an instant, Carter understood that Jack was the father of his other two daughters. He knew who their brown eyes and dimples belonged to.

"I'm sorry," Jack said. "I'm so sorry. But you should have told me. How did you think I would react?"

"I didn't think I'd see you," I responded, anger in my voice. But it wasn't Jack's fault. I knew it even then. This was a situation I had created.

"I know you don't really owe me an explanation, but—"

"Of course I owe you an explanation, Jack," I said. "After all these years, Carter and I are having our own baby."

There was a thinly veiled sadness in Jack's eyes, and I could feel him thinking about what might have been. I would be lying if I said I didn't think about it, too. But I was old enough to know that what might have been was never as good as what was. It just wasn't. I had moved on. I didn't fantasize anymore about what would happen if Jack had decided he did want children, that we did want the same things in life. Because I knew that Carter was the man I was supposed to marry, raise a family with, be with forever.

But I loved Jack, of course. Always. And I don't know what it was about that moment, when I should have been running after my husband, that made me say, "You have given me everything I ever dreamed of. I will love you until the day I die."

"I will love you even longer than that, Ansley."

I nodded and headed down the dock, into that cotton-candy-colored sky. I knew that Carter and I would carry on. We would get through this. It had been naive of either of us to think we could make it through an entire lifetime and never run into the true father of our children. It had been ludicrous to think it was a secret we could keep, even from ourselves.

Dockmaster Dan didn't speak to me that morning, simply tipped his hat, his eyes viewing me like he knew I needed to be alone with a secret, a secret that, I had to consider, maybe wasn't as secret as I believed it to be.

But Peachtree Bluff was a town of hidden truths, of stolen moments, a town that had borne the clandestine, the furtive, the surreptitious tales of the sea since well before the Revolution.

I knew, as the wind caught my hair just so, making me feel like that little girl who had come here when her heart was so innocent and her future so wide, that this town, with all its gossip and chatter and crazy characters, might thrive on a little good-natured fun. But when it mattered, when it was important, this place, this corner of the world that time seemed to have forgotten, would bear the big secrets, the earth-shattering ones, until the tide washed it over and, like time itself, it existed no more.

WHEN I LOOK BACK on my life, I know that I will remember my summers in Peachtree Bluff with the most fondness. Bringing my girls when they were tiny to visit my grandmother. Driving Boston Whalers over to Starlite Island, collecting shells, admiring the wild horses from the widow's walk, playing tag in the front yard, having water-balloon wars. And my childhood summers here, when the world was so pure, nothing was scary, and I was so full of innocence, were the closest, I think, that one could ever get to heaven on earth.

Those were the good times, the times that would always fill my heart with the most gladness. In some ways, this year, even with all of its troubles, would be one of those times. No matter how difficult it had been, whether Adam was lost or found, we were a family again. We were together. We had always loved one another; we had always held one another in our hearts. But something deeper had happened over these past few months. We had become family in the way we were when Carter was still alive, in the way we were always meant to be. And I knew that all of us would treasure this time for the rest of our lives.

My heart felt so heavy that chilly night, as I sat wrapped in a blanket on the outdoor sofa, looking out over the water, at the way the moon reflected and danced and spun, the way the stars glowed here in a way I couldn't remember seeing anywhere else in the world. A part of me knew that this was wrong, that I should be watching these stars with Jack. A part of me knew that I was protecting myself from something I didn't need to be protected from. And that I was protecting my daughters from a threat that wasn't a threat at all. But opening your heart after it has been closed for so many years is hard. It's unthinkable at moments, actually. Right now, my plate was full. So if my heart was a little less full than it could be, that was something I was going to have to be OK with. It seemed that night that Jack had closed the door on a possible future for us. That hurt. But I knew it was nothing compared with the hurt I had caused him in our life together—or lack thereof.

Taylor and Adam burst through the front door, an ecstatic Biscuit running behind them. None of Mr. Solomon's family wanted his little dog, and when I heard that she had been taken to the shelter, I couldn't stand the thought. She had spent her entire life on this street. I would make sure she spent the rest of it here, too. It was my final mea culpa to Mr. Solomon, and I hoped that he would rest easily knowing that his best companion was royally taken care of.

Biscuit had been a terrific distraction for the boys, who didn't understand, thank goodness, what was happening.

"Is Mommy still sick?" Adam asked, crawling up beside me. Taylor followed suit and scampered onto my lap, resting his head on my chest, that thumb popping right into his mouth.

I kissed the top of his head. "Mommy is still sick," I said, trying to hold back tears.

"Will she still be sick tomorrow?" Adam asked.

I nodded. "Mommy might be sick for a while. But she's going to get better," I said. Then I whispered, "I know she will," more for my benefit than for his.

"Mommy sick," Taylor repeated.

"Taylor was sick one time," Adam announced, and Taylor turned his head to look at his big brother with curiosity. "He threw up all over the car."

Biscuit wiggled and squirmed, gathering all of her strength in her hind legs until she popped up onto the couch, covering Adam's face with doggy kisses.

Adam burst into giggles, and Taylor followed suit.

You couldn't help but join them, no matter how hard your heart felt. It was too much joy not to take part in. The moments that sneak up on you, the little surprises that keep you guessing, make life so worth exploring, even when the unthinkable happens.

I barely realized that hot, angry tears were flowing again.

Adam patted my arm. "It's OK, Gwansley. I love you."

Nothing is better than having one of the smallest loves of your life say that.

But the hardest thing about being a mother is the uncertainty. Not knowing. Not being able to fix it. As the breeze blew warm and I caught a whiff of salt, I realized that there were a whole lot of things that I didn't know. But there were two that I did. One, I would love those girls with every cell in my body until my heart stopped beating. Two, as sure as one season is here, the next is right on its tail, about to arrive with a vengeance any day.

As I sat on the front porch, Adam under one arm, Taylor on my lap, I could feel it coming. With Sloane a heap of devastation in the upstairs bedroom and Adam God only knew where, our house felt as icy cold as the depths of winter. But, if you closed your eyes and listened, you could almost hear it. No matter how bad things seemed right now, it wouldn't be long until a gentle breeze carried in the sweet serenade of summer.

THIRTY-SIX

from here to eternity

caroline

The day Adam went missing was the night James made an offer on the house on the corner. I saw something in my sister's face that morning when she got the news. It wasn't only a look of distress, one of sadness and anger and horror over losing her husband. It was also one of simply wanting her life back. She wanted to get out of bed the next morning and have life go back to normal, have Adam come home. Maybe she'd make some waffles, maybe little Adam would whack Taylor with a toy, and he'd have to go to timeout. But that was OK. Because that was normal life, and it was wonderful.

When I saw that look on her face, it was one I knew, because I wanted the same thing. I wanted, more than anything, for my life to go back to normal. The only difference was that mine could. My life could go back to normal. It would take time and work and an unimaginable amount of pain, but I could rip up the papers, forgive my husband, who I truly believed was sorry, quit worrying about what people I didn't even care about were going to say, and try to go back to normal. Just normal. Not perfect, not wonderful, not June Cleaver. Just normal.

I had been planning to tell James it was over that day. I was firm. I had decided. In Peachtree Bluff, everything seemed a little suspended in time, reality was lost. But I knew that I couldn't bear to be the laughingstock of New York. I was going to ask Mom about the money again. If I had something to fall back on, I knew I wouldn't have been quite as worried. It was part of the reason I drank so much the night before, part of the reason I worked out so hard the next morning anyway. I was moving on. And it was scary as hell. But as we all know, life changes in an instant. Mine is no exception.

When I called James to tell him what had happened, he rushed over, of course. I told him that I was going to sleep with Sloane that night and asked if he could stay with the kids. He nodded. He understood. And when I handed him the papers back, he understood that, too.

"Vivi, Preston and I are going to stay here a little longer," I said. "I need more time. I'm not positive we can fix it. I'm not sure about anything." I bit my lip. "But I'm willing to stay in the ring and fight."

He smiled and hugged me. "I can't go back to New York without the three of you, Caroline. I can't bear it. Would it be OK if I got a place here?"

I nodded and smiled. "Sure." I thought about telling James

about the house next door, but I saved that for Jack. I wanted it, sure. But I wanted my mom to have it more. I believed that she was in love with Jack. She deserved the chance to realize it herself. So, instead, I said, "There's a beautiful house for sale down the street. And I know a great decorator."

We both laughed. It felt good.

"I just want to be us again," I said, my voice breaking so quickly after the laughter that it shocked me. But this is the nature of healing, I believe. It is the part that I hate the very most, but you have to feel it all before you can move on.

He nodded, tears filling his eyes. "Me, too. I'm so sorry I hurt us."

I couldn't promise that I wouldn't bring it up from time to time, that I wouldn't occasionally punish him in my own way, that I wouldn't be bitchy or tired or short-tempered. But I knew that one day, my daughter would look back and understand that I had fought for our family. That we all had, really. And my son . . . Well, frankly, I hoped my son would never know.

As the years went on, as life eventually returned to some semblance of normalcy, I would even come to grasp, in part, why James had done what he had done. I would begin to view it as something that couples go through sometimes. It was just that mine was going to be available on Netflix from here to eternity.

My friends, who had sworn to kill James, make his life a living hell, get him kicked out of society as he knew it, last name be damned, wouldn't understand why I made the decision I made. They wouldn't get why I would be so weak.

But lying in bed beside Sloane that night, Emerson on her other arm, the three of us softly breathing but none of us asleep, I knew that didn't matter. I took Sloane's hand and squeezed it. She squeezed back. And I knew that there were some things in life, quite a few of them, in fact, that only a sister could understand.

acknowledgments

Being an author is one of those dreams that you can't make come true by yourself. So many people played an integral part in bringing this book to life, and I am grateful to each of you, named here and unnamed, every day.

Lauren McKenna and Elana Cohen, I knew from the first minute we talked that we spoke the same language. I have loved every minute of working with you two. Thank you both for your insight and your vision not only for *Slightly South of Simple,* but for my career. Thank you for your advice and your peerless editing. I am already a better writer because of you, and I can't wait to do this all over again.

To everyone at Gallery Books, especially Louise Burke, Jen Bergstrom, and Kristin Dwyer: You are the dream team. No doubt about it. I can't express how thrilled I am to be a small part of the amazing things you do.

acknowledgments

My fairy book mother, Kathie Bennett, there are really no words to thank you. You are a champion, a friend, and a defender of all that is good in the book world. I am so lucky to have you in my life! Susan Zerenda, thank you, thank you, for your tireless effort, beautiful writing, and, maybe most important of all, incredible organization.

Sabina Hitchen, you are like a big handful of glitter mixed with genius. Thanks for your tireless work and fantastic ideas.

Bob Diforio, can you believe this is our third book together? Time flies. Thanks for taking a chance on me and for believing in me always.

Elizabeth Fletcher, you are one of those unique people who is wonderful at the big picture and the small details. I can't wait to see your vision come to life.

Thanks to everyone who opened their homes to the *Slightly South of Simple* book tour. What a gift! You are, quite simply, amazing!

To my husband, Will, who has tirelessly supported my chasing of this dream: You are always the hero I write.

Tamara Welch, you are a true jewel and I couldn't do this without you! Andrea Katz, your unflagging support has meant the world to me. Thank you for sharing your expertise. Kristy Barrett (Sweet Bee!), Jennifer O'Regan, Jim Himes, Susan Walters Peterson, Courtney Marzilli, Susan Roberts, Jenny Collins Belk, Kristin Thorvaldsen, Judy Collins, Donna Cimorelli, Kathy Murphy, Nicole McManus, Jill Hendrix, Wanda Jewell, and Shari Smith, you have been champions for me since the day I announced my first book deal and have

acknowledgments

helped me believe in myself. Thank you from the bottom of my heart.

Thanks to my *Design Chic* readers for being so amazing every day and for embracing my books as much as the blog. To my blogger friends who have been here for me and helped me every step of the way, it is because of you that my books are out in the world and that people know to read them. I am in awe of all you do and so grateful for your help.

Mary Alice Monroe, my "big sister," thank you for your guidance, your advice, your generosity, and your huge heart. How blessed I am to know you!

Elin Hilderbrand, there aren't enough "thank yous" for your incredible endorsement of my work. You are such an inspiration!

And, of course, my Tall Poppy Writers—you have taught me everything about this business and always have my back. I love being on this journey with each of you.

Special thanks to all the booksellers who have adopted my book babies as their own. Thank you for recommending me to your readers and for fighting to keep our industry strong. You are incredible, and I am honored to work with you.

Donna and Jerry Henderson, thank you for letting me do what I love, for being the home away from home for my son. You are our family, and we couldn't do this without you.

Thank you to my parents, Beth and Paul Woodson, who have stepped up in every imaginable way to help me do what I love—and for raising me to believe that I could do anything.

Thank you to my mother-in-law, Dottie Harvey, for spend-

acknowledgments

ing hours on the phone with me dreaming and plotting out every detail of this entire series so that I could pitch it. I love your stories and am so appreciative of how much you love mine!

My son, Will, you will always be the very best thing I will ever do with my life. Thank you for being the best little traveler when you go with me, and saying, "I missed you, but I had fun," when I have to leave you at home. I hope you look back on these years as an adventure!

Thank you to my family for making me who I am and for always encouraging me to do what I love. Your support means everything.

You, the reader who holds this book, we may not be blood, but we are family now too. Thank you for spending time with my words. I am forever indebted to you for not only reading, but also for taking the time to write reviews, send me emails, write me notes, come to my talks and events . . . It means the world. I hope to bring you just an ounce of the happiness you have brought to me.

slightly south
of simple

THE PEACHTREE BLUFF SERIES #1

Kristy Woodson Harvey

introduction

The last thing Caroline Murphy expects to hear when she's seven months pregnant is that her marriage is falling apart. In the wake of this news, she packs up her bags and flies south with her eleven-year-old daughter to her mother's home in Peachtree Bluff, Georgia. But Caroline isn't the only Murphy girl who's returning home: both of her younger sisters, Emerson and Sloane, find themselves right back in their mother's arms for one reason or another. *Slightly South of Simple* is a chronicle of sisterhood, motherhood, marriage, and all the ways secrets weave themselves in and out of one's life, filled with Southern charm and plenty of heart.

discussion questions

1. Discuss the title of both the book and the series. By the novel's end, do you think the title fits the work? Is there another title you would select?

2. Discuss Caroline as the novel goes on. Do you think she comes to any sort of epiphany before the end of the novel? Does she come to appreciate her hometown? Can you relate to her relationship troubles, parenting style, or values? Why or why not?

3. Ansley admits to the reader early in the novel that her financial situation after her husband's death was quite dire. In the pursuant chapter, Caroline mentions that she has a "nest egg" to fall back on and is less afraid of leaving her husband because of it. Do you agree with Ansley's decision

to keep these secrets from her daughters? What other secrets do the members of the Murphy family keep from one another? By the time the book is complete, have any of these secrets been resolved?

4. Rumors are a prevalent motif in the novel, from rumors of James's affair with Edie, to rumors of a love triangle between Kyle, Caroline, and Emerson, and beyond. Do you believe that there is a difference between the rumors spread amongst the group in Peachtree Bluff versus New York City? What is the root of these respective rumors in the novel? How do the characters respond to gossip? Do you think any of them handle it better than the others?

5. Caroline determines the best way to resolve the feud between her mother and Mr. Solomon is by tearing down the fence between their yards. How do the neighbors resolve their issues and reconcile their differences in the novel? Have the other characters mended other figurative fences between one another? Discuss the different boundaries, both physical and figurative, that the characters may have placed between one another and why they may have done so.

6. Discuss the lingering feelings of loss experienced by the Murphy women by losing Carter in the 9/11 World Trade Center attacks. Why do you think Caroline was so comfortable with moving back to New York so soon after the

attacks? Why do you think her other sisters, Emerson and Sloane, stayed away? By the book's end, do you think any of them will return? Why or why not?

7. On page 283, Caroline says, "[. . .] I knew that no one else would ever measure up. I would spend my entire life comparing every man with the one I had fallen so hard for. Young love is only for the young. Nothing else compares." Take a moment as a group and discuss your first loves. Is your current partner someone you met as a young person? Do you think this statement is true for Caroline, Ansley, or the other women in the novel? Why or why not?

8. Sloane's husband, Adam, is serving in Iraq throughout the course of the novel. Discuss the ways she seeks to keep him present in her sons' lives and consider the greater effect that a parent's absence has on her family.

9. "Mothers are supposed to know what to do, but there's no handbook for this. There's no appropriate response for something this horrible." (Page 341) In *Slightly South of Simple,* there are many variations of loss. As a group, discuss the ways Ansley supports her daughters. How would you handle the circumstances? As a group, discuss the different ways your own parents or siblings have helped you through hard times. Do you think it's different when the support is from a mother versus a father, a sister versus a brother? Why or why not?

10. Forgiveness is a major theme in the novel. Are you surprised by Caroline's decision to forgive James? What would you do in her shoes? Similarly, discuss the ways Jack has forgiven Ansley, Caroline has forgiven her sisters, and beyond. Do you feel that Caroline has grown as a character as a result of having moved to her home in the presence of her sisters and mother?

11. The narration alternates between Ansley and Caroline throughout the novel. How does this push the plot along? Do you think it gives you greater insight into the characters or their lives? Why or why not?

12. Jack has given Ansley ample time to come around to his wishes. Do his intentions seem genuine? Does your impression of him change over the course of the novel?

13. Betrayal plays a large role in the novel, from James's affair to Emerson's acting role. How do the characters move forward and seek forgiveness for their wrongdoings? Are they largely successful in achieving forgiveness?

14. Of all of the women in the book, who do you feel you relate to the most? The least?

15. *Slightly South of Simple* is the first book in a three-book series. Discuss what you think may happen to Ansley, Caroline, Emerson, Sloane, and the Murphy family in the next few books.

enhance your book club

1. Neither Caroline nor Emerson have particularly "Southern" diets. Consider sharing some gluten-free and vegan sweets or smoothies for your book club. Great (and delicious) vegan recipes can be found at ChefChloe.com and gluten-free recipes can be found at GlutenFreeGirl.com.

2. For your next book club, read Kristy Woodson Harvey's other novels, *Dear Carolina* or *Lies and Other Acts of Love,* Mary Alice Monroe's *The Summer Girls,* or Elin Hilderbrand's *The Rumor.* Do these novels remind you of *Slightly South of Simple*?

3. Interior design is a big part of Ansley's life. Talk to your fellow book club members about a possible renovation you've been considering. Take the time to research new in-

terior design techniques and processes or take a class together at a local art school.

4. Connect with Kristy Woodson Harvey on Facebook, Twitter, and visit her official website at: KristyWoodsonHarvey.com. Consider inviting her to Skype in with your book club.

a conversation with the author

1. **Have you ever lived in the Northeast or in New York? Do you think there's a real appeal for Southerners to leave for another place and return home? Is this something you saw with your own family and friends from North Carolina?**

   Yes! We lived in Manhattan half the time when I was a little girl. I always thought that I would move back. Even now, I'm very comfortable there, which might be a little surprising considering every town I've lived in since had a population of less than 50,000. I think there is definitely a tendency for Southerners to grow up and move to the big city. There's something very exciting about the unknown, about the idea of "making it" in New York. But I think sometimes it's just too big of a change! I read somewhere that the average Southerner makes it about eighteen months in New York. Maybe it's the winters. Who knows!

2. You studied journalism at UNC Chapel Hill and also have a master's degree in English. Is your process in researching your novels at all similar to any of the skills you learned while studying journalism? What is different for you about your process?

Oh, absolutely. I learned from writing columns how to find my voice as a writer, and that is definitely a skill I have used as an author. I learned how a story "feels" when it is complete. In addition to that, that's where my love of storytelling comes from. I still love telling true stories, but it's so much fun to get to make them up. I also have a long list of research "dos and don'ts" in my head from journalism school and am always keeping in mind what are acceptable sources. On the flip side, it's very nice to know that, from time to time, I can make something up if I need to.

3. In that vein, you keep a design blog, *Design Chic*, with your mother. What is your process for researching new posts for the blog? Do you think you'll open a design shop like Ansley's in the novel?

The "research" is the most fun part because it's usually just Mom and me and some coffee and a lot of chatting. We both read tons of magazines and are always searching for new designers, new trends, new brands, new things we think our readers will love. It's so much fun to look back six years when we started the blog and see what we were writing about then and what we are writing about now. It's like a working time capsule of the evolution of our tastes and design trends. I never say never . . . I do have this thought in the back of my mind that it would be so fun to open a bookstore where all of the displays are antiques for sale. But, in reality, I know what it takes to run a business, and it's always more fun in your mind than in reality! But you never know!

4. **Further to the above, can you tell us a bit about working with your mother? Does this change the dynamic in your relationship?**

My mom and I have always been very good friends, so working together has been great. There is definitely a business side to our relationship that wasn't there in the past, but we live five hours apart from each other so brainstorming ideas, choosing new designers to profile, even negotiating with advertisers, keeps us close.

5. **"Gransley" is a unique way to refer to a grandmother. The combination of Ansley's name and "Grandma" are sweet. Was this nickname inspired by someone you know personally?**

No. But grandmother names are very important! Speaking of my mom, she picked the names for this book. I told her about the characters and she went to work finding the perfect names for them. She suggested Ansley for the mother, which I loved, and when I started writing I realized that "Gransley" would be a fantastic grandmother name. Then I was totally sold!

6. **Your portrayal of Caroline, Emerson, and Sloane's relationship is a vibrant picture of sisterhood. Do you have sisters or brothers? Is their relationship inspired by people in your life?**

I am an only child, actually, so I feel like, in some ways, I've been studying family dynamics my entire life. My mom has three sisters, and we are a very close-knit family, so I spent a lot of time with them growing up. I've always been fascinated by how close they are, and a lot of those dynamics played into writing the Peachtree sisters. These characters aren't like my mom and her sisters, but that bond between them is very true to life.

7. **Where did you spend your summers as a child? Did you travel to a place similar to Peachtree Bluff? Where in the South would you recommend your readers travel to experience a similar place of beauty?**

We went to Debordieu, South Carolina, every summer, which is an incredibly beautiful part of the South Carolina Lowcountry. But Peachtree Bluff is heavily inspired by Beaufort, North Carolina, where I live now. The islands and sandbars, the small town full of quirky characters . . . It's all a part of where I live, and I have been dying to write a town like this for some time. More than any of my other books, Peachtree Bluff becomes a character. I hope that readers love it as much as I do.

8. **You come up with a pretty clever way to force reconciliation between Ansley and Mr. Solomon. Where did you**

get the inspiration to literally have the fence removed? Was this inspired by an event in your life, a friend's, or perhaps another book or film?

Don't we all have a fence in our lives? Mine happens to be, literally, a fence. Let's just leave it at that.

9. How did you come up with the title, *Slightly South of Simple*?

In all honesty, I don't know! I usually write the book and then choose the title, but this book was unique in that I brainstormed a huge list of titles before I was finished writing. *Slightly South of Simple* struck me right off the bat and, when the editorial team at Gallery picked it from a huge list immediately, we all knew we had found a winner.

10. What inspired you to write contemporary fiction? Do you think you'll explore another genre, say historical fiction or fantasy?

I read a lot of contemporary fiction, so I think when stories started coming to me that was the genre I was daydreaming. But I also love historical fiction, and I do have some historical characters that have always fascinated me. I can't imagine that I would ever write fantasy or mystery simply because I think that's a whole different type of imagination! For now, contemporary fiction is perfect. I think I'll stick with it for the foreseeable future.

11. Do you have a favorite book that you return to year after year? What makes a book special to you? Do you find

yourself more interested in plot-driven or character-driven works?

Yes! *A Tree Grows in Brooklyn* by Betty Smith. I read it for the first time in third grade and have read it every year since. It wasn't until much later that I realized Betty Smith actually lived in North Carolina. I was this North Carolina girl who had never had any real problems and I felt so connected to Francie Nolan, a Brooklyn girl with an alcoholic father living in poverty. We thought and felt so many of the same things. I think it was the first time I realized the power of story to connect us. I've been fascinated by it ever since, and every year, I find something new to love about this book. I am for sure most moved by character-driven stories, and I think I write them as well. The inner workings of people's minds, even as they pertain to the simplest things, always fascinate me.

12. **Is there a particular reality show you modeled *Ladies Who Lunch* after? Are you a fan of reality television programs? If so, which ones are you currently watching?**

Well, it was supposed to be a bit like *The Real Housewives*. I'll catch an episode of *The Real Housewives of New York* from time to time, but I'm not a devoted fan. I have to admit that I have watched every season of *The Bachelor* since it first aired when I was in high school. All of my high school friends would get together every week to watch it, then my college friends, and even in grad school. Now, I always tell myself that I won't watch the next season, but I always do. I'm not sure if it's the good memories or what, but I can't stop myself!

13. **Can you share a bit about your next project or the next book in the Peachtree Bluff series?**

The next book in the Peachtree Bluff series is Sloane, the middle sister's, book, and I am so excited about it. She is going through quite a bit of turmoil in her life in the present. Her love story, which takes place through a series of flashbacks and letters, is one of my favorites I've ever written. We also get to delve deeper into Ansley's relationship with her mother and her brothers, which is fun—and a little tricky. I also haven't been able to keep myself from writing just a bit of Emerson's story. Let's just say, the future for the women of Peachtree Bluff still might be *Slightly South of Simple*. But it's looking bright all the same!